To Rahul & Krish

Thank u

HOW
to be a
HERO

Nick Sharma

A novel by

NICK SHARMA

Penman
PRODUCTIONS

A novel by

NICK SHARMA

HOW
to be a
HERO

FIRST Edition
Penman Productions, Gleneden Beach, Oregon
Copyright © 2014 Nick Sharma

All rights reserved under International
and Pan-American Copyright Conventions.
No part of this publication may be reproduced, stored in a retrieval system,
or transmitted in any form by any means, electronic, mechanical,
photocopying, recording, or otherwise, except brief extracts for the purpose
of review, without written permission of the publisher.
Published in the United States
by Penman Productions, Gleneden Beach, Oregon.

The events, people, and incidents in this story are the sole product
of the author's imagination. The story is fictional and any resemblance
to individuals living or dead is purely coincidental.

Printed in the United States of America
Library of Congress Control Number: 2014901515
ISBN: 978-0-9914804-0-1

Cover and book designer: Liz Kingslien
Editor: Mardelle Kunz
Cover illustration: Jud Guitteau, judguitteau.com
Back cover photo of Nick Sharma by Innis Casey

Penman
PRODUCTIONS
P.O. Box 400, Gleneden Beach, Oregon 97388
penmanproductions.com

Dedication

*This book is dedicated to my loving cousins
Karishma and Shaneel, who shared the
most wonderful moments of my childhood.
I love you both with all my heart.*

*It is also dedicated to my mom.
Thank you Mom for making everything in my life
possible and allowing my dreams to never die.*

*Special thanks to Ron Lovell for
making this dream a reality.*

~Nikku

CHAPTER 1

A Dream

IT WAS A SCARY DREAM, ONE THAT WASN'T NORMAL. *The pitch blackness of the dreadful skies suffocated the entire landscape. The storm roiled and churned disturbingly, while releasing menacing laughs of thunder that exploded through the air. The storm had won, and it stared down boastfully at its handiwork. But that's not how it started; that's how it ended.*

It started just like any other day for Dulom Village, a village on the outskirts of the Arunachal Pradesh region of India. It was a day of sunshine, sweat, and happiness galore. Rich crops of rice lay in flat paddy fields that were worked by farmers in the hot, baking sun. The flat area around the village quickly grew into hills that ranged as far as the eye could travel. The surrounding hills stretched for miles toward the infinite horizon, and if it weren't for the massiveness of the mountains beyond, they wouldn't be seen with the naked eye from such a distance. But they were colossal and their heights soared into the clouds, showcasing their dominance. Not to be outdone, at the other end of the village lay an even more impressive spectacle: the mighty Indian jungle.

The jungle was a sight unmatched by any around it, a vision of sheer awesomeness. The canopies of the warring jungle and forest trees created a lush, green landscape that blanketed the majestic land and made it look like an emerald jewel glistening in the sun. Only in a few spots did the entwined kingdom of trees open up to

1

show a road carving its way through before being engulfed back into the overgrowth.

It was in front of that raging battle, on the edge of oblivion and the unknown, that Dulom Village was founded. A quaint village nestled in the nook of the line of trees, its villagers tended to their daily tasks, carrying goods and supplies and anticipating a fruitful day. It was paradise, a paradise that was soon to be lost.

First, a shrill sound made its way in from the hills—its resonance resembling the racket of war. Then the sound rallied from the sky and rocketed over the village. Soon it became deafening and war drums of thunder blared, one after the other, shaking the very ground with a powerful rumble. Yet, the rolling thunder was only a flag bearer, only the beginning.

It started with a single cloud above the hills, a scout for what was to follow. It seemed small and insignificant but not for long. Before the villagers knew it, the single cloud quickly grew into many, each cloud darker than the one before, following in a march of darkness from the hills that eventually blocked out the sun.

The largest clouds rolled in like phantoms from the deep, spiraling out of the abyss that was nowhere and everywhere all at once. But these dark clouds that loomed overhead weren't normal clouds. They were not white or fluffy or even grained with dust from the roads. Instead, they were a sheer, sharp, crisp, dark color that closely resembled black—not just any black, but a red that was so pure, so dark, that it appeared as black. This enveloping sheet of blood-stained darkness covered the once sunny, bright skies. It reigned over the fields and swallowed the village in its pitch-black jaws.

Next, a gust of wind blasted in from the jungle and blew through the village, a wind that was much stronger than anyone had felt before. It blew down all loose structures, threw everything unshielded onto the ground, and overturned empty wagons. Then it became deathly quiet, and the villagers were befuddled. They started putting back their fallen goods and turning over their wagons. They thought it was over, unaware of the inevitable truth, the truth that was as clear as the storm was dark, the truth that the storm was only taking its first breath.

The second gust came through much stronger than the first. It knocked down merchant stands, threw wagons full of goods into the streets, and blew doors off village huts. The villagers searched for shelter, but shelter was nowhere to be found. Something was coming, and it was coming from all sides.

There was an iciness in the air, a sharp prickling cold that made the skin tingle. It also made the people wonder what was to come. They didn't have to wait long. The third wind came, and it was the worst. It splintered solid doors, shattered brick walls, and dissolved brave men to tears. They didn't have worry about what was coming because it was already there.

The village was soon abandoned, with no one in sight except a single soul who stood in the middle of the road: courageous little Amith. He was a small skinny boy, only seven years old, but regardless of his size, his heart was larger than a giant's and he stood firmly in place.

The darkness watched, biding its time, seemingly surprised that such a little boy would try to brave its wrath, that such a little boy would stand up to its unending fury. The dark clouds spun, inhaling and exhaling, growing larger with each movement as tendrils of lightning flashed through its innards. Amith knew that this was no ordinary storm, but still he stood as immovable and unyielding as the sun on a scorching hot day.

Angered by the boy's insolence, the darkness let out a roar of thunder, a roar so strong, so forceful, that it could push over an elephant. But not brave little Amith, because Amith was no ordinary boy. Amith was destined to be a hero.

That's when it started, a tingling in the pit of Amith's stomach. An uneasiness that grew stronger and stronger. It was a feeling that Amith was not familiar with. It was a feeling of being lost, powerless, of having no hope, only despair. It was the feeling of fear.

A trumpet of thunder jetted across the sky just before the storm began its assault. Amith watched from the ground as the very air became heavy and dense with moisture. Then the first drops of water began frothing from the mouth of the storm. The storm became more and more intense, revealing more of its anger, and it wasn't long before the blood-soaked skies began pummeling the ground with bullets of rain.

Amith began quivering as the terror started to get the best of him. He trembled from fear as much as from the assault of the cold. His eyes became expressionless and empty of hope. Only sheer will kept him in his spot, but even that was quickly fading. His face became paralyzed, and his strength drained with each pellet of rain that struck him. The loneliness, sorrow, and overpowering pressure that soon followed were crushing. The storm was beginning to make its move.

It was at that moment, in the pit of deep despair, that Amith remembered what he had always relied on for help: Amith thought of his mom. He saw her sorrow-filled eyes from the tough, troublesome times, but he also saw something else. He saw her smile, her gleaming smile that could brave the evils of hell and bring forth the fruitful light of heaven. It was this smile that gave him strength; it was this smile that gave him hope.

Suddenly, the rain no longer struck Amith. Instead, it evaporated as if it had never existed in the first place. The lightning seemed to have lost its luster, and the wind died down to a gentle breeze. The strength of the storm seemed to be sapped right out of the air.

The storm reeled back, surprised at the boy's spirit. It let out another roar of thunder, but Amith stood unshaken and glared at the vicious skies, as a mountain does when it braves the wind. He started to welcome the deafening roar that escorted the darkness, because he knew something that the storm didn't know: Amith knew that his strength was immense, that he could withstand all the storm had to throw at him, and that his fortitude was unbreakable, because he knew that he wasn't alone. His mom was always with him.

But just like Amith, the storm too was unyielding. It held its position high above in the air, judging the situation. Soon its strength returned, and it slowly crept forward, closer and closer, ready to pounce. Amith knew what he had to do to defeat the storm, the one thing that he always saw his mom do in the face of adversity. Amith started to smile.

But the storm bared its teeth, and a flash of lightning ripped the image of Amith's mom from his mind. It bolted down, crackling the air and ripping the ground in half from the force of its strike. Amith was thrown into the air.

The storm let out a hearty laugh of thunder as it approached for the kill. It knew it had bested its prey. It knew that nothing stood between it and the boy. It knew that the time to strike had come.

Amith stared up again, but with no image to protect him. The determination in his eyes was gone; his smile faded and was replaced with quivering lips. Another flash was triggered—this time *it was headed straight for Amith. The lightning cracked the skies as it approached, the sound of it broke the air, and Amith awoke screaming from his nightmare.*

¤ ¤ ¤ ¤ ¤

Amith's mom runs to Amith, her hand quickly covers his mouth just enough so that his loud screams don't wake the entire village. Then she holds him in her arms, rocking him back and forth, as a mother does with a newborn child. Tears pool from Amith's eyes and stream down his chest.

"Bête!" *(Son)* she says in concern and then starts crooning to him. "Bête, it'll be okay. Bête, it'll be okay."

She touches his forehead—it's warm. A fever must have hit him. She holds him tightly in her arms, soothing him with her head on his, slowly rocking back and forth. She repeats the same words over and over again, "Bête, it'll be okay. Bête, it'll be okay," as the dark night slowly slips away.

CHAPTER 2

Friends

HERO TRAINING TIP #1

"A hero never cheats."

~Amith

MORNING SHINES; IT'S VERY BRIGHT, a hot and sunny day like the usual that hits this village. At least it's not scorching. Well, not yet, but it will be, like always.

Amith's eyes flutter open, and he lazily rolls out of bed. Oh, what a beautiful day it is, a perfect day for adventure! With that thought, Amith springs to his feet and gliding from one area of the tiny little hut to the next, he grabs his shorts, steps into them, and goes through the motions of brushing his teeth. He would feel bad if he didn't, never liking to disappoint his mom. He rushes toward the door but stops mid-step. Why, he can't forget his trusty sidekick, his amigo in arms, his compadre, his one and only lucky red scarf! It's not much of a scarf really, just a long piece of thin cloth that Amith wraps around his neck. It's sort of a scarf/cape combo. Although Amith likes to feel the wind on his bare chest and arms, and usually goes shirtless, he does love the warmth of his stylish red scarf. Besides, it just plain looks cool. At least, Amith likes to think so.

Now, the door of the quaint little hut that Amith lives in is flung open. Amith steps out heroically, leaping into the air and standing with his hands on his rib cage, posing as if the paparazzi of the world were waiting for his dazzling arrival. But the world doesn't notice. The streets are starkly empty, in fact, as he watches a tumbleweed roll by. Hmmm . . . They must be saving their adoration for when he saves the day, Amith thinks. He sports a large smile, tosses the end of his red scarf into the wind so that it flutters like a cape, and gallantly strolls into the vacant street.

"Good day, citizen," he says as he bows to a stick resting on the wall.

"At ease, soldier," he says as he salutes an ant trailing by.

"Keep up the good work," he says to a cat rummaging through some garbage piled near the street corner.

Yes, it's a beautiful day in this village, or at least it is to Amith. He is unaware of the poverty and despair visible around him, the meager lifestyle of the people in this village with its dirt roads, mud-brick walls, and tin-and-straw huts that house the ever-poor. It is still beautiful to Amith. In fact, to Amith this is the greatest place on Earth. To Amith, this is where dreams come from, because Amith doesn't see what the world sees. Amith sees something far more impressive, far more magical. Amith sees a world where a lone kid can save the day. Amith sees a world where possibilities are endless and hope never dies.

It is time for the first test of performing his heroic deeds, Amith decides, as he comes up to a small mud courtyard. It might be muddy and brown, and it hardly seems like a pleasant place to play, but Amith sees it differently. Amith may be a prisoner to his surroundings, but his mind is free to imagine. So he does, and Amith starts his play.

To any townsfolk walking by, it might look like a boy playing on a pile of rocks, but to Amith, he is climbing the evil tower of Bad-guy-iz-toh to rescue the poor innocent victims that were captured by the evil dragon pirate. Amith is very adept at using his surroundings as the starting point of his awesome adventures—from turning wooden carts into acid-spitting bears to mechanical constructs made out of cow dung. To Amith, it is all the same, they are mere challenges. Challenges like all those that came before, just waiting to be overcome by a brave little boy such as him.

Amith is the kind of spirited boy who fights and plays in a world uninterrupted by the normalcies of life. He is in his mind a hero—unchallenged in his domain. The only one who comes close is Shaneel.

"Areh *(Hey)*, Amith!" Shaneel yells as he comes rocketing around the corner, waving his hands in the air and wearing a big smile on his thin face.

Shaneel is Amith's best friend. He is the sort of boy who's not good at anything but he tries really hard, even if it means failing miserably in the process. Shaneel is a kind and gentle soul who can't kill a fly without feeling some sort of remorse. That is his greatest asset—a golden heart—although at times it also makes it easy to walk all over him, sometimes even by Amith. Shaneel shares the epic goal of being a hero, but he is also a lover of sorts. Whenever he and Amith would sneak into a movie theatre to watch old forgotten films, Amith cheers the bloody battles and violent duels to the death. Shaneel has a different taste for the flair of heroism; although he would never mention it, Shaneel secretly favors the part where the hero gets the girl.

9

This is the story of Amith and Shaneel, two friends as close as any can be. And although they aren't brothers, they act like it. They share their dreams and play off each other's imagination, creating a rich fantasy in the poverty-stricken world around them. Amith is the hero and, to him, Shaneel plays a sidekick role, but Shaneel doesn't want to be. Shaneel feels that he is as much a hero as Amith. Even though he can never live up to Amith's caliber, he still tries.

The boys begin their play trying to fall onto the same page. Amith has chosen to pretend to be a knight and they duel in the orchard of the great sky castle. Shaneel has no option but to follow.

"Take that, you villain!" Amith shouts as he slashes at Shaneel with a stick he picked up from the ground.

Shaneel looks around confused for a moment. "So who's the villain?" Shaneel asks.

"Your words won't trick me!" Amith says as he moves in for another swipe, but Shaneel dodges the blow.

Shaneel is shocked. "Wait! I'm the villain?" he yells, pointing to himself.

"Defend yourself!"

Shaneel reluctantly does so, and their fantasy begins.

The mud-brown courtyard is suddenly changed. It is no longer a dismal vision of sickness and poverty. It is now the setting of a beautiful castle, flying across the land on mystical, giant, angelic wings, above a sea of clouds.

Inside the flying castle, a plethora of admirers perched high above in the stands watch the annual tournament. They cheer and root for the two dueling knights inside the square far below.

The knights are supposed to be equally matched, although many think that the brash young one with the red scarf has a slight advantage in skill. He expertly wields his longsword, waving it in circles in the air and showing off to the audience's delight, while the other one seems more timid, more calculating, and wields a long spear—his weapon of choice. The two knights circle each other, ready for battle.

Amith moves in for a strike with his stick, pretending it's a longsword. He strikes quickly but Shaneel leaps to the side, just barely missing the wallop of the stick. This is to be expected of Amith whenever Shaneel plays with him. Amith never gives Shaneel a chance to prepare himself. Shaneel knows that Amith always plays the hero, but for some reason, Amith's heroes always play dirty.

Not to be outdone, Shaneel comes in thrusting with his pretend-spear at his devious little nemesis. Amith quickly dodges the attack. Shaneel pretends with his hands to flare a scarf of his own that is flowing gently in the air.

"What! You have a scarf too?" Amith wails.

"Yup, a white one!" Shaneel yells back.

And it is! A velvety white piece that is embroidered from top to bottom—a masterpiece of sewmanship, a prize of clothery, a fine work of artistry. It is nice indeed, but a little too nice. Amith will not be outdone.

"Fine, then my scarf is on fire!" Amith yells back.

And it is! A bellowing flame springs from Amith's neck and flies like a fiery phoenix behind the knight. It follows his every movement. The castle spectators watch, all in awe.

"You can't have a fire scarf!" Shaneel argues, while Amith continues to make roaring fire sounds and flailing his real scarf as if it were a flame. "It will burn your back!" Shaneel continues.

And it does! It is quite scorching hot, and the burning hotness of the flames heats his armor to the point that the knight has to pat it down, killing the flames.

Amith goes through the motions of the knight putting out the flame. "Okay fine! No burning scarf, but you can't have a white scarf either!"

"Fine!"

"Fine!"

Both knights' neck accessories disappear, as the audience members let out a disappointed sigh. But it wasn't to last. The dueling knight championship must continue. The two knights spring to their feet, engaging each other as they perform combination moves back and forth, each one dodging or blocking the other and coming in with an attack of their own. It is a stalemate many times, but still they persist.

Amith and Shaneel play fight with their sticks in the little dirt area of the street, each trying to best the other's move. A figure stands leaning against the wall, holding a basket and watching the boys with amusement.

"Take that!" Amith says as he lunges forward with his stick.

Shaneel parries it with his thin branch. "Easy," Shaneel taunts back and comes in for a hit. He hits with a small thwack. Amith quickly jumps back, repositioning himself. Shaneel sports a gigantic smile, baring teeth. He has the upper hand in the fight; he never gets the upper hand.

An equal opponent—that cannot be, Amith thinks to himself. He must remedy this situation. The hero never loses; the hero always wins. With that thought, determination fills Amith's face, and he comes in with a flurry of hits, each deflected by the impressive Shaneel. They stand in front of each other—Shaneel finally has Amith in a draw.

"Wait, look over there!" Amith quickly says.

Naïve little Shaneel turns and whack, Amith knocks Shaneel off his feet and onto the ground. Shaneel knows it was a dirty trick, but he should have known better. He feels just as much to blame for believing Amith in the first place.

Amith sports a mischievous smirk as he saunters his way over to Shaneel lying on the ground. He sticks out his pretend sword to Shaneel's throat and says, "Who's the hero?"

Shaneel hates those words. Every time he hears them, he knows he's lost. One day he will win and throw it back in Amith's face, but today is not that day.

"You're the hero," Shaneel mutters between his teeth, irritated.

Amith grins widely and parades around the courtyard, caught up in his own victory. He raises his hands up and down in the air, as if there is a crowd of people lifting him up. Shaneel sits with his shoulders slumped, sulking, and glumly watches Amith's boastful behavior.

"You're both my heroes!" a voice calls out, interrupting Amith's little self-parade.

Amith stops in his tracks and turns to look. He sees the one sight that he always loves to see, the one sight that gives him strength and that is the best part of his day: Amith sees the smiling face of his loving mom.

CHAPTER 3

Rheka

RHEKA WAS ALWAYS A STRONG WOMAN, even when her husband died and left her all alone with Amith. At those times life without a husband in the poor village was a death sentence. Women didn't work and were the product of their marriage. Without it, they were hopeless and considered worthless to their society. Once Rheka lost her husband, she lost a piece of herself, yet her smile would never show it. She never shed a tear in front of Amith but instead, smiled at him as if everything would be all right. There was something to those smiles that truly beamed the essence of power and could overcome any element of fear during the most perilous times. Those moments showed her great strength. When the world was stacked against her and there was no way forward, her smile sliced through the darkness and opened a path—as if she knew it would not defeat her, as if she knew that whatever the world could throw at her, she would stand firm and bear the burden of the assault . . . with only her smile as her sword.

Those were the most important moments for Amith and his mom, when she would look at him with that smile, and even when her eyes gave away her sorrow, her smile would give him strength. For there is great power in smiling when there is no hope, only sorrow. Power enough to create the very hope that was lost, however little it may be. And with that hope, there is a way out.

In any situation, Amith remembers that memory most when he thinks of his mom. Maybe it's why he is so fearless, as if her smile guides him and gives him strength to handle any obstacle put in front of him. Her smile is his path, and maybe that's why Amith always smiles and never feels lost. And maybe Rheka knows this, knows that she is raising a brave son able to handle all hurdles put in his path. She uses those smiles strategically, as if she is preparing Amith for something momentous, as if her premonition for his life is as a ruler or a king, not a poor peasant, which he is.

That same powerful smile greets Amith that day. She looks at him and then Shaneel and greets them both with her loving eyes.

"Bête, ap log both huma heroes heh." *You boys are both my heroes,* she announces in Hindi.

Amith immediately drops the stick and runs to her, hugging her like he hasn't seen her for ages, and then quickly steps back to argue.

"Areh, Ma. There can only be one hero," Amith says defiantly. "The other is a villain."

Shaneel sits up, but those last words from Amith have drained his willingness to play. Shaneel wares his emotions on his sleeve, and he doesn't want to be the villain. Rheka sees Shaneel's sadness.

"Well, Shaneel doesn't look like a villain to me," Rheka says and smiles at Shaneel. "He looks like a great hero."

With those words, Shaneel grins from ear to ear, jumps up recharged, and brushes himself off.

Amith's mom has that ability, the ability to breathe new life into people when they feel beaten, as if she had undying soldiers to do battle against the daily attack of the real world. It was just another one of her mysterious powers that would heal the spirit of the sick. She is a powerful woman indeed.

Rheka hands the basket of washed clothes to Shaneel, and he eagerly carries it as they walk down the street. It is a pleasure for Shaneel to help out, especially after the delightful comment from his much beloved aunty.

"Ma, if he is a hero, who am I supposed to fight?" Amith snaps back.

"Bête, you don't have to fight to be a hero," Rheka explains. "Heroes do good deeds. It is their actions that make them real heroes."

Shaneel smiles and nods enthusiastically at her wisdom. However, Amith understands little meaning in her words and stays silent, pondering the obscure, nonsensical idea. After a while, he responds.

"Ma, that makes no sense," Amith says.

Rheka lets out a hearty laugh and almost topples over from it—it is a rare moment when she gets to laugh, so when it happens, she takes full advantage of it, not knowing if another one will ever come again. It is funny to her to see the innocence of a child. It reminds her how truly pure children really are and how life hasn't touched them yet. In the sorrow of the world that surrounds them, it is that joy that makes her happy. She leans against the side wall of the mud hut, tears rolling down her cheeks as she tries to compose herself. When she does, she turns to the grinning boys, who are surprised at the change in her daily character.

"Bête, I love you," she says, quickly bending down to hug Amith and to kiss the top of his head. Then she grabs Shaneel and includes him in the union. Not wanting to fail in the task she has handed him, Shaneel hugs back with his shoulder, while still holding the basket firmly with his hands.

"Love you too, Aunty," Shaneel mutters with his cheek pressed against his aunty's hand.

"Why don't we go inside, and I will make some hot rotis for my two little heroes!" she says.

The boys light up with excitement. The moment they hear the word roti, they forget all about heroes. Now they fantasize about something else—the delicious taste of the tortilla-like treat.

The three enter their mud-walled hut and a gust of wind blows the door shut behind them.

CHAPTER 4

Secrets

HERO TRAINING TIP #2

"A hero always gets up early."

~Amith

MORNING. THE HAY-STITCHED DOOR BURSTS OPEN. Shaneel stands in the door frame. He breathes deeply, almost hyperventilating, as if almost drowning. His eyes focus on Amith, who is sleeping on his meager bed. Shaneel rushes to him and starts shaking him violently.

"Amith!" he screams.

Amith's eyes pop open in surprise. "What?" Amith yells back as he smacks Shaneel's hands away, fighting for his sleep.

"We're going to miss it!" Shaneel says grimly.

Amith sits up with a yawn as he gathers himself and says, "Miss wha . . ." But before Amith can finish, he realizes the importance of the day. His eyes widen and a look of worry crosses his face. Amith quickly jumps out of bed and runs to the door. He pauses at the door, looks back and yells, "Come on!" to Shaneel, then dashes out the door. He almost runs right into his mom who is carrying her basket into the hut.

"Sorry, Ma!" Amith yells as he continues sprinting forward. Thoughts of missing it flood Amith's head, but something else comes to mind—the weather. The air is cool today, he thinks, and there's a crisp feel to it, more than usual. But weather will never stop a hero, no matter how cold it is, Amith thinks to himself.

"Bête, wait!" Rheka calls out.

Amith stops dead in his tracks. Even with his great desire to make it on time, he is always at the mercy of his mom's call. He knows if he doesn't stop, he will spend the entire day thinking about how he didn't listen to her. It's a nasty thing—regret—and Amith will have none of it. So he stops, turns around, and sways side to side, impatiently waiting in place as if he has to pee.

"Areh, what Ma?" he anxiously whines.

His mom pulls out a pair of his freshly washed shorts from her basket of clothes and waves them in the air.

It's at that same moment when the cold air and breeze start making sense. It's not the weather that's the problem—it's his lack of pants. Amith's face turns a bright red as he realizes that except for his red scarf, he's completely naked and standing for the whole world to marvel at. This is not the way that he wants to get attention. But his ambitions about being a hero are high, and starting an adventure early in the day will put him ahead of the game. Amith waits a moment and thinks to himself: does a hero really need pants? A moment passes before he comes to a conclusion. Yes, a hero must have pants; otherwise, no one will take him seriously.

Amith quickly runs back to his mom, yanks his shorts out of her hand, and masterfully puts them on while running. But halfway down the street, Amith stops again—he has forgotten something else. Amith sprints back to his mom, stops, gives her a kiss on the cheek and says, "Love you, Ma," and then darts off again.

19

Rheka stands there smiling, very proud of her mischievous yet loving son. She turns around to go into the hut, but Shaneel comes barreling out the door. He shoots past Rheka, racing after Amith. He yells back, "Hi, Aunty. Bye, Aunty."

Rheka watches as the two boys disappear around the corner. Suddenly, she starts coughing violently, and it takes all her strength to not double over. Then she takes a moment to regain her composure. She takes shallow, painful breaths as she pulls a rag out from the basket and wipes her mouth.

There is sorrow in her eyes as she looks at it. She buries the rag in the folds of her clothing, making sure no one can see the specks of blood that are splattered on it, keeping her secret hidden from the world.

CHAPTER 5

Alley Brothers

THE DUST-COVERED ALLEY APPEARS DEAD to the world, one of the old, run-down places in the village. The bustling shops that once lined the street have disappeared into obscurity. Its only purpose now is to harbor old, forgotten memories of days full of joy, when happiness wasn't lost and the place wasn't abandoned.

It seems like a gloomy day for the alley, but something changes, a flicker of life emerges. Two figures come dashing down the alley: Amith in the lead and Shaneel following behind.

"It's almost time!" Amith shouts back to Shaneel, who is rapidly closing the distance between them.

"I don't know how you could have overslept. I barely slept at all!" Shaneel replies, huffing and puffing.

Amith arrives at the crates first. He starts expertly crawling from one stack of crates to the next, making his way higher and higher along the wall. It would seem he has done this many times before, and the stacks of crates could just as easily have been rungs on a ladder to him.

When the crates no longer ascend higher, Amith coils his legs and, with a powerful spring, leaps up into the air and pulls himself onto the top edge of the wall. Then he swings his legs over the top and sits with them dangling on the other side, not having the faintest care that a fall from this height would mean certain death.

Shaneel lags behind, struggling up the first stack of crates, while eyeing the others that lie ahead. He almost loses his balance as he makes his way to the next stack, and the stack after that is even more menacing—and then there's a gap, a big one.

Shaneel stares at the empty space between where he is and where he wants to be. It's a jump, a long jump, and Shaneel is not as athletically gifted as Amith. Unlike the fearless Amith, Shaneel's mind is full of worry. The thought of falling is overwhelming, and Shaneel sweats profusely as he tries to force himself to make the jump. He looks at it again, determination in his eyes, but vertigo starts to kick in.

"You're going to miss it!" Amith yells down, transfixed by the scene on the other side.

Shaneel looks up and sees Amith, comfortable on his high perch, without the faintest care in the world. "If he can do it, so can I," Shaneel thinks to himself. A defiant look crosses his face, and he takes a step back, trying to fight off the vertigo. Then Shaneel closes his eyes and, with a deep breath, takes a step forward and lunges with all his might.

Shaneel flies through the air as a monkey jumping from tree to tree, but unlike a monkey that is in its environment, Shaneel definitely isn't in his. And there is a problem, a big one: his leap is too short.

Luckily, he catches the side of a crate but unluckily with only one hand. Shaneel's face smashes into the side of the crate as his body swings like a pendulum. The impact is painful but Shaneel hardly notices. His only concern now is to not let a moment of misjudgment be the end of him, as he realizes that he might not be able to do something that Amith so easily accomplished a few seconds ago. All those thoughts race through his mind at once, and the thoughts only grow more powerful as Shaneel's grip fails.

The thumb is the first one to go as it slides off the crate, but the four fingers still hold. The next to go is his pinky, which loses the strength to latch on like the others. Three fingers left.

Then the index finger slides off, and with it hope. Now, down to just two fingers—two fingers that cling to life.

Shaneel's last two fingers slip off, and he begins to fall.

Suddenly a hand bolts down and catches his wrist. He didn't fall very far—less than a foot—but to Shaneel, it felt like a thousand.

The saving hand belongs to Amith, who had made his way down to help Shaneel, to stand at his side, to be his hero, which in this moment he is. The hands of the two boys lock—two beings of the same nature connected to each other through sheer will. Right now, they both need each other and have something on the line: Shaneel for the life he was about to lose in a fatal fall, and Amith for the brotherhood of a childhood friend.

Amith grits his teeth and his face strains as he pulls Shaneel up onto the top crate, and Shaneel breathes a sigh of relief. Amith looks at him with a smile and mutters, "You're getting fat," and gives him a wicked grin before scrambling up the wall once again, like a spider returning to its nest. Shaneel looks up the wall again, but this time Amith reaches down to help Shaneel up. Shaneel smiles as he grabs his friend's hand.

The two boys sit on the top of the wall with legs dangling as they stare out at the other side, at the once grand theatre.

CHAPTER 6

Where Dreams Are Made

THE MOVIE THEATRE, if it can be called that, is more like a place of broken dreams. The quaint little open-seated theatre is arranged in auditorium-like fashion. At the back, the seats are nestled in rows that curve in a half circle. The last row of seats backs up to a large, crumbly wall that is supposed to offer privacy. In front hangs the only screen, a gigantic, tattered white canvas where the pictures are "painted" across its patched surface. All the visions are brought to life by a noisy projector , sitting in the center of the theatre where a section of seats have been removed, that serves up a palette of fantasies for the audience. Next to the screen is an office where the films are stored.

Much like the alley, this place is a relic of lost prosperity—but that wasn't always the case. When movies were first introduced to India, they quickly became a sensation that spread like wildfire. And the rise of the film industry brought many riches to the country, as more and more movies started coming out. Musicals and the Bollywood phenomena hit the screens and captured the hearts of the people. The desire to see these movies created a fever that spread all across India, even to poor villages such as this.

A wealthy man who saw the potential in movies built this outdoor theatre—majestic for the times—trying to make money while the demand was high. It was the pearl of the village for many years, but most of the people were so poor they barely had enough to eat. They couldn't pay for tickets to watch the movies, and the theatre suffered. It slowly fell into ruin—seats broke down and screens tore. The theatre owner had no money to fix it. With the changing times, the theatre barely earned a few rupees, so finally the owner sold it off in trade for a few goats and a sack of rice for his family. Once a wealthy man of great ambition, he now walks the land a broken man, a man who has drifted into obscurity.

Today, the theatre is just a shell of its original splendor. Once a week forgotten movies are played on its single screen, usually ones that have been passed from theatre to theatre until finally reaching this quaint unknown village. Some weeks it repeats the movies. Luckily for Amith and Shaneel, this is not one of those weeks.

The boys sit with radiant smiles as the distorted opening music of the film hits the tiny speakers twice as loudly as they can handle. Then gunfire blazes across the screen as the title appears. The two boys look at the title in anticipation, waiting for what they hoped it would be. When the first cowboy appears, the boys cheer loudly.

It's a Western, their favorite kind of movie, and it's an American one—even better!

The first movie the boys ever saw from their perched seats was an American Western. They had discovered this run-down, open-seated theatre by accident one day while daring each other to climb higher and higher up the crates. Most people wouldn't consider it worthwhile to watch a movie in this poor excuse for a theatre, for the wall is too high and the screen half covered by the awning that protects it from the sun. But the boys don't care. To them, this is paradise, and their high seats on top of the wall are their skybox. If only they had popcorn, they would never leave.

The boys marvel as cowboys and Indians gallop across the screen, in scene after scene. Sitting quietly, they try to make sense of the action. They listen intently for the words they don't know and repeat the ones they do with excitement, using the broken English that has been passed down from other villagers who've encountered American tourists.

But in reality, it doesn't matter what is being said. It's all the same story to the boys: a hero versus a villain, and the hero always wins. It's a story where the hero overcomes overwhelming odds and comes out on top. To them, it's about vanquishing "bad men," as the boys put it, and "saving the day" in dramatic fashion. This is what the boys aspire to achieve—to attain a moment of glory so great that it affects the lives of all the people around them; to make something great of themselves when they are, in fact, insignificant and may never be known to the world. The boys don't understand the deepness of these thoughts for they are just children. But still, a yearning lives within them, a yearning that is the reason they sit here and dream. They dream with open eyes for a possibility that can never be, for how can two poor boys in an unknown village accomplish anything of significance, any act of heroism, any act to be noticed?

As the film progresses, the two boys become enthralled by the heroes on the screen. The story plays out like it always does: The hero finds a reason to fight, the cowboys go after the villain, the villain goes after the cowboys, and a few of them die, but the hero never does. Instead, he gets up, dusts himself off, defeats the villain, and rides off into the sunset with a damsel in hand—the perfect story. The boys watch with their jaws hanging open, their hands clenched in excitement, and their unblinking eyes fixed on

26

the dream playing out in front of them. They watch and watch until the projector whirs to a full stop.

Then the boys look at each other with a sigh of complete satisfaction, as if they had just eaten a large meal. Yup, it was a good movie. It always is when you're with your best friend. They smile at each other and think, if only it could stay this way forever.

CHAPTER 7

Showdown

HERO TRAINING TIP #3

"A hero thinks of others before himself."

~Amith

THE SETTING IS A WESTERN TOWN, *one filled with old saloon buildings and taverns. The air is musky and usually thick with the fumes of gunfire, but today the town is empty. There's an eerie silence, like before some big event—a showdown!*

Through the musky air, a man appears—dressed in full cowboy gear oddly similar to the western heroes that Amith and Shaneel just watched in the film. The lone dark figure walks slowly down the dusty road, his long coat grazing the ground and red scarf blowing in the wind.

The faces of the townsfolk disappear behind closed curtains and shuttered windows, only their eyes are showing as they watch the red-scarfed man. As he leans against the saloon wall, he holds a gleaming silver revolver, just like the one the boys saw in the movie. He pops open the six-bullet rolling cylinder and reaches into his pocket.

Amith stands near a large log, leaning against it. He wears a banana leaf fashioned into a hat and has rubbed some dirt on his upper lip to resemble a mustache like the hero wore in the movie.

He wields the stick in his hand like a gun and finds some pebbles to be bullets.

The red-scarfed man takes a handful of bullets from his pocket and places them, one by one, into the six chambers of the cylinder. When he places the final bullet into the cylinder, he snaps it shut and whirls the cylinder with two of his fingers. It purrs in his hand. The red-scarfed man stops it, and cocks the gun; the bullet enters the firing chamber. He raises his head and glares out at his surroundings from just under the brim of his hat.

Amith starts strutting like a cowboy down the edge of the road, his legs moving wide and heavy, as if he is wearing spurs. He walks past the tree he used as a saloon wall. He looks around at his surroundings, searching for something, but nothing comes to him. He sees only the dense forest trees that line the road. They just stand there, gently blowing in the wind. Amith thinks he should go in there and check, but he knows that area has always been off limits. He's not supposed to go in there. From what everyone has told him, it could be dangerous. Then again, Amith rarely listens to what he's told.

Amith starts walking toward the trees. Suddenly a pebble flashes by from behind him over his right shoulder and stops him in his tracks. Amith retreats behind the large tree.

The red-scarfed man shifts his left shoulder against the saloon wall and sneaks a peek around the corner. Another bullet flashes by, making him retreat quickly, but he could see that the bullets are coming from another mustachioed man standing with a revolver much like the one in the movie and much like the one the red-scarfed man is wielding.

Shaneel stands across the road with a handful of pebbles in his hand. He too wears a silly dirt spot on his upper lip representing the mustache worn by the hero on the big screen. It looks terribly goofy, especially with the folded banana leaf on his head, but Shaneel is in full-blown character mode, his eyes are stern and his "pebble finger" is ready for the shot.

The second mustachioed man looks down the barrel of his gun and yells in his broken English, "Put hands up, varmint!" to the red-scarfed man.

Amith yells back in his equally broken English, "Never! You are the varmint. I am the hero!" Amith quickly glances around the corner, only to be nearly grazed by another pebble. He ducks back.

"If you're the hero, why am I winning?" Shaneel shouts. "The bad guy never wins. Remember?" Shaneel mocks Amith by waving the stick he pretends is a gun at Amith's location.

Amith thinks about this for a moment. There is truth to Shaneel's words, a truth that Amith must change, but how?

Amith sets his feet in place, ready for his next move. He leans back on his right leg. At the same time, Shaneel circles outward to get a better view of Amith. With a powerful thrust of his right foot, Amith launches himself into the air, tumbling to the ground as gracefully as an expert acrobat.

The second mustachioed man fires at the tumbling red-scarfed man but misses with both of his quick shots. The red-scarfed man disappears behind another small wooden building and quickly regains his footing. He pauses. Sunlight shines through his hat into his eyes. The red-scarfed man takes his hat off and examines it; there are two holes in it.

"I almost got you," Shaneel calls out. "I told you: today, I'm going to be the hero."

Amith stares at the holes in his banana leaf hat with troubled eyes. "No, you're not," he argues, as he sits there in childlike frustration. Amith kicks a rock on the ground. It goes bouncing across the field, kicking up dust as it rolls—and sparking an idea. Amith grabs a few more rocks from the ground, bigger ones this time.

Meanwhile, Shaneel starts creeping closer. He is so close, right behind the large tree and ready to pounce. A smirk crosses his dirt-mustachioed face as he readies his pretend gun to take the win. He quickly spins around the corner and points the gun, ready to catch Amith unprepared.

But Amith has vanished! Where is he hiding? A rock that flies at him answers that question. Shaneel quickly dodges it, and it strikes the tree.

Soon a rock whizzes past; the second mustachioed man spins around and shoots it out of the sky with his revolver. He looks at the spot where it came from and for the first time sees his opponent: a man who looks just like him, right down to the same silly mustache. Everything is the same except for the red scarf, that infernal red scarf.

It's a classic showdown, like the ones the boys wait to see in all the movies—the finale, the big bang that is the masterpiece of cinema. Today, the boys will have one of their own.

They stand still, ready to pounce, ready to make a move, but Shaneel hesitates. He knows that Amith is up to something. They've played this game a thousand times and Shaneel always comes out the loser. But he is determined today, because this day will be different; this day Shaneel will be the hero and Amith finally the bad guy.

31

Shaneel suddenly crouches, his stick-gun still drawn. Amith gives a smirk. No, that's what he wants, Shaneel thinks. Quickly, Shaneel starts to back off.

Amith just stands there, watching Shaneel try to think of the right move. All the while, Amith playfully throws a rock up and down in the air with his free hand, helping build Shaneel's anxiety.

"Lucky shot, partner," Amith taunts Shaneel, breaking the tension. Shaneel starts to relax.

"Oh, yeah?" Shaneel responds, as he wildly points his pretend gun at Amith.

"Yup. I bet you can't do that again," Amith insists, while throwing the rock higher and higher in the air.

"Yes, I can," Shaneel shouts, eyeing the rock.

"*Okay, let's see,*" *the red-scarfed man says and puts his gun into his holster, smirking.* "*You wouldn't shoot an unarmed man, would you?*" *He raises his eyebrows up and down mockingly.* "*Not very honorable for a hero.*"

"Hey, that's not fair," Shaneel yells. "Draw your weapon, and let's finish this. I'm almost winning."

"*Sure, on one condition,*" *the red-scarfed man says.* "*I want to see you shoot a rock in midair again.*"

This is the moment that Amith has been waiting for. He has thrown out a challenge to Shaneel, and Amith knows him all too well. If Amith says that Shaneel can't do something, it only drives Shaneel to try to do whatever he can to do it. Amith realizes that this is the moment for him to take the upper hand.

The reverse psychology starts playing its trick. Thoughts of grandeur and winning in a heroic fashion cloud Shaneel's mind. In this moment, Shaneel must decide—either he takes out an unarmed man as only a villain would do, or he accepts the challenge. And heroes always accept challenges. This is the moment when Shaneel's true nature is put to the test, and Amith knows Shaneel's true nature.

"Okay, but don't try anything. I'll show you I can do it," Shaneel asserts with confidence.

And this is also the beginning of the end of Shaneel's chances for winning. Each time they play heroes, as soon as Shaneel gets the upper hand, Amith thinks of some shrewd way to turn it around, even if at times it's more devious than heroic.

The red scarfed-man grins mockingly and throws the rock sky high. As the rock travels into the sky once more, the second mustachioed man glares at it and with lightning speed, he flashes a shot. The only thing that returns to the ground is dust from the obliterated rock. The red-scarfed man stands there in awe.

"Told you! I'm a faster shot than you, varmint!" Shaneel spits out as he quickly points his stick revolver back at Amith.

Amith starts to show that conniving little grin that he always does when he is about to win. Shaneel begins to worry, knowing that something just happened and the future just became bleak.

"Yeah, but you have one problem," Amith taunts.

"What?" Shaneel inquires, his gun still drawn, unsure of his misstep, waiting, but knowing the inevitable outcome.

"You're out of bullets, varmint," Amith boasts with a ghastly smirk.

A look of shock comes over Shaneel's face as he stares at his six-shooter revolver, just like the one the hero used in the story. Shot one: Amith behind the tree. A miss. Shot two: Amith peers to see Shaneel. Another miss. Shots three and four: Amith jumps out from behind the tree. Shot five: The shot that blasted the rock out of the air, triggering Amith's plan. And the final, sixth shot, the one that Shaneel just gave up to Amith because of his word.

Suddenly, a rock glances off the stick, knocking it out of his hand—and knocking Shaneel down in surprise.

Amith slowly struts up to Shaneel, his fake gun drawn.

"I told you that you were the varmint," Amith boasts as he steps over Shaneel, who is still lying on the ground.

The red-scarfed man pushes the barrel of his gun into the mustachioed man's chest and demands, "Say it."

Shaneel and the mustachioed man in his fantasy both turn their heads away in unison and reluctantly respond with a sigh at the same time: "I am the varmint."

"And who is the hero?" Amith asks teasingly.

"You are the . . ." Shaneel starts to say, but before he can finish, a dark figure tackles Amith to the ground and breaks up the boys' Western fantasy.

The boys are back in the real world of dirt roads, tree stumps, and discarded logs—not their make-believe Western world. Shaneel lies on a dry patch of grass near the road, his face and hands covered with as much dirt as the silly mustache he painted on. A few feet away lies Amith, also just as filthy as Shaneel. Standing triumphantly above him is a six-year-old girl.

"I am Karishma, queen of the Amazons!" she announces to the heavens, and then points to Amith with sureness in her voice, "and YOU are my husband."

CHAPTER 8

Karishma

HERO TRAINING TIP #4

"A hero is nice to others."

~Amith

JUST MOMENTS BEFORE, Karishma had been in her room, inside her family's nice small home. Karishma is a vibrant girl, full of life and determination. She is small framed and stands at a height of three-feet-awesome. Her hair is as frizzled and wild as her intense personality; she is always fast to act and think later. Her features are soft and doll-like, making even her temper tantrums seem cute; of course, this only triggers more anger, for what's more irritating than to have someone pinch your cheek when you're mad?

Just moments before, she had stood in front of a mirror and tried to destroy the careful styling her mom had so diligently done to her hair. Karishma hated it; she even hated her nice clothes. Instead, she wanted to wear clothes that were old and torn. Nice things weren't what she wanted. And she wanted to be around someone as rough and tough as her, someone like her dreamy little Amith who was rugged and handsome, and untamable, just like her.

And then, while at war with her own hair, she had heard the two boys playing outside. Amith and Shaneel ran past her house and down the streets of the village, playing cowboys. It looked like fun and Karishma wanted in, so she found a way. She had watched and waited for the right opportunity, and then made her surprising entrance.

Amith squirms away in disgust from under Karishma's feet and scurries to Shaneel's side.

"You can't play with us," Amith shouts.

"Why not?" Karishma asks Amith with cute but angry eyes.

"Because . . ." Amith replies, trying to come up with an excuse.

Karishma turns to Shaneel with the same look. Shaneel smiles shyly—he is never comfortable around girls, especially cute ones.

Amith becomes agitated and blurts out, "Because you're a girl, and girls don't know how to play!"

The words hurt Karishma, but instead of responding from the pain, she responds the best way she knows how: she fights back with anger.

"Yes, we do!" she snaps.

"No, you don't," Amith snaps back.

They stand there arguing with each other—face to face, going back and forth, saying yes and no—until finally Shaneel is forced to jump in.

"We're playing cowboys," Shaneel explains in a calm voice.

Karishma is quiet for a moment, thinking about this before deciding what to do.

"Fine. I'll be the cowboy queen . . ." Karishma replies, once again pointing at Amith, ". . . and you are my cowboy husband."

Amith, shocked at the response, stumbles back. "No, that isn't it at all. See! You don't know how to play."

"Come on, Amith. Maybe we should let her play," Shaneel pleads, trying to put an end to the conflict.

Amith thinks about it for a moment. He's outnumbered two against one. If he decides not to let her play, maybe Shaneel won't play either. Then he would be bored all evening, and evenings can be pretty long in their village. And what if he does let her play? Well, she might just win! Who will be the hero then? It's a dilemma with only one option left.

"Fine," Amith blurts out, and then the mischievous smirk follows. "If you can catch us."

Amith bolts off, leaving Karishma and Shaneel in the dust. Shaneel looks at Amith and then Karishma. It's a tough choice, with only seconds left before Amith disappears. Does he do the right thing and stand by Karishma, or does he follow his best friend to the bitter end? With a remorseful look, Shaneel utters "Sorry," and chases after Amith.

Amith's mastermind plan is in full effect. Now, the only choice for Karishma is to go home or to lose by not being able to keep up with the faster boys. But this is Karishma, and running away from a challenge is not what she does, instead she runs at it, and so she does once again. Karishma takes pursuit.

CHAPTER 9

The Beach

*"Psychic powers are a very effective way
to vanquish evildoers."*

~Amith

IT'S A NEW DAY, Amith thinks to himself, as he rolls himself awake. He sits up with his legs folded underneath him and rubs his eyes. The room is filled with waves of sound from his mom sweeping the ground with a broom made of sticks woven together. It sounds like the ocean slowly cleaning the shores for a new day.

Amith's eyes blur as he takes a deep yawn, muffling all sound for a moment. Then his ears pop and fill with the whooshing sound of the broom again. His eyes water for a second, but he rubs them clean.

He watches as his mom stops sweeping and puts something in the basket on the wall—their version of a laundry hamper. On the table, Amith sees his carefully folded shirt, a shirt that he only wears for special occasions. It's his only one, so he is forced to take great care of it. Besides, it's more pleasant to feel the warm sun directly on his skin without any interruption from a barrier such as a shirt. At least, that's his excuse and he sticks with it.

His mom returns to sweeping again but she's almost done. The ground is made of dense dirt and dried clay, but it does get dusty, and on those rare days when the wind blows hard, the dust gets into everything. A whole day can be spent at the river just cleaning the dust out of their sheets.

Amith's mom stops for a few moments and takes a deep breath as if she's winded, and then continues sweeping. He notices something different about her today; she looks tired and her face is covered with sweat. She must have been working very hard, he thinks. Then suddenly some magical force compels Amith's mom to turn her head and give Amith that empowering smile of hers, as if she knew he was concerned about her. Amazing, he thinks. Another talent she possesses—she can read minds. Wow!

"Bête," she says, her broom still keeping its rhythm, "today is an important day. Get ready."

So Amith does. It's at these moments, when his mom's voice is full of seriousness, that he does anything she asks without objection. Could be another power, maybe mind control? Amith starts to wonder if, of all the great powers she possesses, some must have passed down to him somehow. After all, he is her only son.

A moment passes as Amith ponders the idea. Cool, he thinks. Then Amith starts squinting real hard, trying to trigger any latent psychic abilities . . . but nothing happens, at least not yet. His mom must have had years of training under a special master, but he must find out soon so he can add it to his hero training.

Before he knows it, he's dressed and ready to go. Amith's mom waits for him at the door as he finishes up. She opens it, and they head down to the beach together.

¤　¤　¤　¤　¤

The sun gets swallowed into the depths of the sea, as a group of villagers stand praying near the water's edge. They wear pure white ceremonial gowns that flow with the breath of each breeze.

Amith and his mom stand with some of the other villagers that have gathered around. The two wear the finest clothes of the ever-poor. Amith's mom's head is covered with a white shawl, and the rest of her body is wrapped in a plain white sari worn in the most modest of fashions. Amith stands next to her in his neatly tucked-in shirt; his ragged shorts unfortunately never stay clean for very long.

Amith spent the whole trip here trying to trigger his mental powers but with no success. Now he grows restless. He impatiently pulls on his mom's sari, but she's in full prayer and it's impossible to break her concentration. Maybe he can untuck his shirt while she's distracted, maybe he can get away with being a little naughty as well as comfortable. He starts tugging at it.

"Stop it," Amith's mom mutters without even glancing at Amith.

Whoa! How did she know? Her power must be strongest near the water, he thinks. He must really work on perfecting his mental capabilities to match his mom's. Then they can be mind-reading gurus and travel the world, predicting the next catastrophic event. He imagines what they'd say to the people: "Wait! There's an avalanche going to happen—nobody go up the mountain. Stop! There's a deadly trap ahead with a thousand warriors who will kill you if you go any further—go tomorrow. Hold on! You will get a stomachache if you eat that." Amith smiles while he plays with these ideas in his head.

An old man dressed in orange garments starts walking toward them. He's bald and wears strange, oversized beads around his neck. He is barefoot like the others, but his frail body barely leaves footprints in the sand. This must be the master; he must know kung fu like in the movies. All the masters do.

The elderly man walks slowly past them. Amith feels disappointment that the master did not recognize him, the chosen one, and announce Amith's significance to the world.

Instead, the elderly man continues up the path to finally stand near a very large bed of woven branches. He pauses there and looks around at the gathered crowd. He must be putting on a show, Amith thinks. The man then starts to speak in a strange language that Amith cannot understand. This must be the ultimate power chant of heroes. Amith senses that it's almost time, so he stands up straight, takes in a deep breath, and puffs out his chest, ready for the anointing of psychic abilities.

"Bête," Amith's mom says, looking straight at him. Her gaze strikes him right in the stomach, bypassing all his armor and weakening him into behaving. Wow! She's very powerful indeed.

Suddenly a woman runs up to the orange-garbed man. She's crying hysterically. An elderly woman with her tries to pull her away from the bed of branches that lies near the water, but she only succeeds in keeping the other woman from moving forward. Then a man steps up to help.

They all look alike, Amith notices. They must be the competition, and Amith bets that they train together. With their combined efforts, they pull the woman back, yet she still reaches out to the bed of branches, as if calling to it with her arms. But it doesn't move. She needs to train more, Amith assumes.

The orange-garbed man says his final verses in the strange, mystic language, sprinkles rice and incense on the bed of sticks, and then throws rose petals and says a few more words. Rice, incense, flowers—got it, thinks Amith. Awesome psychic mental powers, here I come. Shaneel's going to be so jealous.

The elderly man pulls up a branch that looks a little different from the others. One end is covered with a black rag, and a dark liquid drips from it, leaving dark, oily spots in the sand. The smell from the rag fills the air. It's foul, and very, very strong, almost nauseating. Amith scrapes his tongue on his teeth, trying to get rid of the taste. Yuck!

Another man comes up to the orange-garbed man; he holds something near the branch. The flicker of a spark triggers the rag, and it bursts into a small flame. Almost in unison, the gathered people start to wail.

Why is everyone so sad? It should be a time for celebration— Amith is about to save all of them, he thinks. The orange-garbed man lowers the flaming branch onto the woven wooden bed. The fire quickly dances along the top, engulfing the surface in fire.

The woman with the outreached arms finally collapses onto the ground in tears. The crowd begins to hold onto one another, and Amith's mom grips onto Amith's hand tightly.

Amith looks up at his mom and sees that her eyes are filled with tears. Why is she so sad? It's just a bed of branches.

Amith looks again, trying to see through the flames that have spread over the bed of woven branches. Then with terror he makes out a man's lifeless body inside the burning pyre. He feels the blood rush from his face, and he clenches his mom's leg.

She pulls him close and then crouches down to Amith, locking his eyes with hers. Normally these dark brown eyes can penetrate the deepest of Amith's fears and beckon him to confess his crimes, but today, they are not full of discipline. Today, they are filled with pure sadness.

"Bête," she says to him in a calming voice, "don't be afraid. There is no fear from dying. The good deeds that you do in your life are what makes you live forever in the hearts of others. And even if you fail when you try your hardest, at least you tried. Okay?"

The words pierce Amith to his very core, yet he doesn't fully understand their meaning. This is the first time his mom has ever talked about failing; Amith doesn't understand her meaning, but he nods his head in agreement.

Then all that fear is wiped away as his mom reveals her smile, that ever-powerful smile with those teary eyes that give Amith infinite strength. She then kisses him on his forehead and stands up; Amith stands quietly next to her, watching the cremation.

The two listen as the shaman finishes his Sanskrit prayers and anoints the burning wooden pyre. The crowd mourns deeply as the funeral fire burns slowly, its ashes traveling into the approaching night sky.

CHAPTER 10

The Vendor

HERO TRAINING TIP #6

"A hero never lets fear stop him from doing anything."

~Amith

THE MUD IN THE STREET FEELS SLICK. The air is damp and musty, and seeps through the walls of the shabby buildings along the street. Yet this place is full of life today. It's a special day for this stale place; today is market day.

People toil endlessly at their menial tasks, getting ready to sell their wares. Poor excuses for shops appear along the road. Most of them are no more than a three-sided stand with pictures carved into the wood to serve as the store's sign. Some don't even have that, because many of the shopkeepers are illiterate. The items for sale range from dried meat to hand-carved statues of various animals. The merchants call out their bargains in desperation to the people passing by. Men saddle themselves with carts, pulling everything from goods to people about the shops. Their weary bare feet leave beaten footprints in the dirt as the rich ride on the encumbered backs of the poor. All the while, the sick and dying lie in the streets, begging for a little morsel of food.

Carefree Amith and Shaneel walk side-by-side through the poor-ridden streets. They have a look of astonishment on their faces from the movie they just watched while sitting on top of the alley wall.

"Did you see that? It was amazing!" Shaneel says.

"I'm going to be a hero just like Chuck Norris!" Amith says loudly as he stretches his hands into the air, punching the sky and ending with a karate kick combo on the ground.

The commotion attracts a nearby street vendor's attention. He quickly shoves his hand out in their direction, surprising the boys. In it he is holding a rather large jaguar tooth.

"If you want to be a hero, you're going to need this," the vendor shouts.

The boys exchange looks, but then are drawn in by the merchant's sneaky sales pitch.

"The finest merchandise brought from the deep jungle depths, all the way from the lost temple of Dhanvantari," the vendor continues, moving his hand in a way that guides the boys' eyes over his table of goods. On the table, carved bone figurines of monks, shamans, and elephants with their tusks raised—symbolizing wealth—are on display.

None of the carvings or statuettes are of any interest to Amith, but something else has his attention. The vendor's merchandise rests on top of an embroidered cloth that hangs off the side of the table. On the cloth, a picture of a large jaguar with two pure black eyes stares out at Amith.

There is something drastically real about this image to Amith; the eyes hold him spellbound and muffle the sound of the vendor's voice. The deep blackness of the eyes resembles those in Amith's dreams, of the always-encroaching terror from the pitch black sky that draws near. Amith takes a few steps back in alarm, unsure of what to do.

"What's the matter, boy?"

Amith has no response.

"Are you okay, Amith?" Shaneel asks with concern.

Amith feels like fainting as the ground starts to spin. His heart beats as though he had just run a marathon. He feels sick, but he can't move. He is frozen in place, and the whole time his eyes never escape the lock of the jaguar's gaze.

"It's just a picture, boy," the vendor says to Amith, noticing the boy's uneasiness.

Shaneel grabs Amith and shakes him with alarm. "Amith!" he yells.

The jolt snaps Amith out of it, as if waking from a deep sleep. Shaneel looks on with concern, his eyes focused on Amith.

Amith looks at the vendor and then Shaneel. Then Amith runs.

🐾

CHAPTER 11

A Promise

THE SMELL OF INCENSE IS VERY STRONG — that's the thought that pops into Amith's mind. It's a unique, pungent aroma that is hard to replicate with anything else. The tiny deity statuettes of various gods sit in the little shrine, in the corner inside their little hut. Amith and his mom sit, each with their palms joined in front of them. His mom is busy with her silent prayers, probably never asking for anything, but thanking God for helping her make it through the day.

Rheka is completely focused on the statuettes she prays to with sheer devotion. Just like his mom, Amith has a focus, but it's on something else. His focus is entirely on his mom. To Amith, it's amazing to see a woman so wronged by the world have so much faith in God. They don't have anything, yet here she sits, thanking God for what little they do have. Amith sits silently wondering, looking around at the dirt floors, the walls made of mud and sticks, a roof made of tin sheets that leak in the heavy rains, and a fire-pit stove that barely keeps them warm during cold nights such as this. He doesn't see anything of importance or wealth. What is she so thankful for?

Rheka finishes her prayer by ringing a small bell near the altar. She looks over at Amith, sitting silently with his legs crossed like hers, his palms joined lying in his lap, waiting in boredom. She pulls him close and gives him a kiss on his forehead, but it doesn't help. Amith is still bored, and she knows it.

"Well, let's see if this will cheer you up," she says. She reaches for a laddoo—an Indian sweet—and feeds it to Amith.

He opens his mouth enthusiastically. The sweet instantly liquefies, releasing its sugars inside his mouth at the same rate that the smile grows on his face. Pretty soon, Amith is grinning from ear to ear.

"I knew that would do it," his mom says as she picks him up and carries him to his bed. Amith lies quietly as she gently tucks him in. Then she sits next to him, seeing how much he has grown. She smiles proudly.

"Ma?" Amith says.

"Yes, Bête."

"Why do you pray?"

Rheka sits back, startled from the unexpected question. There is a moment of silence as she wonders how to answer him. When she finally does, she says, "Bête, you can lose everything, but you can never lose prayer."

There is a silence as Amith thinks about the answer, then he says, "Yeah, I know, but why do you thank God?"

There is another pause from Rheka as she searches for the correct answer to his tough question. "Because I have a lot that I'm thankful for," she finally answers.

"But we don't have anything," Amith argues.

"I have you."

Amith smiles at the answer. She, in return, kisses him on his forehead. "And I would thank a thousand gods and say a thousand prayers just to give thanks for having you," she says as she rubs his nose with hers.

Amith smiles broadly once again and closes his eyes, satisfied with the response. As they sit there, Rheka watches her son in silence, waiting for him to fall asleep.

"Ma, I'm going to be hero," he proclaims, as if destiny itself had said it.

"I know, Bête, and you will be an excellent hero and save many people," she says encouragingly.

Amith slowly drifts into sleep. "I know who I'm going to save, Ma," he says, yawning.

"Who?" she asks.

"You."

Rheka sits there in silence, awe-stricken by his words.

"I'm going to save you from this life, Ma. I'm going to give you a better one . . ." he mutters as he drifts further and further into sleep, ". . . the best one, the . . . one . . . you deserve."

Rheka sits there quietly.

Amith is sound asleep.

A tear forms and rolls down Rheka's cheek. She tries so hard to hide the cruelty of the world and the situation they are in from Amith, and now she realizes that she has failed. Amith has seen through all the ruses, all the clever ways that Rheka has tried to hide it all from him—the tragedy, the hunger and the sickness, the death looming at the door, the fear of uncertainty, and all the other hardships of the poor.

He has seen it all, but still he isn't angry for the situation they are in. He doesn't hate her for not being able to give him everything that he wants. Instead, he wants to give her everything.

CHAPTER 12

Ninjas and Space Marines

HERO TRAINING TIP #7

"A hero is never greedy."

~Amith

THERE ARE THOUSANDS OF THEM, *and Amith and Shaneel are completely surrounded. The exits are blocked and the only thing to do is to fight or die. There is little hope that they will make it out of this alive, but they must survive—they must survive for all of mankind.*

"You will not win, alien!" Amith yells at some broken sticks that are leaning against the alley wall. Three pieces are splinted to each side, and Amith imagines them as arms of the alien. "I will not let you enslave all of mankind!" he continues.

"They're getting closer!" Shaneel yells to Amith, while pointing his hand like a gun at a puddle of muddy water.

The three-armed alien—tall, green, and mean—stands towering over the boys. Its three arms stretch all the way to the ground and its fingernails curve in like the talons of an eagle. Its gaping mouth stretches halfway down to his chest, ready to take a bite with its razor-sharp teeth. The alien monster slowly opens and closes its clawed hand, beckoning them to attack and mocking the two heroes known as Space Amith and Space Shaneel.

A *few yards away, Space Amith stands ready, his ninja laser sword vibrating in his hand. A few steps back, Space Shaneel points a ray gun at an alien of gelatinous ooze that slithers closer and closer.*

The three-armed alien monster steps back at the sight of Amith's laser sword. It yells something in its alien tongue. Soon, the troopers that were waiting behind it start coming forward in an unstoppable charge.

"You can't beat me, alien. I am the hero!" Amith taunts.

"We will save all of mankind!" Shaneel yells in support.

The three-armed alien monster laughs its alien laugh, deafening to the ears of men. Then it motions forward with one arm, initiating the alien blitz.

"We have to get out of here, Amith," Shaneel yells as he fires a shot at the advancing alien ooze, blasting it into two separate pieces. The pieces of ooze begin to glow a neon green and then become two complete alien oozes.

"Heroes don't run, Shaneel. We will fight!" Amith yells as he runs forward, using his sword to slash his way through the charge of a thousand alien monsters. He runs past the last monster and leaps into the air, his sword aimed straight at the three-armed alien commander. The alien commander's jaw drops in surprise at Space Amith's awesome ninja might.

Amith runs down the gravel-filled road, grabs the three sticks from the wall, and hurls them down to the ground with great showmanship.

The three-armed alien commander shrieks and falls to the ground as Space Amith's sword goes through its torso.

Amith lets out a monstrous roar, pounding his chest in victory. An alley cat, curious about the commotion, wanders around the corner.

"Look! An innocent bystander!" Amith screams, pointing at the cat.

"We will save you, innocent bystander!" Shaneel yells at the cat, while kicking dirt into the puddle that is supposed to be the alien ooze.

The cat shrieks, its tail standing up in shock and confusion. The poor cat doesn't understand that it is no longer a cat. Today, it is an innocent bystander, whether it likes it or not. Today, it has become part of the boys' game, and its part is to be saved—and what better person to save an innocent bystander than a hero.

Amith tumbles toward the cat so quickly it doesn't have time to escape. He scoops up the cat in his arms and carries it to a nearby crate. Amith pulls himself up the side of the crate, with the cat in his hand. Once on top of the crate, Amith seats himself. But the cat jumps off and hides behind the crate.

"Shaneel! Let's go before the super space bomb goes off," Amith screams.

"Right!" Shaneel yells back and turns around to blast his jetpack into the ground, vaporizing the last remaining alien ooze into smoke.

"Good thinking," Amith congratulates Shaneel as he makes his way inside the spaceship's cockpit.

"Thanks," Shaneel says as he settles into his co-pilot seat.

They check their gear and all the dials—they are all set to go, and it's time to take off.

"Are you ready?" Amith yells.

"Let's go, Amith!" Shaneel responds.

"Meow?" says the innocent bystander.

The spaceship fires its thrusters violently into the ground, kicking up a large cloud of smoke and debris, as they try to escape the planet's atmosphere. Below, the alien planet implodes and then turns into a supernova. The blast radius flames up, trying to grab the spaceship with its fiery fingertips. It almost catches the spaceship, but finally loses the chase at the last moment.

Amith and Shaneel shake the crate they are seated on, as their make-believe spaceship rockets through space. They rock left and right, pretending that they're dodging meteors, all the while imitating rocketing sounds.

"We made it!" Shaneel yells in excitement and throwing his hands up in the air.

"Yes, we did . . . barely," Amith says gravely, his mind on something else.

Today both boys won. They share the glory of the victory. That means there are two heroes who equally saved humanity. But wait! Two heroes means two victors, and whatever great treasure is bestowed upon them will have to be split between them. This is the dilemma Amith ponders.

"Wait! There's an alien monster on board!" Amith yells out in panic.

"Where?" Shaneel yells in terror, searching the crate for any sign of a monster.

"You!" Amith yells as he pushes Shaneel off the crate and onto the ground.

Amith sits on top of Shaneel in conquering victory; he'd completely blindsided him again.

"Who's the hero?" Amith asks, seated on Shaneel's chest.

"You are . . . the hero." Shaneel responds by pushing Amith off him, getting up, and dusting himself off. "I have to go," Shaneel says and walks off.

CHAPTER 13

Those in Need

HERO TRAINING TIP #8

"A hero helps those in need."

~Amith

THE BEGGAR SEEMS CLOSE TO DEATH. His eyes are hollowed and his skin is almost transparent from the lack of fat in his system. His bony rib cage protrudes so much that it looks like you could almost put your hand completely around each rib.

He doesn't have the strength to speak or even ask for help. His hunger is so great, his skin hurts. He just sits there sulking, his head down and his chin resting on his chest. His eyes are squinted, fixed on something. He is staring at an ant trailing its way toward him.

The beggar puts his hand in front of the ant. As the ant slowly crawls up his hand, he lets it. He lifts his hand slowly, not letting the ant walk off. With transfixed eyes, the beggar watches as the ant creates a new route by tracing the lines on his palm. How ironic that it chooses the lifeline to follow, the beggar thinks. The ant's not going to get very far; it's a short line that ends abruptly— too bad. The beggar picks the ant up with his two fingers before it reaches the end. He stares at it, almost inspecting it for a moment, as the ant squirms between his two fingers. Then he puts the ant into his mouth. He grits his teeth on the tiny ant body, breaking the exoskeleton, and gulps it down. His eyes return to the street, looking for another ant, but nothing comes. He rests his head back against the wall that he has been leaning against and waits for certain death.

Amith comes walking around the corner. He munches on a piece of naan bread his mom had prepared fresh this morning. It's delicious, but he can't be bothered by that at the moment. He's thinking about why Shaneel didn't come out to play today. Was Shaneel mad that the monster got him last time? No, that couldn't be it. He should be used to losing. Wait! Does that mean Amith has to do his hero training alone? Can he be a hero without a sidekick? Although it is true that they are far stronger together than divided, a hero never falters. A hero must stand against all odds and defy all challenges with his mighty strength, even if he is alone. Amith takes a step back and puts his arm in the air, flexing his bicep at the thought.

Then he accidently bumps into the beggar.

It's a tiny bump, but it sparks life into the beggar. He slowly turns his head to see what stopped his quiet descent into oblivion. His eyes widen and fill with clarity and aliveness.

Wait! This beggar wants to play, Amith thinks. He must be bored sitting here all alone and very excited to see a young strapping hero like Amith appear. What fortune for the beggar to have a playmate bump into him today.

Amith is caught up in his thoughts and unaware of the focus of the beggar's stare: Amith's hand holding the naan bread.

Very well, the beggar and Amith shall face off, and the naan shall be the prize. It's a challenge, and heroes must oblige. But

Amith will not go easy—Amith plays hard, and he plays to win. We'll see who needs Shaneel, Amith decides.

The beggar reaches for the naan. Amith quickly dodges back. Amith holds out his naan and yells playfully, "You will not get my food, monster!"

The beggar looks confused, but he's too hungry to think. He lunges for Amith's naan again.

The well-fed Amith is too quick, and he evades the beggar's reach. Amith gets ready for another pounce but then nothing happens.

The beggar's eyes drain of the life that filled them moments before. The cruelty of the world is almost humorous, the beggar thinks, so much that if he had the strength, he would laugh. Instead, he relaxes back against the wall, moving even less than before having just expended all of his energy. The fortune-tellers were right, the beggar thinks. The lines don't lie. All his life he thought palm reading was just a way to steal money from the naïve. Now, the only thing left was the cold hard truth, that death was at his doorstep and it just started knocking.

Amith holds out the naan again, but the beggar doesn't move. He doesn't make any attempt—he just looks at the sky and the clouds that move slowly past. Amith tries again but the beggar doesn't do anything.

Hmm, I must be stronger than I think, Amith decides, and victorious once again.

"Who's the hero?" he asks himself.

"I'm the hero!" he announces in celebration. Then Amith skips off in triumphant conquest.

The beggar continues to look at the passing clouds. His eyes aren't fixed on anything except the light. He whispers something with the last strength he has, "Ma-duth." *Help* in Hindi. But the streets are empty, and no one is there to hear his request. All is silent. The clouds slowly move past but the beggar's eyes stay fixed, fixed on a lost hope, fixed on the emptiness of the sky, until his eyes too are empty.

CHAPTER 14

The Mystery of the Fake Monks

IT'S JUST ANOTHER DAY, and the sun's beauty shines all over the village. Amith's mom is out working in the rice paddy fields, Shaneel's parents are at their little store. The two boys are free. There isn't an adult in sight. This can only mean one thing: a perfect day for adventuring. Amith and Shaneel are already out, playing near the road again. This time, they made sure the way was clear of any sign of Karishma. After a full uninterrupted morning of playing heroes, the boys lie on their backs, exhausted, and bask in the sunshine.

"Bhā'ī (Brother), this is the life," Amith says as he smiles over at Shaneel.

"I know," Shaneel says as he rolls side to side, scratching his back.

After a while of playing what-does-that-cloud-look-like—where half of Amith's answers are his mom and half of Shaneel's answers are girls—they sit and admire the wonderful day.

"What do you want to do next?" Shaneel asks.

"I don't know. We can go into the village, or we can see how far we can go down the road before we turn back."

Amith loved to play that game, to slowly creep down the road where they were told never to go, to see how much he could bend the rule. Shaneel would always be scared, but nevertheless he would follow Amith. Shaneel might not be the bravest boy, or the most athletic, but he is loyal and always sticks by Amith, no matter how much trouble he gets in afterwards.

The two stare at the road. It travels down a long curvy path and then disappears into the jungle rather quickly. It seems very serene, but they know better. Things hide in the jungle that can swipe you away at any moment. At least that's what they've been told.

Shaneel, like a good boy, heeds those words, but Amith always felt the adults used that as an excuse to make sure nobody runs away from home. He would travel down the road tiptoeing his way farther and farther, all the while watching Shaneel squirm until he doesn't have the heart to make him suffer anymore and turns back. Regardless of Amith's antics, he really cares for Shaneel. He might not know how to show it, but he has a soft spot for his friend and worries about him in his own way.

"Nahhh," Amith says, not wanting to test Shaneel's limits today.

Shaneel lets out a relieved sigh under his breath.

"Let's go see what's going on in the village," Amith says and darts off toward the village center.

¤ ¤ ¤ ¤ ¤

In the village center, there are some locals who dress up as monks. They walk around and con the unsuspecting tourists who travel this far up the road to their village. The fake monks pretend they are from the temple of Dhanvantari, which is supposed to be an ancient temple hidden in the Arunachal Pradesh region of India, but no one has ever seen it. They weave tales and paint pictures of how glorious and holy the place is, while swindling money from the tourists by asking for donations, sometimes even resorting to pickpocketing those unbeliever-types of travelers. Tourists can rarely escape the preying hands of these swindling monks. If only Amith could prove to everyone that they are fakes, the people would be safe.

What a great mystery to solve, Amith thinks to himself with an inward smile. So, Amith walks around, squinting his eyes and hiding inconspicuously behind bushes and shrubs, all the while observing his targets, the fake monks.

Shaneel tries to keep up, unaware of Amith's ongoing fantasy.

Amith starts mumbling to himself. "What are these fake monks up to? They must be fakes." Amith suddenly stops. He juts out his jaw and starts stroking his chin as if in deep thought.

How to prove they are fakes, he thinks to himself. For one thing, the temple does not exist. The second thing Amith wonders is, why would monks need money? And the final affirming point, to hit the nail on the head, is that none of the monks here know any kung fu. And everyone knows that all monks know kung fu.

"The case is solved. They are fakes." Amith shouts, pointing into the air with his index finger. He looks over at Shaneel, who is taken off guard, and says, "Did you get that, Watson?"

"What?"

Amith breaks out of his character. "Areh yaar *(man)*, I am a Sherlock." Amith points to himself. "You are a Watson," he says and then points to Shaneel.

"Oh, yeah, got it!" Shaneel says, sporting a smile as he finally gets a clue about Amith's detective fantasy.

It's been a good morning for Shaneel. Today he didn't have to be the villain at all. Instead, he became a sidekick to the famous detective. Not exactly what he had in mind, but it sure beats playing the villain all the time.

"Okay, shall we tell the police?" Shaneel asks, getting into his sneaky detective mode.

"No, the police are corrupt. We must handle it our way." Amith sneaks up close to one of the monks. "You are a fake monk!" Amith screams loud enough for everyone in the area to hear.

The con artist is taken off guard and looks around to see where the voice is coming from. He sees Amith, standing right behind him making a face, but before he has a chance to say anything, Amith dashes down the road. Shaneel runs after him.

¤   ¤   ¤   ¤   ¤

Before long, they are in the safety of Amith's home, panting and out of breath.

"That was good," Shaneel says, happy at their heroic deed.

"Yeah, it was," Amith responds smiling, still gasping for air.

"So, what now?"

"Areh, we still have all night!" Amith says with delight, as he puts his arm around Shaneel.

The two stroll down the street together, happy at their little victory. Happy to feel like heroes, even if no one else thinks they are. Because to them it was a perfect day, for what better way to end the day than to have your best friend next to you.

CHAPTER 15

Mom

MORNING COMES, and it must be a cold one as Amith gets a chill down his spine that wakes him up. He looks over and sees his mom curled up next to him. She's still asleep with her hand over his chest, snuggling him in her arms—it's an excellent time to test his escaping skills.

Amith starts carefully moving free from her grasp, his motions fixed on not disturbing her. First, he frees his shoulder. As her hand slides off, it falls gently on the bed. Amith pauses.

Great! She's still asleep—time to move the legs. Amith slowly pulls his legs to the side of the bed, his body angled like a triangle, but his legs are free. Time to sit up and get out of this boring hut. Amith sits up and swiftly hops off the bed.

He stands ready to be shouted at to go brush his teeth before he leaves, but nothing happens. No movement, his mom is still silently asleep. He is free to run off and get into all sorts of adventure, with no brushing, maybe even no bathing. Oh, the possibilities, Amith thinks excitedly, shaking his fists in silent glory.

Seems easier today than other days. Most of the time, she spots him before he can make it to the door. She has that ability to always know where he is, or even what he's up to. It's a strange connection that can only be shared between mother and son.

It's one of the reasons why Amith never feels alone—he knows that his mom is always there, to save him, to protect him. That connection always wakes her up when he tries to sneak away in the morning. And he is always stopped and greeted with a little breakfast and a kiss on his forehead. It's a nice punishment and if it wasn't for brushing his teeth and combing his hair, Amith would gladly accept the consequences. Yet today is different, the connection doesn't seem to work. The spark doesn't make her sit up and tell him to go bathe before he heads out. Today he is free to roam.

With that final thought, Amith quickly heads to the door, but he trips. The small table slowly rocks and it would be fine, but there's a tin teapot on the edge, and the pot is about to fall.

Amith quickly lunges for it, but it's too late. The teapot lands with a clang against the hard ground. The ring from the clang vibrates through the little hut instantly. A thousand alarms couldn't be worse. Amith flinches and grasps his head, cowering from the noise.

But just as quickly, all is silent. Amith braves a peek. Nothing! His mom is still asleep. What luck! Amith heads to the door, his escape skills intact.

Amith opens the door—only one more step and he's made his getaway. But something stops Amith at the door, some magical force that tells him to turn around, calling him to his mom. Could be her mental powers, maybe they work better when she is asleep, he thinks. But the feeling is too strong to ignore, too strong to just walk away from. Amith heads back to his mom's side of the bed.

She looks pale, her lips look dry, and she's still in deep sleep.

Then the door bursts open. It's Shaneel. He stands in the doorway and says, "Come on, we don't want to be late again."

Amith starts to head out the door, but he stops again. Something is wrong, something doesn't feel right. Amith goes back to his mom's side. He holds her hand in his.

"Ma," Amith calls out to her.

His greatest nightmares cannot equal his fear in the quiet that follows. She does not respond. Amith stares at her. Is this some sort of game? Why is she not waking up? She always listens to his call. She's always there for him.

"Ma?" Amith calls again.

The silence is deafening. Shaneel stands frozen at the door.

CHAPTER 16

The Village Doctor

THE SMELL OF DISINFECTANT IS OVERPOWERING. It fills the nostrils with burning air, but at least it feels clean. The rest of the place is in much worse condition. This is no hospital or even a doctor's office, but instead a shabby little house turned into a medical clinic, and it shows. The walls are covered with splintered pieces of wood that function as shelves. Medicine vials, many empty, sit on top of them. Hospital beds line the walls in rows as soldiers' barracks would. What equipment there is looks old, handmade, and decrepit, but it's the best the poor can afford.

The village doctor is a stern man. He doesn't talk much because he's busy with his overwhelming situation. There is so much sickness in this little clinic, more than even a small hospital could handle. How is one man going to do it all?

The doctor wears small, round wire spectacles that wrap around his ears and accentuate his intelligence. Coarse white hair circles his head but is gone in the middle, maybe lost from too much thought or regret. He makes his way around, meeting with the medical helpers who attend to the patients' needs. The patients wait quietly on their cast-iron beds—some with railings, some without. Their issues range from persistent coughs to missing limbs. The thin, worn-out mattresses they lie on barely offer any comfort or protection from the broken springs beneath. But then, comfort is more than what the poor are used to.

Rheka lies on one such bed, one with no railings. It makes it easier for Amith to hold her hand while the doctor wipes her head with a wet cloth. It's hard to tell if it's sweat or water from the cloth that runs down her face. There's so much of it, but at least she's breathing.

Is this a dream? Is this another one of those nightmares that seem so real? But you eventually wake up from those. Amith wishes to wake up from this nightmare, but never does. This is his reality now, his fate, and it is, unfortunately, very real.

The only reassuring thing for Amith is that he is not alone. Shaneel is here, so are Shaneel's mom and dad. They stand in support, listening intently to the doctor's words.

"She has a very high fever," the doctor says. "The saline is not helping bring it down."

Amith stares at the saline solution IV stuck into the crease of her arm.

How can this be true? How can a woman so powerful and full of amazing abilities be put in this condition? She's unstoppable, but here she is weak, at the mercy of a merciless life. It seems impossible, but it is true.

"We need to keep her hydrated. I don't know how long before her symptoms get worse," the doctor continues.

Amith's eyes tear up. He's never cried like this before. It's something unnatural to him. He's always had his mom next to him to give him the strength to cope, so his tears were always short-lived or even sometimes nonexistent.

The doctor crouches down and looks into Amith's eyes. "Listen, Amith, I will do everything I can for your mother," he says. He's a nice man, and there's a sincerity in his eyes that makes the words extremely comforting. "But you have to be strong—not for you, but for her. Show her your strength."

Amith nods and holds back his tears. The doctor gives him a smile and pats Amith on his head, then stands up.

After the doctor examines Amith's mom, Shaneel's father talks to him. "What do you think, doctor?"

"Truthfully, I've had a few patients here in her condition," the doctor replies and then pauses before continuing, as if deciding whether to tell the truth. "It didn't go well. I'll keep her here for a week, but if her fever doesn't go down soon, we'll need a miracle to save her."

A commotion from the other patients fills the building as the double doors swing open. A patient is being wheeled in; he's badly hurt, bleeding from head to toe and clutching where his arm is missing. He is in terrible pain and tries to scream, but no sound comes out—his voice is lost. The woman beside him is crying, and much like Amith, there is fear in her eyes. "Doctor, help!" she screams.

"Stay with her, keep her cool," the doctor commands Shaneel's father before rushing to the new patient.

"What happened?" the doctor asks, as he starts lifting the injured patient onto a bed.

"Tēndu'ā!" she yells.

"In the village?"

"No, in the jungle."

"I'll do everything I can for your husband," the doctor says again, just like he said to Amith.

Those same words ring in Amith's ears, with the same sort of sincerity, but they seem tainted now. It feels as if the doctor spoke those words a thousand times, but never delivered, as a

68

memorized recitation of encouragement to the crying patient, man, woman, child, or whoever he was talking to at the time. And it must be a lie because how can he save that man? A man who is so close to death, bleeding profusely from the attack, how can a village doctor with no real equipment stop it? It's a false promise, and empty words won't turn into bandages, but the doctor grabs his tools and gets to work. There is utter chaos as the nurse runs around, grabbing towels and water. All their attention focuses on the newly admitted man.

Amith stares at his mom.

His eyes well up with tears. He must be strong, the doctor told him to, even if he was lying. If there is a faint chance that it's even remotely true and somehow it gives her the strength to endure, he must try to follow the doctor's advice. But Amith can't help it—the tears don't stop. Amith dashes out of the clinic.

"Amith!" Shaneel's mom calls out, but he's already gone.

Shaneel looks at his mom and dad. They nod. Shaneel runs after Amith.

¤ ¤ ¤ ¤ ¤

Shaneel walks down the familiar alley behind the theatre. It's getting dark already, but he climbs, making his way up the crates; the fear of falling has disappeared. Today, Shaneel is filled with courage and strength because he needs it. For today, he has to have enough for the both of them.

Amith sits on top of the wall in his usual spot. He stares with blank eyes at the old movie that is playing on the screen. Shaneel finally reaches the top and joins him. They sit together in silence and watch the movie for a while. After some time, Amith lays his head on Shaneel's shoulder. Shaneel puts his arm around Amith, comforting him. The movie plays.

CHAPTER 17

The Cup

THERE ARE A LOT OF PEOPLE HERE, hundreds of them. They walk around in a beautiful temple with golden spires, decorated with flower arrangements, elaborate ornaments, and colorful lights. Statues and statuettes of gods and deities fill the little shrines that are set into the large, beautiful marble walls. Equally gorgeous are the colors from the banners that hang off those walls, indicating a matrimonial event. Glorious shades of yellows, blues, and reds adorn beautifully painted pictures showing a celebration of life. Because today is a special day—today is Amith's wedding.

Servers dressed in flowing orange robes walk among the people. They serve hot chai and Indian sweets, such as laddoos, to all the guests. Everyone seems to be having a good time, a picture-perfect moment.

At the far wall, a large flower curtain hangs from the ceiling to envelop a large square area. The flowers are strung on thin threads that gently sway as people enter and exit the enclosure. Amith sits inside, on a red velvet pillow near a stone fire pit. The people come in and congratulate him on his special day. Although he's much older now, a grown man ready for the world, he still has that same spark in his eyes. His mom sits next to him. She looks the same, her beauty frozen in time. She smiles proudly toward Amith and feeds him a laddoo. His face lights up like it always does in response.

The two sit quietly watching a group of girls get their hands and feet decorated in henna in preparation for the wedding celebration.

Not a word is exchanged between them as they sit next to each other, one with each other's thoughts.

Then the girls start giggling as the music blares, a traditional Indian song signifying the arrival of the bride. Amith looks at his mom, and she looks at him.

"I love you, Bête," she whispers in his ear while they wait for the bride to come down the long hallway.

"Love you too, Ma." Amith responds by kissing her on the cheek.

First, flower girls enter, covering the carpet with red rose petals. Then the groomsmen walk in, Shaneel in the lead. He holds one side of a large flower-covered sheet over the bride and mimics every step she takes with her beautiful henna-covered feet. It's hard to make out who she is since her face is hidden by a beautifully embroidered red veil, but her flowing dark hair shines through. She is breathtaking in her gorgeous red sari and stunning gold jewelry that jingles with her every move.

The flower curtains part to the side, pulled open by the two servants as the group makes their entrance. The bride's elegant flowing red sari trails behind her as she approaches Amith. She stops in front of him. It's hard to tell, but she's smiling shyly underneath her veil. Amith can only look in awe as she takes her place next to him.

The priest gets ready and says a few words of blessing as he raises a jewel-covered golden cup into the air. Then they all sit down in unison around the fire pit. Amith and his mom send a smile to each other. The wedding is about to begin.

Later. . .

In keeping with tradition, the guests dance all through the night to Indian wedding music played on loud speakers sounding like a live band. The music suddenly stops; people wait in anticipation:

it's time for the groom to take the bride away. There's something about this moment that always makes people cry, a moment when the daughter's sense of ownership changes permanently. She is, in fact, no longer a daughter but instead someone's wife, and in this case, Amith's wife.

The relatives of the family start crying as the bride says her goodbyes, making her way to all the members of her family. Amith stands next to her while she greets the relatives, waiting to finally take his wife to his mom, to the woman who taught him everything. Rheka stands nearby but not with tears like the others. Instead, she shows her magnificent smile that's filled with pride. The crowd of people seem not to matter, they disappear into the background as Amith and his new bride make their way to her. Amith's focus is on her; she is timeless, ageless, and rightfully so, since a mother's love is undying.

Amith bends down and touches his hand to his mom's feet and then to his forehead, as is traditionally done. It's an age-old tradition for Indian men and women to show respect and ask for a blessing from their elders. This is very important, because there is no one in the world that Amith respects more. After Amith stands up, Rheka reaches over and kisses Amith, first on his forehead and then on his cheek, then she takes a drink from the jeweled golden cup. She leans over and whispers in his ear, "Thank you for saving me."

Amith's face lights up as he sees the glow of his mom; her radiance is magnificent. This is his big day, and she is here to see it, to see her son become a man. Rheka then raises the jeweled cup in the air, and everyone cheers. Applause fills the room.

Then, like a hazy dream, all is gone. Amith stands completely alone. The only visible thing from horizon to horizon is pure white. It's an infinite emptiness. But something gleams next to him, and Amith looks down. On the ground where his mom just stood moments before sits the empty jeweled golden cup. Amith reaches for it.

Flashes of light break up the dream. Amith opens his eyes. He had fallen asleep watching the movie. It's already night, and a chilly wind is blowing hard against the wall where they sit. But it doesn't bother him. A bright light shines on Amith's face; it's from a movie but not the one they had been watching before his dream. This movie is in black and white, like the ones that Amith never really likes. The absence of color made it too bright during certain scenes and too dark in others, a constant battle of light and dark. This must have been what Amith had seen in his dream.

Amith looks around and sees Shaneel beside him. He's still here. He never left, though he too has fallen asleep. It must have been hard for Shaneel, knowing his fear of heights, but that's what a good friend is for, although Shaneel has been more than a friend. He has been like a brother to Amith, and times like this prove it.

Another flash of light flickers brightly from the movie screen, so much that Amith has to squint his eyes. A strange image appears. It's an image of the jeweled cup in his dream, the same cup his mom was holding, the same cup she drank from, the same cup she raised. Except this time, it isn't in a dream. It is real, and it is in the movie. Amith watches intently.

The cup on the screen is sitting on a table; it's adorned with holy symbols all around it. A knight in shining armor walks up to the table. The monks that guard the table move aside and allow the knight to pass. The knight reaches for the cup and holds it high in the air, just like Amith's mom did in the dream. The people cheer.

73

Amith is awe-struck. He quickly shakes Shaneel, but Shaneel resists. Amith starts shaking him violently. "Come on, wake up, Shaneel!" he yells.

Shaneel finally opens his eyes, either from his fear of falling or Amith's frantic cries. "Whaaaat?" he says, yawning.

Amith grabs Shaneel's face and points it toward the screen. "Look!"

Shaneel watches.

A new scene of the knight riding off to a dark abandoned castle fills the screen. The knight makes his way through the now-drained moat and rides slowly up to the castle doors.

"I don't get it," Shaneel mumbles with Amith's hand still on his face.

"Keep watching!"

The castle doors creak open with a sturdy push from the knight. Dust and debris fall from the edges—it must have been closed for a long time. The knight leaves his horse there and heads down a long hallway, then up stairs that spiral upward. Once at the top, he comes to a door. He tries it. It's locked. The knight unsheathes his blade and breaks the lock with a swift slash.

"Finally! Some action," says Shaneel.

"Just watch, man."

The room is nearly empty—only a bed sits in the middle. Cobwebs ornament the bed's four spires, but the cover on the bed is untouched by time. On the bed lies a beautiful woman, who is sleeping. The knight stares at her, mesmerized by her beauty.

And so does Shaneel, now silent and completely focused.

The knight reaches into his bag and pulls out the jeweled cup from the previous scenes. He then kneels down, next to the sleeping maiden, and takes off his helmet. He's much older than she—the lines on his face show a man who has suffered sorrow and pain. He looks like an old man, but for some reason he reminds Amith of himself.

The knight pours some water from his iron canteen into the cup. The cup gleams as it works its magic. Then the knight lifts the woman's head and pours some of the water from the cup into her mouth. Instantly, her eyes open as the cup's magical powers start to take effect. She is lifted into the air by a magical force that stands her in front of the aged knight, as if she were a goddess.

She smiles at him and says, "What took you so long?"

The knight smiles in relief and his shoulders slump. It must have taken his whole life to find the relic, and now that he has, he can finally rest. He's tired and exhausted, but then a miraculous thing happens: he drinks from the cup and he too becomes young. The room around them changes and all the dust and debris vanishes. Everything is of pristine elegance. He stands up straight and holds his goddess in his arms. The jeweled cup sits next to the couple, gleaming as the sun passes through the window.

Words unknown to the boys appear on the screen—The Maiden and the Holy Grail—then the movie fades to black.

Amith looks over at Shaneel and says, "Did you see that?"

Shaneel nods his head in awe.

CHAPTER 18

Tēndu'ā

THE HOSPITAL ROOM IS UNCHANGED, although most of the people have left. Amith's mom still lies on the bed, a wet towel on her head to keep her fever down. Amith stands next to her, holding her hand. She's still unconscious.

"Ma, I don't want you to worry," Amith says. "You remember when I told you I was going to be your hero?"

She doesn't answer.

"Well, I found a way to save you. There's a cup that heals sick people. I'm going to find it, Ma. I'm going to find it and use it to save you."

Still no response.

"I'm going to be your hero, Ma. And then on my wedding day, you can stand next to me and feed me laddoos like all the other moms do."

Maybe those last words had some deep power, because his mom's head moves a little. She's still unconscious, but that's the first movement she's made all day and Amith is excited to see it. She must be getting better already. He knows that she is very powerful, and a small fever can't hurt someone with so many great abilities, now can it? He was a fool to think otherwise.

Amith leans over and kisses his mom's forehead, much like the way she did to him all his life. Now their roles have switched. For now, he is the one in charge. He is the one who will have to take care of someone while they are sick. He is the one who will have to sacrifice his food so another can eat, and he is the one who will spend sleepless nights so another can rest. He must live up to all the sacrifices his mom has made for him; he must follow those same footsteps. He must become the hero that his mom always knew he would be, because at this moment, she needs a hero, and Amith is it. This is the moment that Amith has been preparing for his whole life.

Amith stares at his mom for a few moments and then whispers his final words in her ear before leaving her bedside, "I love you, Ma. I'll come back and save you, I promise." He kisses her head once more and then leaves.

As Amith starts out, he walks past the other hospital beds and something catches his eye. It's the wounded man, the one the doctor said he was going to save. The one who should have been dead, but here he is: alive. He must be alive since his chest moves up and down rapidly with each breath, as if he is having some sort of scary dream.

Amith goes over to take a closer look. The man's wounds still smell of burned flesh; it's repulsive, but Amith stands steady. They must have had to cauterize the wound. Amith saw it in a movie once—it was horrible. The tool they used lies on the table: a piece of flat iron that was heated up in the furnace and held to the gash. It must have been painful, but it worked. He must have been a tough man to endure such pain. What sort of thing could do this to such a tough man?

Amith stares at where the injured man's right arm used to be. It's bandaged up very well and it no longer bleeds. Could the doctor be telling the truth? Were the recited words not a lie? Can the doctor really save his mom? He must be able to since he saved this man, and he was far worse than his mom. At least he can keep her healthy while Amith searches, while Amith looks for a cure, while Amith becomes the hero he is destined to be.

Suddenly, the injured man sits up, his eyes darting around the room in horror. He grabs Amith's arm with his left hand, clutching it in his powerful grip. Amith is shocked and stares back at him. But the man's terror doesn't come from Amith—it comes from something else, something immense.

The man locks his eyes on Amith and says, "Tēndu'ā, Tēndu'ā." And with that the man lets go of Amith's arm and falls asleep, back into his nightmare.

Amith stands trembling, wondering why the man said what he said. But there is no time to waste—he must go and save his mom. He takes off running out of the clinic. Still, his mind is filled with the man's words, repeating over and over again: Tēndu'ā, Tēndu'ā, the Jaguar, the Jaguar.

CHAPTER 19

A Book

HERO TRAINING TIP #9

"A hero never gets scared."

~Karishma

THE MOON IS HALF FULL and beams a weak light into the otherwise dark and gloomy night. There is a cool breeze blowing in from the woods, and it snakes its way through the dark streets. On this night, the entire town seems void of any life, except for Shaneel who waits by the rubble where the boys played cowboys. He wears a backpack crammed with all sorts of things, but mostly food and water.

Amith comes running up to Shaneel. "You have everything?" Amith whispers, huffing and puffing.

Shaneel nods in response, but Amith rummages through the backpack to double-check. Inside there are some rotis, some pieces of bread, one large Coca-Cola bottle filled with water, some dried fruit, and one candy bar that Shaneel got from his parent's store. Upon completion of his inspection, Amith returns a thumbs-up.

The boys run down the street toward the theatre. They pass the same huts, including the one Karishma lives in, and soon they disappear into the empty streets. Unknown to the boys, the ever-observant Karishma watches them from her window.

¤ ¤ ¤ ¤ ¤

For the first time, the boys stand inside the theatre's multiple-seat arena. It's desolate, but it seems full of life, as if the essence of the movies has bled into the very dirt around the seats. No one is there tonight, and it was relatively easy for them to make it through the gate—just a simple task of digging a foxhole under the gate and crawling through. Now the boys stand marveling at the giant screen, the source of their dreams. They had never seen it up close, and the sheer vastness of the screen is incredible. To them, it is always in the distance and out of reach of the hands of the poor, but now, standing so close, they can fully appreciate the immense screen in all its glory.

Although weathered and tattered, the screen covers the entire walled area, only disappearing just below the cloth awning that is being used to protect it from the harsh rays of the sun. Hanging on the wall, on each side of the screen, are two lights that are rarely on except on those darkest nights to allow people to exit the area safely. Tonight would have been one of those nights. How the boys wish the lights were on so they wouldn't be stumbling around in the dimly lit area. It's so dark that, if it weren't for the moonlight bouncing off the screen, they might have missed the wooden turquoise door that leads to the owner's office, right next to the screen.

"There has to be something here about the movie," Amith says.

"Are you sure?" Shaneel asks.

80

"Yeah, they must have sent a map or something with the film."

"A map?"

"Yeah, all we have to do is find it, and then we find the cup," Amith says with assurance.

"Where?"

Amith looks around. "Some place safe, some place people wouldn't be able to get into." Then he points to the office and says, "That must be where they keep it."

The boys head over to the door, but it doesn't budge when they try to open it. The door is locked on the inside and won't be as easy to open as breaking into the theatre was. That's a good sign that there's something important hiding inside, but it's a problem for the boys as well. They look for another way in and find a small, shuttered window on the other side of the building. Too bad, it too is locked but only with a loose chain.

Amith throws his scarf over his shoulder and motions to Shaneel to give him a lift up. Shaneel kneels down and Amith tries to balance on his shoulders. Shaneel wobbles up to a standing position as Amith straightens himself just enough to pull on the window. It budges only a little bit, but it's enough space for someone small to squeeze through, someone smaller than Amith and Shaneel.

"Can I play?"

The unexpected voice frightens Shaneel into wobbling with Amith still on top of his shoulders. Amith desperately tries to catch himself, but it's too late. Shaneel and Amith come crashing down, and the loud noise echoes through the alleyway. Luckily, the sound only alarms a cat that has no intention of being involved with the boys again and runs speedily away down the street. Calmness returns as Amith and Shaneel hold their breaths and wait for the police and sirens. No one appears.

Amith gets up cautiously, dusting the dirt off his clothes from the fall. He looks over to see where the voice came from.

Standing a few feet away, Karishma comes out of the shadows and stands there eagerly. She has a small satchel slung over her shoulder, and she holds her arms behind her as she sways back and forth.

"So, can I play?" she enthusiastically asks again.

"What are you doing here?" Amith yells as quietly as he can.

"I want to play."

"You can't play with us," Amith whispers as loudly as he can.

Shaneel moves in, trying to relieve the tension before it gets out of hand. "We're not playing, we're working."

"Fine, I want to work then," Karishma replies with a grin.

"It's not work for little girls. It is work for boys," Amith states before walking back to the window.

Karishma looks disappointed. Normally, Karishma would never let Amith win so easily—it would be a fight to the bitter end. But for some reason, the seriousness in his voice tells her there is no hope.

Karishma walks off. She goes back to the gate and doesn't even bother using the foxhole. She just slides between the bars of the gate instead. Shaneel sees this.

"Wait!" Shaneel yells.

¤   ¤   ¤   ¤   ¤

Inside, the small and desolate office is quite scary. It seems larger than life to tiny Karishma as she cautiously creeps around. It's hard to make out anything of major significance. A table stands in the corner to one side of the room, a walking stick leans against it. Next to that sits a garbage can, full of who knows what. The rest is a blur of dark shadows that seem to dance on the walls from the thin line of moonlight dribbling through the shutter opening.

Just moments before, the two boys helped her up onto the window ledge and pushed enough on the shutters so she could wriggle through the narrow opening. Now, they stand nervously outside, waiting for Karishma to come out with the riches. They know she's on her own and also that she's their only chance.

"Do you see anything?" Amith quietly calls to Karishma.

"Not yet," Karishma whispers loudly through the small opening in the window.

Karishma looks around again. It's dark, very, very dark, and she wonders if she's alone. Then she freezes at the first thought that springs into her mind: monsters. But the second thought is about how much she doesn't want to disappoint the boys. She wants to prove her worth in order to find her place in their boy-dom. So Karishma takes a deep breath, then another and another, until she gathers enough strength to start thinking positive thoughts. She convinces herself that there couldn't possibly be anything in here with her. If there were, she would at least hear it. Finally satisfied, Karishma takes a small step forward.

The wind blows hard on the shutters from outside and makes a taunting moan as the shadows again come to life on the wall. Karishma stands mortified. They stop moving.

"Can . . . we . . . play . . . Amazon . . . instead?" she squeaks slowly.

"No!" the two boys whisper loudly back in unison.

Too bad. Amazon warriors would be so much more fun than this dreadful situation, Karishma thinks.

"No way out, I have to go through with it," she mutters as she pumps her little fists for courage.

Karishma takes another step forward, but her shadow moves on the wall with her. Karishma freezes up, yet her mind is racing. Is something behind her? Is someone trying to grab her? No, no, just a shadow, her shadow. Ha, ha, funny . . . but not really. Okay, time to collect and rethink. Build up that courage again and make another move. Come on, Karishma, time to move. Don't disappoint Amith.

With that thought, Karishma takes another step and stops. Time to check; a moment passes . . . nothing happens. Okay, safe to move again. Karishma takes another step and another.

Outside, the boys wait impatiently.

"Areh, what's taking her so long?" whispers Amith.

Shaneel shrugs an "I don't know" look.

"Pick me back up."

Shaneel kneels down and Amith starts climbing onto his shoulders again. Shaneel wobbles over to the window, grunting from the effort; Amith braces himself, trying to balance against Shaneel's movements.

Karishma stands frozen, but then her mind picks up again. What was that noise? Is that outside? Was it human? It better be human. She could be playing princess right now, but nooo. Now she's stuck here with the boys, stuck in a very dark and scary room, and she's all alone. She better find what she's looking for and get out quickly.

With each step, Karishma becomes more tense. The room is so quiet that she almost prefers the strange noises that scared her.

She moves close to the table and sees something on it. Looking closer, Karishma can make out that it's a journal or a book of some sort. She grabs it.

The book is filled with words, facts, and lists that would be interesting to someone who could read. Too bad Karishma can't read. She turns the book upside down, then to the right, then to the left, but still the words don't make any sense. She stares at it with an intense concentration, trying to call forth all her intelligence to decipher the script, but she comes up short. There's nothing there that makes any sense to her.

Outside, another gust blows through the alley, causing Shaneel and Amith to lose their balance again. Amith braces himself on the wall with his left hand, trying to take some of his weight off Shaneel. His hand makes a loud thud as it strikes the concrete surface.

Karishma swings around to see where the noise came from. But she also bumps into the walking stick, which hits the ground, clanking loudly like an angry old man walking up right behind her.

Karishma frantically bursts through the office door screaming, still holding the book, her hair standing on end, and quickly disappears between the outside gates.

"What's wrong with her?" Shaneel wonders.

"And that's why I don't play with girls," Amith replies, letting out a deep exhausted sigh.

With no other choice, the two boys shrug their shoulders and chase after Karishma.

CHAPTER 20

Public Enemy Number 1

HERO TRAINING TIP #10

"A hero always follows the rules."

~Amith

THE COLORS OF DAWN ARE A BEAUTIFUL SIGHT, with its deep orange and red soaking through the clouds and into the heavens. It's a beautiful sight to behold, but Amith is fixated on something else: the book Karishma found in the office.

"Is this all you got?" Amith asks as he inspects the book.

"Yes, that's all I got," Karishma responds mockingly, feeling unappreciated for the heroism she just showed.

"Let me see," Shaneel says as he grabs the book.

The two boys fumble with the book as they exchange looks. Such a strange thing with so many words, they think. It's a mystery to them as much as it is to Karishma. They turn the book sideways, staring at the lettering, but still they understand nothing. It would be a lot easier if they knew how to read. They would have found out that the book is just notes about the owner's favorite scenes, the delivery schedule of last year's movies, and other insignificant facts and doodles. But the boys don't know how to read, so they stare at the book, clueless, trying to break its code.

Karishma watches the two boys enviously, wanting to join them. Amith notices.

"Karishma, go home," Amith says and scowls in frustration. "We have work to do." He focuses back on the book.

"But I want to help," Karishma pleads.

Even Shaneel disagrees with Karishma's wish to join them. He knows that this journey might be quite long, quite dangerous, and the last thing he wants is to see Karishma get hurt.

"You can't come, Karishma," Shaneel replies. "It's too dangerous for girls."

Shaneel also fixes his attention on the book, leaving Karishma to her own lonely misery. But if there is one thing that Karishma hates more than anything, it is being told what not to do.

"Fine, I'll leave," Karishma grunts and stamps her feet.

The boys pay no attention to her tantrum. There is no use. It seems like the boys have made up their minds. If it was just Amith, Karishma could haggle her way in, but having Shaneel against her also gives her little hope in winning. Karishma turns and starts walking home.

"What does it say?" Amith whispers to Shaneel.

"I don't know. I can't read," Shaneel answers.

Those whispers don't go unnoticed. Karishma overhears the boys' conversation, and it triggers a little spark of an idea in her mind. The spark turns and twirls and becomes a full-fledged plan in Karishma's head, a plan that could make her one of the boys and maybe even get Amith to fall in love with her.

"I guess you don't need anyone to tell you what's in the book," Karishma teases, as she casually walks away, putting her devious little scheme to work.

The boys turn their attention to Karishma. It's working, just like she planned.

"You know how to read?" the surprised boys say in unison.

She stops and turns and gives an innocent grin back.

Suddenly, a police siren blares off in the distance.

"Oh, no! The police!" Shaneel yells, scrambling around and almost dropping the book. "They must be after us for breaking into the theatre!" Amith screams as he clasps the book in his arms, close to his heart.

The kids start to panic, unaware that the police have no idea of any wrong-doing in the theatre, and even if they did, nothing of value was "borrowed." In reality, the police would have far less interest in solving any crime that wouldn't benefit them. But to the kids, they have just committed the biggest crime in history, and in their minds, they have each just become public enemy number one.

The sirens continue to sound far in the distance, but to guilty minds it seems to be right around the corner.

Shaneel looks around for a place to hide. He sees nothing but the jungle, and he's not supposed to go there. Maybe the village? No! For certain, the police will check their homes and investigate all the people close to them. If the police find them, they will hire the army to pull them out, so they can face the music for their most terrible crime. Someone will snitch; it's just a matter of time. Shaneel starts to sweat as he wonders where in his life he went wrong.

Startled and worried, Karishma doesn't know what to do, so she reverts to her last line of defense: she starts to cry. Such a little mistake, she thinks, and now she will have to spend her whole life in jail with other boys—mean ones too.

But Amith does not falter. He just keeps staring at the book. He is more afraid that they will take away his last chance to save his mom than of serving life in prison. He knows he will do anything to save her, and he is not letting go of the book—his only hope—even if it kills him. This is his chance, and he will do everything he can to make it work.

"I want to go home. I want to go home," Karishma cries.

Amith rushes to Karishma with the book. "No one is going home," he commands. "We have to find out what the book says." He holds the book in front of Karishma's face. "Karishma, what does it say?" he asks eagerly.

Karishma takes a look, but of course she doesn't know. She does know that her lie is about to be discovered, though, and that she's going to be in trouble with her parents for stealing, and now, with the boys for lying. They will never let her play with them again. She can't hold back the tears and starts to wail.

"I can't . . ."

"Yes, you can," Amith interrupts. He knows the book has something to do with the cup. Otherwise, why would they have found it? "Just look at the book," he yells, holding it closer to Karishma's face so she can't look away.

Karishma tries to read, but the words have no meaning for her and her eyes fill up with more tears. She pushes the book away.

The sirens are getting closer and closer. Shaneel scrambles on top of a nearby log to get a better vantage point. "Amith, we have to go!" he yells.

Amith doesn't move. He continues to force the book in front of Karishma's eyes, demanding her to answer him. "Karishma, look at the book. Tell me, where does it say we have to go? What does it say about the cup?"

"Amith, we have to go now. They'll find us if we're in the vill . . ."

"Shut up, Shaneel!" Amith yells back, silencing Shaneel.

The rude outburst upsets Shaneel, but the fear of being caught is overpowering. It's the most prominent issue on his mind. The dilemma for him is simple: does he run and save himself, leaving his best friend to take the full assault of the police, or does he stay and endure the hardship with him. Shaneel decides to stay.

Karishma stares at Amith. He's not giving up and is even more determined to get the answer. But Karishma has nothing to tell him. All the while, the sirens are getting closer.

"Karishma, tell us!" Amith snaps.

She has no choice. She has to do something. She has to say something.

"The bo . . . book tells us . . ." she stutters, "to go far away from the village." She points in the opposite direction from the sirens, a direction that heads straight into the jungle. "That way!" she screams.

Amith lights up, assured of his success now, and snaps the book closed. He starts running into the jungle; Shaneel and Karishma follow after him.

A few moments later a police car passes without stopping, headed for an unrelated emergency in the village, and totally unaware of the turmoil the sirens have caused the kids.

It's not long before all is silent once again. The dust clears from the dirt road, but the kids are nowhere to be seen. They've gone into the jungle, blindly following Amith's lead into the unknown—led by a lie made out of fear, all in the name of hope.

CHAPTER 21

The Lie

HERO TRAINING TIP #11

"A hero always tells the truth."

~Karishma

THE SOUNDS OF NATURE ARE ALL AROUND, unfamiliar sounds that come from every direction. The birds sing high above, and the crickets chirp near the ground. Frogs hop from leaf top to leaf top, as they watch the air for their next meal. Such is the way of the jungle, but the usual tranquility of nature is disturbed when the kids come dashing into a small clearing within it.

It takes a moment for them to get their bearings as they catch their breath from their exhausting sprint. The police sirens are long gone, but the sense that they will be ambushed at any moment remains.

They take a moment to look around and find themselves surrounded by hairy bushes, twining branches, and large sulking trees. They've never been in the jungle before, and even those few villagers who have only enter the edges of its boundaries and return with stories of dangers and warnings to stay away. To the boys, it doesn't seem so bad. The thought of the police finding them was a far worse ordeal than this. What dangers can the jungle have that would be worse?

Amith leans against a tree and stares at Shaneel, who stands bent over, taking deep panting breaths. Amith walks up to Shaneel and gives him a jab on his arm. "You were scared," he says.

"Hey, no I wasn't. You were scared," Shaneel says, quickly defensive.

"I wasn't scared. Nothing scares me," Amith boasts, holding his hands at his sides in his heroic pose.

"Oh, yeah? Why were you in the lead the whole time then?" Shaneel laughs.

Amith tries to think of a good comeback but comes up with a terrible one. "I was just making sure the way was safe for you two."

"Well, I was the hero that time," Shaneel says as he slaps Amith back.

"We'll see who the hero is," Amith shouts as he tackles Shaneel to the ground. The boys wrestle with each other for a while, enjoying themselves in the laughter and fun and forgetting their recent squabbling.

Karishma is shaken from the incident, her thoughts still on the recent events: almost getting caught by the cops, Amith's fury, and Shaneel's cowardice. She wonders if she is in the right place, or if she should run back home before it's too late. But watching the two boys play changes her mind. It is something about them being together all the time, forgetting their fears and risking it all for each other, that is very calming. She decides to stick around.

Shaneel notices Karishma's uneasiness and frees himself from Amith's bear hug. Amith continues to wrestle by himself on the ground.

"Karishma, are you okay?" Shaneel asks her.

"Yeah, I'm fine." Karishma lies.

"I'm a bear!" Amith yells as he springs to his feet with his arms spread wide to tackle Shaneel again. They stand like two bears poised to fight each other.

"We should go back soon, before we get lost," Karishma says, trying to interrupt the wrestling boys.

Amith stops and grabs Shaneel's fallen backpack from the ground. "No, we can't go back," he says, handing the backpack to Shaneel. "We have to find the cup." He smiles, picks up the book, and opens it to the first page. He looks at it in another attempt to decipher the writing, but it's still no use. Karishma is his only hope.

"But . . ." Karishma tries to explain but is quickly interrupted.

"No, Karishma, we have to find the cup," Amith says firmly. Then he closes the book and hands it to Karishma. "We need to find it so we can save my mom." Amith smiles.

Karishma doesn't want to take the book, but she does. She stares at it, knowing that from now on her lie has made the book part of her. There is no way out.

"Yeah, Karishma, it's important to find the cup for Aunty," Shaneel says with a delighted nod, ". . . and you're the only one who can read the book," he continues, while pointing at the book.

The lie she told stings her heart, and she wants to confess her sin before it goes too far. She has lied before, but never about something as serious as this. She stands there sulking as Amith approaches her. He walks up to her, puts his hands on her shoulders, and stares straight into her eyes, the windows to her soul.

"I need you to help me find the cup, Karishma," Amith says. "We need you," he continues, as he smiles that powerful smile of his.

Karishma has a hard time holding the gaze and she looks away, but the enticing words travel from her ears down to her heart. Amith has never formerly invited her to play before. He always found a way to sneak out of it, or only played with her when he was forced to. Maybe that's the reason she wanted him so much, because she knew she couldn't have him. And something about those first few words—"I need you"—makes the request hard to resist. Could it be that he is finally warming up to her? Could there be a chance for the two of them? Is this the start of a blossoming love?

Karishma thinks it over and her worries, as well as her guilt, quickly subside. Boys do take longer to develop than girls, she has heard, and Amith is surely a boy. Maybe he will make a great husband someday, he just needs a little bit of fine-tuning to come around. Karishma runs through the event in her imagination, as only a six-year-old can.

"Will you help us, Karishma?" Shaneel asks, breaking into her daydream.

Karishma looks at Amith. He stands smiling at her, waiting for the answer that he wants to hear and showing that same powerful smile that his mom radiates, the one that makes it impossible to say no. So Karishma has little choice but to give in. She doesn't have the heart to disappoint Amith, and she doesn't have the strength to beat that incredible smile. "Okay," she says, mesmerized.

With that Amith spins around and tosses his red scarf over his shoulder, in his dramatic cape-like fashion. "Let's go," he commands, as he points into the jungle ahead. Amith marches forward, then stops and looks back over his shoulder. "It's time for me to be a real hero," he says.

Shaneel rockets to his feet, gripping his flimsy backpack straps. "I heard there was some sort of road ahead," he says.

Amith is happy to hear that. "Great! Let's go," Amith says, taking gigantic steps deeper into the jungle.

Shaneel follows behind. "Come on, Karishma," he calls.

The two boys disappear into the jungle. Karishma stands alone.

Karishma stares at the book in her hand, the one that was supposed to guide the way, the only salvation for Amith's mom. She doesn't know how she will ever get out of this; the only sure thing is that it's going to get worse. She can't have Amith lose hope, or his mom, due to her poor actions. She has little choice but to follow, to head into the unknown, down a path paved by her little lie that grew so quickly that it became a monster. And now she must travel its course and find a way to tame the beast.

Karishma walks into the jungle, ready to face the obstacles that are to come, knowing that one day she will have to face the truth, to bear the burden of her words and expose what she now has to hide. As of now, giving Amith his hope has taken all of hers.

CHAPTER 22

The Delivery Truck

IF IT WEREN'T FOR THE TRUCK that they hitched a ride on, they would have thought the road deserted, a forgotten line of dirt through the jungle. Its path is carved in a wavelike fashion and makes the truck sway from side to side as it moves along as if they were on the sea.

On most trips, the delivery truck carries hay bales piled on top of one another and fitting snuggly into the truck bed. Today, unknown to the driver, it also carries three stowaways—Amith, Shaneel, and Karishma—who snuck into the partly filled truck when the driver stopped to take a break on the road.

Traveling this way makes the journey much easier, and it is a relief to see another human after spending an uncomfortable night and early morning in the wild. The kids are energized and feeling more sure about their journey. Amith confidently holds onto the side rail of the truck with one hand. As the truck sways with the curvy road, he rocks back and forth, waving his free arm in the air as if he is fending off pirates. Shaneel sits next to him, a little queasy compared to his swashbuckling friend. Neither sea-faring nor sitting in a shaky truck is his cup of tea. Karishma sits on the other side, resting between two hay bales with her back against one and her feet on top of the other.

She continues to look through the book, searching for a clue to what it says or where they are supposed to go. She doesn't fare too well, and staring at the shaky lines gives her a headache.

It's not clear whether the rocky truck ride or the frustration of being lost makes Karishma feel sick to her stomach; either way, Karishma can't take it any longer. She heaves over the side of the truck.

"Yuck!" Amith cries out. He turns to see if the driver saw anything, but he is focused on the road. Besides, the roar of the rusty truck engine and the hay bales hide the kids very well from detection.

Shaneel can't hold it any longer either, after seeing Karishma get sick, and he too pukes over the side.

"Double yuck!" Amith says in disgust.

It's at this moment that the truck makes a sharp right turn, causing the kids to be thrown to one side of the truck bed. Amith grips tightly on the railing. Shaneel manages to also.

"Shaneel, you okay?" Amith yells as he gets to his feet.

"Yeah. How about you, Karishma?" Shaneel asks as he gets back up.

There is no answer.

They look at where Karishma was riding, but there's no sign of her, only the two hay bales that she had been lying on just a few moments before.

"Where's Karishma?" Amith yells to Shaneel.

The realization that she's gone starts to sink into the boys' minds. She must have been thrown off at the sharp turn. Karishma out in the jungle alone—she won't last a day.

What should they do? Shaneel thinks. A hero would jump after her. A hero would stand and risk his own life for a friend. A hero would make the leap, and a hero is what he should be.

"We have to jump off," Shaneel yells.

"What?" Amith snaps.

"We have to find Karishma," Shaneel yells as he courageously readies himself to take the big leap over the side of the truck.

"You're right," Amith says as he stands next to Shaneel.

Shaneel smiles at his friend's show of honor.

"She has the book!" Amith yells.

Shaneel's smile disappears.

The boys squat down, ready to make the jump.

"Okay, on a count of three," Amith yells.

"Okay," Shaneel answers back, taking a deep breath, as if it were his last.

"One!"

"Two!"

"Thr . . ."

"Wait!" Karishma yells.

Shaneel falls back into the truck bed from surprise, but Amith is quick enough to hold onto the railing.

They turn to find that Karishma has been buried under some hay bales that tumbled onto her, with only her tiny feet sticking out. She waves her hand in the air to show that she is okay and tries to push the hay bales off, but they are heavy, and she struggles. Shaneel quickly rushes to help. Amith stays by the railing, watching.

"I can't believe that we were going to jump off a moving truck for you!" Amith screams nastily.

Karishma is delighted to hear those words. As Shaneel gets the last hay bale off, Karishma sees Amith standing near the railing. Her heart melts.

"You would do that for me?" she says, blushing.

"Of course I would. That's what a hero would do," Amith says, as he lets go of the railing and puts his hand on his chest as if he was taking a pledge.

To Karishma, her brave little Amith now seems dreamier than ever before. Shaneel, bothered by her reaction and from being left out of the conversation, sits back. While Shaneel sulks, Amith enjoys basking in the glory of a hero. He leans on the railing and gives Karishma a smile. She starts to blush again.

All of a sudden, the truck takes another sharp turn, and Amith disappears off the railing. Horrified, Karishma and Shaneel jump to their feet.

The wind hits Amith in the face hard, and for a brief moment, falling feels like flying. If it wasn't for the fear that he might die from the impact, Amith would have enjoyed the experience. But any joy he might have felt quickly disappears the moment he hits the ground.

It is a while before Amith regains consciousness. Karishma sits cross-legged next to him—she has been there the whole time. Her face lights up as Amith opens his eyes. He lets out a pained groan as he sees her.

"Karishma, what happened?"

"You fell off the truck," she replies coyly, now fully relieved of her concerns for Amith.

"Where's Shaneel?"

"Over there," she points.

Shaneel stands near a group of trees, looking at something in the distance. He knows that Amith is okay. Shaneel's been in many tussles with him, and one thing he knows about Amith is that he is as tough as he is stubborn—and boy, is he stubborn.

"I jumped off when the truck stopped," Karishma explains as she starts checking Amith for scratches. He pushes her prying hands away with disgust. She gives up and continues explaining. "There's some sort of farmhouse or something over there," Karishma says and points just past Shaneel.

Amith slowly gets to his feet. He rubs the back of his head— nothing bad, just a little tender and a minor headache. Then he stretches his arms and legs. It seems like he suffered no major damage, just some minor scratches. Relieved, he gives a thumbs-up to Karishma, which delights her.

Then Amith walks over to Shaneel, who welcomes him with a pat on his back. Amith turns to look at what Shaneel has been staring at.

Karishma was right. There is a small farmhouse down the road. The delivery truck that they were riding on is parked in front of it. Amith visually inspects the farmhouse. He doesn't have to say anything; Shaneel already knows what Amith is thinking.

"You think the cup might be in there?" Shaneel asks.

A mischievous smile crosses Amith's face.

Shaneel lets out a pained sigh.

CHAPTER 23

The Farmer

HERO TRAINING TIP #12

"A hero never retreats."

~Amith

THE WAY IS CLEAR, but who knows what danger lurks in the depths of the farm. Amith ponders these thoughts while readying himself for his assault on the field, an assault as if he is going into battle.

This is the normal way of his daily routine: get up, get ready, be a hero. And today, he will be the hero once again. Today, he will find the salvation for his mom. Today, he will not rest until he vanquishes the army of darkness that dares to stand in his way. Shaneel is onboard too, ready and determined. His face is stern, like a battle-hardened soldier. As Amith ties his red scarf around his forehead like a bandana, the boy's fantasy begins.

Smoke and debris cloud the vision of the shocked soldiers and their civilian companion. That was a close one, a blast that deci-mated the very ground it landed on, leaving a cavernous hole in the world that went to its very core. But Amith must continue for the good of the mission. He must continue to accomplish his mis-sion, a mission that is more important than his life at this moment. He must find the holy cup. In order to do that, he must reach the enemy's military base and search for any clues within. For what better place to hide a magical artifact than the very depths of an isolated enemy stronghold?

Amith readies himself, takes a deep breath, and then leaps into the air so high it's as if he had springs on the bottoms of his feet. Amith glides gracefully in the air from his kangaroo jump to the other side. He falls and tumbles along the ground, channeling the shock of the impact through his body, all the while never letting go of his weapon: a machine gun, the likes of which only the buffest heroes can use. He quickly rolls to his feet and points his massive gun in front of him.

Amith jumps over a small divot in the ground. He waves his stick in the air as if instructing his troops of a battle plan. Shaneel and Karishma follow in a similar fashion, although Karishma is not as interested as the others. Her mind is on solving the riddle of the book, the riddle of reading. They close in on the farmhouse and the delivery truck.

The enemy base is up ahead, not too far away, maybe a couple of meters, but it's a dangerous few meters. The supplies of enemy weapons have arrived, and the truck that carries them waits near the entrance, with the battle soldier known as "the Butcher of Children" in the front seat.

The door swings open and a husky, heavy-set man gets out of the truck. His exit removes the strain of his weight from the truck, and the wheels creak and return to their original shape after being squished from the pressure. The giant man stretches; his cracking joints sound like snapping bamboo sticks. He lumbers into the house, unaware of the children soldiers who are ready to strike.

Amith, Shaneel, and Karishma stand watch, hidden behind some bushes and a tree. They wait for the burly truck driver to enter the house. When the way is clear, Amith looks back and whispers, "Wait here. I'll clear the path."

Shaneel and Karishma nod in unison.

The enemy fire is drawing ever near. Jets and helicopters have filled the skies now and bombard the very ground in front of the enemy base. Advancing would be an impossible task for anyone else but not for the super soldier known only as Amith.

Amith makes his way through the treacherous and forbidding terrain with his trusty machine gun in hand. Another bomb whistles on its way to the ground, and this time the blast is close, too close. It knocks Amith to the ground and his weapon out of his hands. Normally, an explosion like that would kill even an elephant. But never fear, Amith isn't normal, and he is okay. For a hero like Amith, this is just a flesh wound, barely a scratch.

Amith gets up and looks around, but sees no gun. It must have disintegrated in the blast. No time to worry—if it must be hand-to-hand combat to survive, then so be it. Amith starts to make his way to the enemy base, dodging enemy fire as if he is protected by some mystical shield.

Karishma and Shaneel watch in amusement at Amith's commitment to his fantasy. Amith ducks, weaves, and rolls through the patches of dying grass and thorny bushes, slowly inching his way closer to the farmhouse.

Amith takes a moment to visually scour the terrain once more. The enemies move from one part of the house to the other, their shadows covering the windows as they stir inside. The Butcher of Children is in there, it's easy to tell, for his large body fills the entire window when he passes. He seems angry from the way he moves his hands in the air. Amith must be cautious; the butcher is a fearsome foe and he must not be seen by him to gain the upper hand. It's

time to put all his super ninja stealth soldier training at the acad-
emy to work. Amith drops to the ground and crawls forward, staying
hidden in the piles of leaves and brush on the ground.

The door opens and the butcher steps outside. Amith flattens
himself on the ground; his body is limp and pressed into the cool
dirt, waiting for the danger to clear.

"I can't keep making trips over here for nothing. I need to make a living too—I have kids to feed," the truck driver shouts as he storms his way to his truck.

"I'm sorry, but the water doesn't flow like it used to and the land doesn't give nourishment, so the crops aren't growing," the farmer replies as he steps out of his house. He looks defeated, all skin and bones, unbelievably famished especially for a would-be provider of food. He also doesn't have the same vigor as the driver, and his shoulders sag, as if the weight of the world rests on them.

"I'm sorry. I didn't mean to waste your time," the farmer continues.

"Areh, I'm not worried about wasting my time. It's my fuel that I'm worried about—petrol isn't cheap," the truck driver snaps back.

After a few more apologetic words, the farmer politely wishes the driver a safe trip.

"I'm giving you one last chance," the truck driver roars as he gets into the delivery truck. The truck's corroded engine clatters to life when he turns the key. "I'll be passing by at the end of the week. You have until then," the truck driver says, leaning out the window. "Don't blow it!" The truck driver turns his truck around and it sputters back down the road.

The farmer watches the truck disappear into the jungle, maybe for the last time. He takes a moment and stares at the sky. There's nothing for his eyes to catch hold of, just clear, empty skies, and then he turns his gaze to the dried dirt that once was moist, rich soil. The farmer lets out a deep sigh, and after a moment goes back inside his house.

That was close, Amith thinks to himself as he gets up. That must have been the mastermind of the whole war, the one who launched the satellite space guns that decimated an entire country and started this whole mess. Amith decides that he must go and investigate—and show no mercy.

Amith sneaks the last few yards to the farmhouse and leans against the wall. Time to see what's going on inside—luckily, there's a small hole in the wall. Amith peers through.

It's sparse inside; a wooden desk and a chair, a beat-up old mattress made of hay wrapped with cloth, and some farming tools fill the small room. The farmer walks to his desk and sits down on the broken chair. A few moments pass as the farmer stares blankly at the wall. He sits there quietly, then holds his face in his hands and begins to pray. But before he can finish, he starts to weep into those very same hands. All the while, Amith watches intently from his peep hole.

A few more moments pass as the farmer collects himself. Then he gets up and walks to a cabinet. He opens it slowly, cherishing every moment, and reaches inside one of the drawers. He pulls out a handgun.

The farmer goes back to the desk and sits in his chair. Tears are streaming down his face, but he is not openly crying. A blank, lost expression hangs on his face instead. He carefully examines the gun in his hand; it's pristine, almost holy in appearance. After he is satisfied that he has taken in all the details, the farmer puts the barrel in his mouth and starts to squeeze the trigger.

Amith takes a step back, tripping on loose rock, and lets out a gasp in surprise. The farmer stops and rushes to the door in an attempt to catch the intruder.

"Hey! Who's there?" the farmer shouts as he runs outside. "I said, who's there?" the farmer yells again as he waves his gun wildly in the air.

There is no one—Amith is gone. There is no sign of anything, just the breeze of the wind and the rustle of the trees.

What was that? the farmer wonders. A person? Maybe it was something else? It could've been an animal . . . or a ghost.

The farmer looks at the loaded gun in his hand. Suddenly he fears it and throws it to the ground. It clangs against the rocks and no longer looks pristine as it did moments before. He starts to weep profusely as he comes to his senses. The dread and emptiness he felt moments before are gone. He no longer feels the need to pull the trigger. Then the farmer has a revelation, and everything starts to make sense.

The farmer looks around once more. There is nothing in sight, but he knows better. The farmer looks to the heavens and smiles and basks in the sun. This is an awakening for the farmer, the dawn of a new day, because he knows that it wasn't an animal, or a ghost, but instead, it was an angel, an angel that came down from the heavens and saved his life.

CHAPTER 24

Because the Book Said So

HERO TRAINING TIP #13

"A hero takes others into consideration."

~Amith

AFTER WHAT SEEMS LIKE AN ETERNITY, the farmer finally goes back in the farmhouse. Amith, Shaneel, and Karishma, watching from their hiding spot in the jungle, let out a sigh of relief.

It is way past noon now, and the morning has slipped away after the day's travel as quickly as most of the afternoon. The sun sinks, and darkness and cool follows. A breeze chills the children's bare shoulders, or maybe it is the thought of almost being shot. Either way, there is no time for Amith to dwell. He starts moving into the jungle again. Shaneel and Karishma follow close behind as usual, while the moon starts to make its appearance.

"How big was the gun?" Karishma asks as they move forward.

"It was bigger than my head," Amith says in exaggeration, holding his arms out wide to create an imaginary gun barrel the size of a telescope.

"Wow," Shaneel responds with excitement.

Shaneel's enthusiasm is almost as big as Karishma's terror. It's no wonder the boys don't want to play with her, since what excites one, terrifies the other. Her mind still on the farmer's gun, Karishma keeps her eyes on the farmhouse as they continue into the jungle.

Amith's red scarf flaps in the wind as he climbs up some rocks as gracefully as a mountaineer. He stops and looks around, then asks, "Where did you say it was again, Karishma?"

Karishma doesn't respond.

"Karishma?"

No answer still—her mind is stuck on the farmer's gun.

"Karishma!?" Amith yells, trying to get her attention. His voice booms and echoes in the jungle, bouncing off the valley loudly enough to warn the farmer of trespassers.

Within moments, the farmhouse door opens again. The farmer comes out, now dressed warmly for the night, but he no longer holds the devilish weapon he once wielded.

Nonetheless, Karishma is still frightened. There's something about the thought of the weapon, so close and so real, that scares her.

The farmer makes his way past the grave of dying crops that riddle the ground and approaches the jungle's edge. His eyes are still adjusting to the change of light from inside to outside, but it will be just moments before he sees them. Karishma tenses with anxiety.

Amith repeats his question, but this time in a lower tone. "We have to go now. Where do we go next, Karishma?" he asks, getting her attention by grabbing her shoulder.

Silence once again fills the area—not because of Karishma's lack of acknowledgment but because she can't think what to say. She doesn't know where they are supposed to go. All that she can think about is the farmer coming at them with the gun, lining them up and shooting them, one by one. That's when an image flashes in her mind of a family hiding in a cave as a pack of deadly animals pass by. Maybe it was from a movie, but it sticks in her mind and she responds with . . .

"A cave, the book says a cave, away from the farm," she whispers as the farmer starts searching the edge of the jungle.

Amith brightens. It might not be the most insightful of instructions, but at least he has a direction—away from the farm—and that's good enough for Amith. He slips ahead and moves deeper into the jungle. Karishma and Shaneel follow close behind.

Soon the farmer gives up his search and returns to his house, because it's no use looking when it's getting so late. Anything can happen. The farmer knows that the jungle comes to life at night, and it's hard to see in the dark. Besides, it's better to check in the morning, when it's not so dangerous.

¤ ¤ ¤ ¤ ¤

Amith is the first to reach the pipe canal. He looks at it from the top of a rock that Shaneel is also crawling up. Together, they examine their discovery from their new vantage point.

The mouth of the snaking pipe stretches as wide as the gaping jaw of a large tiger—not big enough for adults but wide enough for kids to enter. Water trails out from inside the dank darkness, trickling slowly down into an almost dried-up creek bed that once reached the farm. The entire pipe appears to have been engulfed by the jungle. Its sides are cracked, and thick moss hangs off the edge where the water used to flow. It must have been of great use to the farm once, but now it looks weathered and broken and only serves as an opening in the side of the hilly terrain, ominous and dark, just like a cave.

"You said a cave, right?" Amith asks Karishma whose eyes are still focused behind them.

"Yeah," Karishma answers without looking, still searching for any signs that the farmer is following them.

"Looks a little spooky," Shaneel says.

"Chicken!" Amith teases as he flaps his elbows up and down. Karishma turns to find out what all the commotion is about and sees the pipe. It's dark, very dark. "No! Not this one!"

"Are you sure, Karishma?" Shaneel asks.

As if on cue, a spider crawls out of the tube. It's tiny, a daddy long legs, but it seems as big as a house to frightened little Karishma. "No, no . . . definitely not this one."

Uncertainty fills Karishma's mind as she wonders what to be more concerned about—the gun-wielding farmer chasing them, or the abyssal darkness of the supposed cave waiting in front of them, along with all the icky critters inside.

"Well, we might as well check it out while we're here," Amith says, adjusting his shorts. "Besides, it'll give us a place to rest for the night."

Shaneel looks worried; he doesn't like bugs either. "You want to sleep . . . in there?" he sputters.

Amith doesn't answer. Instead, he turns his head and shows them an impish grin. Karishma is a little perplexed, but Shaneel knows that grin very well, and it usually spells trouble.

CHAPTER 25

The Tunnel

IT'S DAMP, AND THE SMELL INSIDE IS HORRID—a mixture of stale water, dead grass, and mold. A few weathered holes on the top of the pipe allow moonlight to shine in, but it only travels a few feet before it's lost in the engulfing darkness of the pipe. Still, the light acts as a beacon for the kids and almost seems to be inviting them to travel, crouched on all fours, farther inside. It's a good thing there's a full moon tonight; otherwise, the kids wouldn't have even that light to guide them.

Amith is in front, the usual leader of the expedition. This is his first major clue, and he'll be damned if he lets Shaneel find the cup before he does. It isn't a problem for Shaneel to follow Amith since he never wanted to enter the pipe in the first place. Karishma lags behind, placing her hands precisely and with great care on each crawling step forward.

A gust of wind whooshes through the tunnel and makes noise when it exits through the cracks above, as if the pipe were a demonic flute.

"What was that?" Shaneel croaks out, immediately stopped by the noise.

"Areh, nothing man," Amith says over his shoulder, "just the wind." Amith continues moving through the pipe.

Shaneel takes a deep breath and gathers the courage to move forward. A clunk sound echoes through the pipe as Amith runs into a piece of a metal can, stopping Shaneel in his tracks once again.

"Areh, you can't tell me *that* was the wind!" Shaneel cries.

"It's just a piece of metal," Amith yells back. He holds up the can in the dim light leaking from one of the holes above. They're not going to make much progress if Shaneel keeps stopping them at every noise, Amith thinks. He must come up with a solution.

"Didn't you say you always wanted to be an explorer? Pretend you are an explorer."

Shaneel nods in the darkness. Escaping into his imagination sounds more pleasant than their current surroundings, so he concentrates on his fantasy.

The long dark path of the tunnel transforms, but not into what Shaneel wanted. His fear overtakes him, and now the tunnel seems more like the jaws of a venomous beast than the tranquil emptiness of a cave. The dampness on the ground is transformed into saliva, and the wind that blows through the tunnel seems like the heavy breathing of an animal just waiting for the kill.

Shaneel quickly opens his eyes.

"That didn't work at all!" he yells, more frightened than ever.

"Okay, fine. Go back and wait for me. I'll go see what's up ahead," Amith grunts in frustration.

"Go toward the noise? Are you crazy? It could be some sort of scary animal."

"Think, bhai," *(brother)* Amith snickers as he continues, "Karishma is behind you. If it is an animal, it'll get her first, and you'll have time to escape."

Karishma shrieks at the idea and clutches onto Shaneel's leg. Shaneel likes this.

"I don't want to go back," Karishma pleads.

112

"Don't worry, I'll protect you," Shaneel whispers, invigorated with courage from Karishma's touch.

"Okay, then, stay here, the both of you. I'll go ahead and see," says Amith.

Shaneel and Karishma nod in unison. Finally, a sound plan. Amith continues full speed ahead. He mutters "scaredy cats" to himself. A noise rings through the tunnel—maybe the wind again, Amith thinks, and turns around to take a look. No one is behind him, just empty darkness. He's all alone . . . alone . . . in the dark. A cold chill runs down his spine.

Amith starts whispering to himself, "I'm an explorer. I'm an explorer," trying to reassure himself like he tried to do for Shaneel. He moves farther ahead. Another clunk and Amith freezes, but there is nothing behind him again. He moves forward but his hand brushes against something. Amith quickly slaps the air, trying to fight it off, but it's too dark to see. It could be a twig, a branch, or a venomous blood-sucking bat. Amith harshly beats the whatever-it-is to smithereens. After assuring himself that he has thoroughly vanquished the creature—or branch—he starts moving forward again.

Amith pushes ahead, looking for the next opening of light in the dark gloom. Eventually, he finds one, and its beam offers a moment of solace, but that moment is abruptly ended as Amith discovers a skin shed from a rather large snake.

In the village, there have always been stories of snakes. The snakes would sneak in from the depths of the jungle and enter the village to eat small prey—mainly rats, cats, and tiny puppies, but he heard they are capable of consuming much, much more. Some are even venomous and have killed a villager or two. Hopefully this is not one of them. Amith starts muttering his chant a little faster and louder.

"I'm an explorer. I'm an explorer," he says as he starts moving ahead only to be stopped by a hissing sound. Amith freezes once again. What to do, what to do? The tunnel is too small to fight a snake. What if it's a cobra? Oh, please don't let it be a cobra, especially the spitting kind. Those things can kill a person in one bite.

All these worries rush through Amith's mind, leaving little hope for anything other than a fight for survival. And there is no way to see what's ahead or to figure out what's making that bone-chilling sound.

Idea, idea! Amith must think quickly and find a solution to his problem. Wait! The piece of metal can—he still has it. Amith finds the next crevice of light. Good, it's a big one. Amith holds up the tin and bounces the dim rays of moonlight up ahead, using it as a flashlight. It's surprisingly effective and lights up the path extraordinarily well.

To Amith's surprise, he doesn't see a snake. Instead he sees a wall of debris ahead, packed like a dam of thorns, twigs, and leaves gathered up from years of neglect. Water leaks from the edges, making that horrible hissing sound as it fights to free itself from the barricade. There's something else there too, that's protruding from the debris. It's hard to make out, but it looks like a handle of some sort, maybe the handle of a cup. Yes! It sure looks like it could be a cup. Is this it? Is this the answer to Amith's problem, the prize for his quest, the victory for his challenge?

Amith rushes for the barrier and quickly grabs the cup handle. He pulls on it as hard as he can, but it doesn't budge. He tries again with no success, only to be followed by attempts three, four, and five, all increasingly unsuccessful. Amith can tell he lacks the strength to budge the cup, as it remains tightly snug in its place, fortified by its surroundings.

Amith takes a break, as he breathes heavily, trying to regain his strength. He stares angrily at the cup handle. It's up to him. One small, defiant obstacle stands between him and utter victory. One solemn act of heroism to accomplish so that a lifelong dream can come true. A hero wouldn't give up, especially when he is so close. Amith will do all he can to win.

Amith takes a deep breath and lunges for the handle again. He grabs hold of it, in an unyielding grip, and pulls. He sits on the floor of the pipe, pushing with his legs for leverage against the debris-filled barricade, and leaning back, pulls with all his might. The hissing gets louder as water seeps from the sides. It's starting to budge.

But before victory can be attained and unbeknownst to Amith, a real snake slithers through a crack in the pipe, the very same opening Amith used earlier to shine light onto the wall and open a doorway to the object of his mom's salvation. Now, that hole acts as a gateway for Amith's doom.

The snake just barely fits its two-foot-long body through the hole and plops into the water, making a small splash. But the sound is masked by the hiss of the water coming through the barricade. The snake looks around to see what has been causing all the commotion and sees Amith up ahead. It flicks its tongue out, as if licking the air. Then it starts to make its way toward Amith.

Amith keeps pulling, still unaware of the impending downfall that lurks behind him, ready to strike, ready to end his journey.

The snake glides through the shallow water toward Amith, the hiss from the water masking the true call of the snake. Soon the snake is within striking distance.

Amith keeps tugging at the handle. His focus is only on the handle and the water that seeps out from the little cracks and onto his bare, unprotected torso.

The snake gets ready—it couldn't have a better target. It contracts and then lunges at Amith.

At the same time, Amith frees the handle from the barricade's grasp. The water blasts forth from the loosened wall, knocking Amith onto the wet tunnel floor and causing the snake to miss its strike and hit the walled-up debris instead. It falls into the slow stream of water now flowing through the tunnel.

Just then Amith catches sight of the snake, and his eyes pop open in shock.

The snake quickly recovers and raises its head for another attempt at its target.

Amith starts scrambling backward as the snake slithers toward him, moving in close enough for another strike. Amith cringes, ready for the bite of the venomous snake, ready to take the hit, ready for what he feared would come true.

Then Amith hears a rumbling in the irrigation pipe. It even stops the snake from its planned attack as the vibrations travel through the pipe. Amith stares past the snake, at the cracked wall, and so does the snake.

The built-up pressure behind the wall is trying to get free. Pieces of debris are rapidly falling off the little hole that Amith made from pulling the cup handle out, and a stream of water gushes out of it. The pipe groans and moans from the water pressure.

The snake turns its attention back to Amith. It rears its head again, knowing this is its last chance to strike. The snake makes another lunge.

Suddenly, the entire wall bursts open from the pressure of the water. The trapped water charges through the tunnel, engulfing Amith and the snake in its powerful surge.

¤ ¤ ¤ ¤ ¤

Shaneel and Karishma sit near the end of the tunnel but still inside, waiting for Amith. They hear the rumble start.

"What's that?" Karishma asks as she shrinks closer to Shaneel for protection.

"It's probably nothing, just some strange noise," says Shaneel, trying to reassure her.

The tunnel starts to shake.

"I hope," he says, not so sure himself.

The rumble gets louder.

"Amith?" Shaneel says, gulping.

Then he hears Amith scream through the tunnel.

"Amith!" Shaneel cries out as he forgets his fear and heads into the tunnel toward the rumbling.

Suddenly Amith appears, but he isn't alone. The full force of the water is rushing through the tunnel at breakneck speed, and riding on top of it is Amith, who continues screaming, as the torrent of water jets its way toward Shaneel and Karishma.

Shaneel turns around, trying to block the tunnel to shield Karishma from the hit, but it's no use. Amith crashes into Shaneel and Karishma, and the three are quickly swept up in the tidal wave of water, sending them rocketing through the opening of the tunnel. They fly out of the pipe and fall into the empty stream bed. The water behind them continues to gush from the opening, quickly bringing the stream back to life.

Amith, Shaneel, and Karishma sit in the stream, drenched from head to toe.

Amith suddenly jumps into the air, screaming, and starts stamping the wet ground.

"Hey! It's just water," Shaneel yells.

Amith takes a moment and looks around. There is not a snake in sight. A moment passes as he considers his luck, then he quickly looks himself over, checking for bite marks. He doesn't find anything and lets out a relieved sigh. The gushing water dies down to a normal stream.

Then he looks at what he is holding. It's a handle all right, but not a cup handle and not the goblet handle. It is the handle of a thin, yellow rolling pin used to roll out dough into rotis—much like the one his mom has at home. Amith sulks, wringing the water from his clothes.

Karishma stares at Amith for a moment before she points at him and starts to laugh. "Scaredy cat! Scaredy cat!" she cries.

Amith stands in embarrassed shock, his heroism questioned. She didn't see any of his heroic battle with the snake.

"No! There was this big snake!" Amith explains.

"Yeah, sure. Just like the gun . . . this big," Shaneel jokes, holding his arms out wide.

Amith reaches down into the now thriving stream and splashes water at Karishma. She gets hit right in the face, and Shaneel laughs. Annoyed, Karishma splashes Shaneel in the mouth, causing him to spit out the water. Karishma and Amith start laughing.

They start splashing each other and laughing, and before they know it, it's a full-fledged water fight between the three kids at night, lit by the sparkling moonlight above.

The water they play in gathers its strength, building into a stream. The stream flows past the playing kids and down its once-forgotten path, all the way back to its original home: the farm.

The strange but familiar trickling noise wakes the farmer from his peaceful sleep. He gets up quickly and runs outdoors to take a look. The farmer's eyes gleam with amazement as he stares at the miracle happening in front of him.

The stream once again flows onto his farm, filling the crop's irrigation canals, and filling his spirit as well, and the parched land takes its first drink after a long, thirsty drought.

The farmer rushes up to the waterway in astonishment. He leans over and touches the flowing water with his hand. He feels the coolness of the life-giving liquid running past his fingertips. His shoulders relax as the tension begins to wash away. He sits down next to the stream and watches the water trickle into his irrigation canals, and for the first time in a long while, the farmer is happy.

CHAPTER 26

Camp

HERO TRAINING TIP #14

"A hero never gets jealous."

~Shaneel

IT'S A COLD NIGHT. The moon is thankfully full and beams its radiance into the jungle. The nighttime song of the land fills the air as wind blows past the treetops, and the crickets sing and dance their ballet to nature's music.

The three kids are gathered in a small clearing, not too far from the road. They listen to the jungle sounds, hoping for another truck to come along, but so far nothing. It seems the road is even less traveled than they thought, and catching one truck was just pure luck.

Amith lies near a tree. He uses his rolled up red scarf as a pillow against the exposed roots. As he lies there he plays with a twig, pulling the bark off in long strips.

Shaneel sits not too far away, staring at the night sky. He had been trying to make a pointy end on a branch to use as a spear, but he's already grown tired of it and tossed it aside.

This night, the kids have failed in their efforts to make a fire, and although Amith was a great helper at doing it in the safety of being at home, he isn't much good at it here in the real world.

Luckily, he knows that the moon stays full for nearly three days before it starts to lose its glow. This is a good excuse to cover Amith's laziness. He tells the others that lighting a fire would make little difference on this bright night and he better save his strength for the real heroic deeds.

Karishma sits nearby, staring at Amith. Shaneel takes notice. He doesn't like it much.

"What do we do when we find the cup?" Shaneel asks, trying to get his mind off their current situation.

"I'll take the cup back to the village, to my ma, and she'll use it and get better," Amith answers, sitting up.

Shaneel smiles as he daydreams about the day when it happens. "Like a real hero."

Amith smiles at the remark. "Yeah, just like a real hero." Amith tosses the twig aside and lies back on his makeshift pillow. "You can be my sidekick," he says as he closes his eyes.

Shaneel doesn't like that image—Amith getting all the glory while poor Shaneel hangs around to do all the dirty work. He's not the only one daydreaming, Shaneel realizes, when he looks over at Karishma. She seems to be picturing what Amith says also, but she's smiling at the thought.

Shaneel grabs his makeshift spear and tests the edge. Still blunt. So he starts working on it again, trying to make it sharp. It's a good way to show Karishma how well he can survive in the wild, he thinks, and that he can be just as rough and tough as Amith. Maybe then she will pay more attention to him.

Karishma gets up and moves close to Amith. "I'm cold," she says as she curls up next to him.

"Aye, get away from me!" Amith complains as he tries to push her away.

121

Regardless, she snuggles next to him. Amith stops pushing her away and takes a look at her. She's already asleep. Kind of cute, he thinks, and smiles.

Shaneel turns his head away, irritated. I guess the hero always gets the girl. If only he was a hero. He grabs the spears and chucks it into the jungle. It sails into the darkness and disappears, much like his chances.

Before long, Amith and Karishma are fast asleep, their little snores whispering in the night. Shaneel moves over to a broken tree stump on the other side of their camp and leans against it. All alone, he closes his eyes and forces himself to sleep.

CHAPTER 27

A Road Less Traveled

IT IS A HOT DAY, but a welcome cool breeze rustles through the trees, and they shed some of their leaves. A day like this is best enjoyed sitting at home with a nice glass of mango lassi, a cool Indian drink. But for the kids, it's time to get to work, as they continue to walk down the empty road to an unknown destination.

Amith takes the lone lead as usual, his red scarf gently flowing up and down in a cape-like fashion. He slashes the air with a stick he found on the ground. Shaneel and Karishma lag behind, busy talking. Shaneel tries to impress her with his knowledge of movies.

"What happens next?" Karishma asks, curious.

"Well, the knight and the maiden go into the forest, and that's where he falls in love with her." Shaneel smiles at Karishma.

"The forest?"

"Yup."

Karishma looks away and closes her eyes and starts to picture the scene.

She sees Amith. He is walking toward her, dressed in gleaming armor, and he holds flowers in his hand.

A smile creeps onto her face.

Somehow sensing that her thoughts aren't about him, Shaneel quickly interjects, "Pretty boring stuff, if you ask me."

Karishma opens her eyes and turns her attention back to Shaneel.

He continues eagerly, trying to keep her attention. "Yeah, pretty boring stuff until the good guy and bad guy fight in the end." Shaneel picks up a stick and slashes in the air, trying to show his fighting prowess to Karishma.

But Karishma looks away again. Her gaze falls on Amith, who is having his own fantasy battle. She continues daydreaming.

The castle sits in a beautiful, ornamented courtyard in the middle of an evergreen forest. Shrubs and vines tiptoe their way up and embrace the wooden walls. Up close, they are even more splendid as they are in full bloom. But these flowers are different from the normal ones that come from these vines. These are roses, red roses.

The serenity of the setting is broken by the sound of metal as two knights' blades clash against each other. One wears a suit of black armor; the other wears gleaming white. It's Amith and Shaneel. Karishma stands nearby, dressed in a flowing white gown, watching the two battle for her heart. A quick thrust here, a dodge there, a swift slash, and another dodge. They match each other's attacks gracefully in a close tango, neither one getting the upper hand. Karishma watches enraptured, not knowing which to root for. Finally the white knight delivers a glancing blow; it's not much, but he has gained the upper hand. Blood trickles down the black knight's arm, but he doesn't stop. Instead, he readies his blade.

Suddenly, they stop their duel and turn to Karishma—first the white knight, then the black one.

"Karishma! Where do we go?" Amith asks.

Karishma snaps out of her dream. "What?"

"Where are we supposed to go?" Amith asks again, now standing next to her.

She had forgotten that she is leading the way, that it is up to her to guide them to their destiny. But Karishma doesn't know what to say, so she fakes confusion to buy herself some time, even though she knows it won't last for long.

"What?" she repeats.

Amith gets annoyed and slaps his head, thinking, are all girls this irritating? "Areh, where does the book say we need to go next to find the cup?"

Should she tell them the truth? Should she finally come clean and tell them that she has been deceiving them the entire time? Should she expose herself as a liar and destroy her only connection with Amith?

Karishma tries for more time as she carefully pulls the book out from her satchel.

"Let me see," she says as she thumbs through the book, looking for an idea. Nothing comes to her. The words are a mess like they have always been.

"Just read what it says, Karishma," Amith says impatiently.

Karishma looks up, lost for words.

Luckily, the conversation she had moments before with Shaneel comes to the rescue and triggers an idea, an idea that can make this whole trip magical, an idea that would make the dire consequences worth it and her dreams come true.

Shaneel's words ring in her ears, ". . . the knight and the maiden go into the jungle and that's where he falls in love with her." She stops on a random page and looks up with a smile and says, "The jungle."

CHAPTER 28

Mud

HERO TRAINING TIP #15

"A hero always keeps his cool."

~Shaneel

IT'S BEEN A LONG TREK THROUGH THE JUNGLE without much reward. The densely packed trees force the children to climb over enormous roots, getting their hands and clothes dirty. Amith makes his way up on top of one of these large roots, sweat pouring down his face. Shaneel and Karishma follow behind.

"Amith, bhai, let's take a break," Shaneel calls out.

"We can't stop now," Amith responds, grunting. "We have to find the cup." Amith charges his way through to the next obstacle.

"Amith, don't worry. We will find it, but we should take a break," Shaneel says, out of breath. "Karishma is tired."

Amith stops and looks back.

Karishma struggles to make her way up, her tiny frame crawling over a gigantic root. She barely manages to clear it and stumbles the rest of the way toward the boys. She is covered with sweat and is breathing heavily.

"Okay . . . let's . . . go," she says with a few gasping breaths.

"No, Karishma, we're going to take a break," Shaneel says, taking charge for the first time.

"Shaneel, she's fine. We should continue," Amith says, challenging Shaneel's command.

"Just a little bit, Amith," Shaneel says. "We just need to rest for a moment, maybe get something to eat," he continues.

"No, we should keep moving," Amith barks as he turns and heads for the next root. He makes his way to the top and then stops. He hears a rumbling. Amith looks down; it's his stomach. He had forgotten that they hadn't eaten anything all day. Moving forward does sound like a good idea, but then again, right now food sounds like an even better idea.

¤ ¤ ¤ ¤ ¤

The air up here is a lot cooler than below, Shaneel thinks, as he sits perched high up in a tree. He tries to take his mind off the height, but what keeps coming back to him is the thought of his "almost-fall" from the crates. That was quite a terrifying experience and not so easily forgotten. This is clearly much higher, and much more dangerous, and also more frightening. But he couldn't say no, not in front of Karishma. Besides, if he is determined to be a hero, he must act like one. A hero doesn't get scared, and she will never think of him as a hero if he chickens out. Then again, a hero is smart, and climbing this tree is not very smart. Shaneel stops his ascent.

"Why do I have to be the one climbing the tree?" Shaneel yells. He waits for a good reason to keep defying gravity.

"Because it was your idea to get something to eat, yaar," Amith yells from below, standing safely next to Karishma.

"Stupid, stupid, stupid idea," Shaneel mutters to himself as he continues his climb up the banana tree. Higher and higher he goes.

The fruit is at the top of a banana tree; the bananas clump together in big bundles and hang down the side. Banana trees vary in how tall they get, depending on the type. The yellow bananas are sweeter and the trees small, while the red ones are bitter and their trees can grow to a dizzying height of forty feet in the wild. Unfortunately, this one has reddish bananas, and it towers into the high canopies of the jungle.

Shaneel makes his way to the top of a shooting, branchlike leaf; its stem is near the trunk, which is usually sturdy and offers some support for his foot. Also, one lone banana remains from a bundle that has been picked nearly clean. It hangs just above him, so Shaneel decides to go for it.

"Hurry up, yaar!" Amith yells from below.

The outburst almost knocks Shaneel off balance, and he has to kneel down quickly and grab the tree trunk to steady himself. The tree starts gently swaying, scaring Shaneel even more.

"Quiet man, I need to concentrate!" Shaneel shrieks from the top as he waits for the tree to stop moving.

"Concentrate? Just grab the banana! It's easy," Amith shouts from below.

"It's easy, just grab the banana," Shaneel mockingly imitates Amith's voice to himself. "Hey, it was your idea. Why don't you climb the tree? Always bossing everyone around." Shaneel continues his mutterings to himself as he stands up again. "I'll show him. I'll show him who the hero really is this time." Shaneel reaches out for the banana—it's just inches away. He stretches and grabs for the banana. All of a sudden, it disappears, swiped away in a flash.

What was that?! Shaneel is extremely shocked at the idea that he is not alone. Who could possibly be up here with him? He cringes at the thought and starts looking around. Then he sees it, the criminal at large.

A monkey in a neighboring tree swings Tarzan-like on a vine with Shaneel's prize in his hand. It's grinning from ear to ear and raises his eyebrows up and down while swinging back and forth on his vine.

As the monkey comes close on one of its swings, Shaneel tries to swipe the banana back, but the attempt makes him lose his balance and he has to scramble back to safety. The monkey swiftly moves away, kicking off from Shaneel's tree and into the neighboring one. Then it jumps off the vine and lands gracefully on one of the branches. Its monkey friends are watching the spectacle. After a bit of monkey-discussion, they look over at Shaneel who is still hugging the tree for dear life. They start flailing their arms and imitating Shaneel trying to catch his balance.

Shaneel stares back in disbelief at their mockery.

Amith and Karishma are watching the whole show from below, and it's not long before they are bursting with laughter.

This only infuriates Shaneel more, especially since this was his chance to show Karishma what a great hero he is, but now he looks like a complete fool, thanks to a gang of monkeys. In anger, Shaneel roughly shakes the tree he is in.

The monkeys, in turn, try to imitate Shaneel by shaking their own tree while they howl in laughter. However, Shaneel's tree shaking yields a surprise. The aggressive move loosens a bundle of bananas high above and they fall to the ground. The monkeys stop their taunting, amazed by Shaneel's fortunate outcome.

Below, an eager Amith and Karishma are equally astonished, but hunger compels them to gather all the fallen bananas before the monkeys can swipe them.

Shaneel witnesses this from above. Then he turns his attention to the monkeys. He shows them a giant grin and starts to tease them back by imitating a monkey. All of a sudden, a clump of mud smacks Shaneel right on the face, covering his gleaming smile.

¤ ¤ ¤ ¤ ¤

Amith and Karishma are dining voraciously on the fresh bananas while Shaneel makes the last few yards down with ease. Once he is on the ground, he uses a fallen banana leaf to wipe his face.

Amith stops eating—there is a pungent aroma in the air. He starts sniffing the air and wrinkles his nose in disgust.

"What's that smell?"

"Stupid monkeys were throwing mud at me," Shaneel replies.

Amith has a peculiar look on his face. He might not know much about animals, but he knows monkeys. He gets up from his fruit feast and walks over to Shaneel. He sniffs Shaneel's face and gags from the smell.

"I don't think that's mud," Amith says in disgust.

"Then what is it?" Shaneel asks.

Shaneel takes a piece of the mud from his face and takes a huge whiff. Now he can smell it—the odor is unmistakable. It's an odor that comes from something that all animals and creatures must do, and something no one talks about. A look of worry comes over him as he becomes aware.

The monkeys above are going wild, howling with laughter.

Amith starts rolling on the ground himself, this time laughing harder than ever. Karishma soon joins in too as she realizes that it's not mud on Shaneel's face but monkey feces.

CHAPTER 29

Heal the Sick

THE KIDS HIKE THEIR WAY THROUGH THE JUNGLE, on a trail of sorts. The path could have been made by humans or even carved out by animals hunting for their next meal—it is extremely hard to tell. It's weathered and short portions of it have disappeared entirely, but the kids follow it anyway because otherwise they would have to wander through the thick, thorny undergrowth. That would only hinder their progress, and Amith won't have any of that.

Amith and Karishma lead while Shaneel follows, still dismayed about what had conspired earlier. At times he stops suddenly, grabs a leaf, and gets an inkling to wipe his face. The very *thought* of the incident is disgusting. And at those moments, Amith and Karishma sneak a peek back at him and let out little chuckles. One day, *maybe*, Shaneel might even remember this and laugh, but today is not that day. Shaneel is not amused.

The three kids slowly make their way through the dense vegetation, helping each other over loose rocks, fallen trees, and debris, heading farther into the unknown. Suddenly they hear a noise and stop.

It's a strange noise, not a growl or a roar, and it's not even menacing in the least. It is a howl, a howl of pain and despair, a howl for help. The children quickly run toward the noise, trying to get close enough to find out what could possibly be causing it.

As they draw nearer, the howl gets weaker and weaker until it resembles a loud whimper, but they know they are heading the right way because the sound gets clearer with each step forward. Soon they spot a small trail of blood-soaked hoof prints which leads to a clearing. In the center of the clearing lies a weak fragile creature, bleeding from one of its legs. It's a deer, and it's dying. Karishma is overcome with emotion. The boys would never have guessed that she was an animal lover. At least, she never spoke of it. It may be the most feminine thing they know about her now. She runs to the injured animal.

The boys cry out, "Wait!" not knowing if whatever did the damage might be lurking around.

Karishma is deaf to their calls. The only call she hears is the one of the animal, the call for help. A call that she gladly answers.

The deer is badly wounded. Its body is over three times bigger than little Karishma, but it seems helpless and frail. One of its legs is bleeding, as if something had taken a bite out of it. There is so much blood on the grass that it even reflects some of the sky. The deer lies with its head on the ground, gulping for air. Its eyes are half glazed over, but they still focus on Karishma as she comes running to it.

Karishma kneels down next to the deer. Their eyes meet with a sort of mental connection. Immediately her eyes stream with tears. She pulls the deer's head onto her lap and starts petting its head and down the back of its neck, which is as far as she can reach. This calming motion soothes some of the deer's painful moans, and its breath becomes somewhat normal. Then the deer lets out a little groan as it tries to move its leg, and as the pain of its wound starts to creep up again, it starts to whimper once more.

Karishma is filled with grief. She sobs as though she feels the deer's pain. She wants to help, but she doesn't know what to do. She looks around, searching for something that can give her a clue as to what to do next.

The boys decide it's safe to approach. "Karishma, we should go," Amith says, displaying little feeling for the injured animal.

"We have to save her!" Karishma pleads.

"With what?" Amith asks, putting up his hands. "What are you going to do?"

Karishma doesn't have an answer; she just looks at the deer. The pain in its eyes seems immense, as it stares back at Karishma as if asking her to do something.

"I don't know. We just have to save her, okay?" Karishma sobs helplessly.

The deer lets out another groan. Hearing the sound, Karishma cries even harder. The two boys look at each other.

"Do something, yaar," Amith says as he shoves Shaneel's shoulder.

Shaneel takes a deep breath and rolls his shoulders, trying to conjure up an idea, but after a moment, he presses them back down with a sigh as nothing comes to mind. He puts up his hands, palms up in defeat.

"I don't know; you say something."

"Fine," Amith says to Shaneel. "Karishma, let's go. It's just a stupid animal," he snaps.

Karishma cries hysterically. Shaneel smacks Amith on the arm.

"What?" Amith yells, rubbing his arm from the blow.

Shaneel lets out a deep sigh at Amith's ignorance, then he goes over to Karishma and leans down by her and the deer.

"Karishma, I'm sorry. There's nothing you can do to help it," Shaneel says and gives her a hug. She leans into him for comfort, calming down a little.

Shaneel stands up and gives Amith a mocking smile, raising his eyebrows up and down, which of course annoys Amith.

Suddenly, the deer groans in agony, and once again Karishma bursts into tears.

Amith returns Shaneel's mocking look. Shaneel is irritated, but his mind quickly returns to being concerned about Karishma. He kneels down by her, but the motion bumps Karishma and the deer's head in her lap. The deer moans again, and Karishma grabs the bottom of Shaneel's shirt, motioning him to stop. Shaneel is startled and freezes in place.

But Karishma doesn't let go of her grip. She turns her head to stare at Shaneel as though she just got an idea. Suddenly Karishma's grip becomes very powerful and her tears stop. She lets go of her grip on Shaneel's shirt and then pushes him back. Shaneel moves out of the way quickly, not wanting to do any more damage.

Karishma slowly takes the deer's head off her lap and puts it down on the ground. Karishma stands up next to Shaneel. They are face to face—at least as much as a short person can be to someone taller. He stares into her eyes. The deep brownness of her eyes fills Shaneel's heart and mesmerizes his soul.

Is this it? he wonders. Is this what he has been waiting for? Is this the time for her to confess her undying love for him, like they do in the Bollywood movies? Is this where the scene cuts to another scene right when the girl and boy are supposed to kiss? He can only hope.

Suddenly, Karishma lunges at Shaneel, knocking him down. Shaneel is shocked. She jumps on him and starts tugging on the bottom of his shirt.

"Hey, stop it! What are you doing?!" Shaneel cries.

As Shaneel yells, Amith watches in fascination at the turn of events. Shaneel tries to wrestle her off, but she is ferociously persistent and oddly powerful. She keeps yanking on the bottom of his shirt until it tears.

"Stop it! You're going to rip my shirt."

But it's too late. With a final aggressive heave, Karishma pulls a long strip of cloth from the bottom of his shirt. Then she quickly runs back to the animal and picks up the injured leg. The deer howls from the movement, but it's a weak howl. Karishma starts wrapping the cloth around the wound.

Amith helps Shaneel to his feet. "You know she just kicked your butt, right?" Amith whispers to Shaneel.

"I . . . I let her win," Shaneel stutters in defense.

As Karishma finishes bandaging the deer's leg, the boys let out an "Oh" in unison.

The bandage seems to be helping—the bleeding has stopped. Karishma sits down and puts the deer's head back on her lap. She starts petting it again with long, smooth motions. It seems to soothe the animal's pain.

Amith and Shaneel stand next to each other, impressed. The boys had never been part of anything like this before. Their medical know-how only includes what they've seen in the movies, which is that when a hero gets shot, he brushes it off and moves on, stronger than ever. Besides feeding the occasional sick dog or cat in the village, the boys know little of what to do.

A moment passes, as a gust of wind travels through the clearing.

"Okay, what now?" Shaneel says to Amith quietly.

Amith shrugs his shoulders. After a moment, he calls out, "Karishma, we should leave."

Karishma gives Amith a fear-provoking defiant stare as she continues to protectively hold the deer's head tightly on her lap.

The boys take a step back and stand there, watching as Karishma continues to nurse the dying animal.

She is looking over the animal's body. It has many cuts, possibly from crashing through the jungle and escaping to this clearing. Karishma tears small pieces of her own dress and starts blotting blood from the cuts. But it's a losing battle; the animal is growing weaker and weaker.

The deer tries to moan in pain, but no sound comes out.

Karishma starts to cry again. It's a sad sight, sad enough to affect even Amith. He kneels down next to her.

"Karishma, don't cry," he says soothingly.

But she still does.

Amith gives her a hug and then he says, "Karishma, sometimes things die so they can start a new life. This animal was meant to do other things. It needs to move on, so it can start a new life."

"I couldn't help her . . ." Karishma mutters with tears streaming down her face.

Amith sits there at a loss for words and meets her gaze with sympathy. He tries to think of what to say, and then the perfect words pop into his mind. He kneels down and looks at her, face to face.

"Sometimes no matter what you do, you cannot change what is going to happen. But what's important is that you tried and did the right thing. Okay?" Amith says.

Karishma nods, her tears stop. Amith stands up and joins Shaneel. They watch as Karishma puts the deer's head on the ground and starts to collect herself.

"Amith, where did you hear that?" Shaneel asks him quietly.

There's a pause as Amith takes a deep breath before answering with a smile. "My mom," he says. Amith looks at Shaneel. "That's why I have to save her." Amith picks up some small pebbles next to his feet and calls out, "Come on," and heads into the jungle, playfully tossing the pebbles up in the air.

Shaneel and Karishma follow, leaving the slowly dying deer in peace.

CHAPTER 30

The Scout

AMITH STOPS AS HE WATCHES a rather large centipede crawl along the jungle floor. He's never seen a bug that big—almost a foot in length. It would be pretty scary if it didn't seem so docile and uncaring of Amith's presence. It's a good thing that Karishma is still lagging behind; if she saw this, she would jump into Amith's arms out of fear. But there is something magical about this creature to Amith, something so interesting. Amith kneels down to watch it walk, each of its family of legs hitting the dirt on unison in a timed march forward. Suddenly, a large black rat appears and grabs the centipede in its mouth, cutting it in half. It hisses at Amith and then runs back into the bushes with both ends of the centipede.

Amith is startled. He stands up quickly, looking around for the rat, but it's gone. A gust of wind blows, giving him a chill. Soon, Shaneel and Karishma catch up.

"What are you looking for?" Shaneel asks, seeing Amith stare at the bushes.

"Nothing," Amith responds.

Shaneel sits down on a nearby log and goes through his backpack. Almost all of the supplies they brought are gone. The coke bottle of water is empty, and the bread was eaten long ago, as well as the dried fruit. The candy bar from his parents' store is still there, and just a few of the bananas they picked up during the monkey ordeal remain all the way at the bottom. Shaneel shudders at the thought of the monkeys, and the memory makes him not want to even touch the bananas.

Shaneel takes out the candy bar. He breaks it into three pieces and gives the bigger two to Karishma and Amith, keeping the smaller one for himself.

They all sit on the log eating the treat, happy to take a break.

"Delicious," Amith says as he gobbles his piece down in one bite, then starts licking his fingers.

"I know," Shaneel says with a smile. "It's my favorite." But Shaneel's smile fades quickly. The candy bar is from his parents' little store, and he can't help but be reminded of them. Through it all his parents have been in the back of his mind, but he's been pushing the thought back. He doesn't want to think about what his parents are wondering. He knows they are worried.

It's been three days since their parents have heard anything from the kids. The kids didn't even tell them where they were going. Their parents are probably worried sick, as well as angry—very, very angry. And if the police have come to their houses, to ask them about the great robbery at the theatre, the kids would be prime suspects. Their parents would be furious at them. It is probably better not to go home right away—they can only dream what punishment the parents have planned for when the kids return home one day.

Yet, Shaneel knows that no matter how angry his parents may get, how badly they may spank him as punishment, he has to be here for Amith. He made a promise to himself a long time ago that he would never let Amith go through anything alone. To this day, he has kept that promise, and it's a promise that Shaneel never wishes to break, no matter the cost to him.

Karishma sits there quietly, still working on her piece of candy. She too worries about her parents, but she is more concerned about the lie she told and how she will get out of it. She knows there is little chance of getting out of trouble, no matter what decision she makes. Her concern is which path to take now.

"Where next?" Amith asks her, breaking into her thoughts. Karishma reaches into her satchel and pulls out the book, which she keeps wrapped and close to her body as if burying a secret— which she is.

She rummages through the book for a while, still clueless. Shaneel tries to take a peek, but she pulls it away from his view.

Interesting, Shaneel thinks. He could have sworn the book was turned around the other way the last time she looked at it. Must make no difference when someone can read, he guesses, as he puts the thought out of his mind.

Karishma closes the book and points forward.

¤　¤　¤　¤　¤

After a long while, the kids arrive at a good stopping spot. They sit down on a fallen tree. Moss, twining vines, and leaves cover the top, as well as a few bugs, which the kids push off with a leaf.

It's a good resting place. Amith finds some bushes nearby that are covered with berries that he recognizes as ones that his mom uses in some of her tasty dishes. One of the benefits of being so poor is that they often must forage for food. All the hunger has taught him the basics of surviving in the wild.

So, they plop down in their spots and enjoy their well-deserved rest. Shaneel stuffs some berries in his backpack for the road. Hopefully they won't get too squished on the journey. Karishma just sulks.

Amith grabs a stick and points it at Shaneel, beckoning him to play. Shaneel meets the challenge by finding a stick of his own.

Soon they are play-fighting an elegant battle of sticks to entertain Karishma, who sits and applauds at the spectacle. It is a moment when the kids can forget where they are. They forget the danger that lurks around them. They forget the great burden they have taken on their shoulders. It is a moment when the kids are, for at least a few minutes, just kids.

Suddenly, a great rumble sounds off in the distance. The shocked kids instantly stop playing, their hearts beating fast. They listen for another boom, but it doesn't come. The first one felt like the entire jungle shook from its wrath, whatever "it" was.

A huge gust of wind blows through the jungle canopy, rustling all the leaves. The kids look up at the sky, but they don't see anything—just a lone dark cloud.

CHAPTER 31

Thunder and Lightning

HERO TRAINING TIP #16

"Heroes don't make fun of others."

~Amith & Shaneel

THE KIDS COME UPON A LARGE FIELD full of yellow grass, mostly taller than the kids. The grass obscures most of the sight and seems endless, but there's no stopping the kids now. They still push on. Only the tops of some scattered trees can be seen in the distance; besides that, there isn't much to look at except the little path they have carved out as they walk deeper into the field.

When the kids reach dense areas, they have to use their sticks to break through, leaving a trail of broken twigs and tattered grass in their wake.

Amith takes a step through another bunch of grass and feels a drop of water. He stops. He looks back at Shaneel and Karishma.

"Did you feel it?" Amith asks.

"Yup," Shaneel says, nodding his head in agreement.

"What?" Karishma asks.

"Rain," Shaneel says, turning around.

A heavy thunder rumbles across the sky.

"Big rain," Shaneel says, staring up in astonishment.

Before Shaneel reaches the end of his sentence, huge drops bombard the kids and then it starts to pour. The sky crackles above, and Amith cannot help but think of the nightmare he had before. The sky growls as the clouds churn into each other, releasing more water as if being wrung out of a wet towel by an evil giant standing high above.

"We should find shelter," Amith yells to the others.

Shaneel looks around. "Where?"

Karishma points to the treetops in the distance, the closest landmark she can make out. "There!"

The kids run toward the trees. In the meantime, the weather doesn't let up. The clouds howl and wail in the downpour. The dirt turns to mud as the kids kick and splash through the field.

They can feel the weather changing, as the rain increases with each step. The skies roar with thunder as the kids get closer to their refuge. Finally they reach shelter under a giant tree.

The tree has many spawned branches that coil out and reach into the air, and those branches are covered with a mass of smaller branches and leaves that provide a haven for the kids. The tree roots sprout up from the ground like seats, but the rain hits there. So the kids start to climb, trying to find a drier spot: Amith first, Karishma second, and Shaneel—always concerned about falling—climbs up last, each looking for a dry spot.

Amith finds a branch high above—it's a large one that protrudes the most and towers over many of the others. It provides a great space for him to lie down and dangle his leg, which Amith kicks back and forth. Karishma finds a cozy little nook close to the heart of the tree. She sits with her back comfortably against it and folds her legs. Shaneel finds his spot on a small branch. His branch is not as sturdy as Amith's gigantic one and Shaneel has to put one leg on each side to keep his balance, but it works. He takes out his empty coke/water bottle and holds it out to catch the rain in it.

The kids sit there, staring into the abyss of the rain and admiring the scenery from their new vantage point. From there, they can see how vast the field truly is. The field stretches very far from the jungle that lies at the far end. The ground it covers looks like a smooth blanket of yellow—the only break in the expanse is the path the kids carved out as they made their way through it.

"It's pretty, isn't it?" Karishma says, admiring nature's pristine beauty.

"Yeah, it is," Shaneel says as he looks back at Karishma.

"Ehhh, it's all right, I guess," Amith says. Amith doesn't care to take in what's around him like the others—to him, there isn't a point. Instead, he is focused on what he has to do, his goal of becoming a hero. And the imagery of being a hero is amazing. To Amith, the beauty of what's in his head vastly overpowers anything in real life. He can even create his own tapestry of nature in his mind that yields to his every command—every color, every stroke made just the way he likes it. For when one has such power in his dreams, what can the real world ever provide that wouldn't pale in comparison?

The rain pours most of the night and never truly lets up. At moments, the storm lessens a little, but then it regains its strength and unleashes it back into the world.

Karishma sits staring at Amith who kicks his foot against the tree, causing little bits of bark to break and fall on the quietly annoyed Shaneel below.

"Amith?" Karishma calls out.

"Yeah?" Amith answers.

"Why do you want to be a hero so badly?"

Shaneel perks up his ears in interest. He never thought to ask *himself* that question. Instead, as they grew up, he got lured in by Amith's imagination and just followed along. Now, Shaneel too holds that dream, but he wonders if he really wants to be a hero or if he just doesn't want to be left behind by Amith.

Amith thinks for a moment before responding. It's an interesting question, one that no one has ever asked him before.

"I guess because heroes can change the world. They can make a difference and be noticed," Amith says, sitting up. "Heroes can do things others won't do because they're too worried about the consequences. Heroes have the courage to do things because they are fearless."

Shaneel and Karishma sit there immersed in Amith's words.

"I'm going to be a great hero one day," Amith continues as he lies back on his branch and describes one of his daydreams. Karishma and Shaneel join him, also picturing his fantasy.

"I will show the world how great a hero I am."

The streets are full of decorations. The buildings tower into the skies all the way past the white clouds. The buildings glimmer in the sun, but a lone, pure beam of sunshine hits the street. It is much stronger than the others, and the beam follows a boy.

A young Amith walks proudly down the road, flaunting a large smile on his face. People line up in the streets, cheering him and calling out his name to come closer.

"Amith, over here!"

"Amith, say hi to my folks!"

"Amith, what's the answer to question six on my test?"

Amith approaches the cheering crowd and shakes hands with the first couple. Next he meets the grandparents of the second couple and says, "Hi folks." Then he walks over to the worried student and answers enthusiastically, "The answer is C." They all smile and cheer as Amith continues his walk.

"I will give people strength."

The people crowd around as they celebrate this special event—seeing Amith. They applaud and offer him necklaces made of flowers and sweet treats like the ones Amith's mom makes.

"I will show them how they can help others."

A very young, lost child cries in the crowd, abandoned by everyone. Amith reaches down, picks him up, rears his arm back, and tosses him like a football to his parents. The parents catch the child with gleeful appreciation. The child starts giggling and clapping his hands together. "Thank you! We will name him Amith!" the parents cry out in excitement.

"I will give them hope."

Amith now reaches a podium. He stands tall and proud. His mom stands next to him. The crowd goes silent in anticipation.

Amith smiles at everyone, then reaches into the podium's shelf and pulls out the cup that he saw in the movie. The crowd begins to applaud. Amith holds the cup high in the air for everyone to see. The crowd reacts with enormous excitement and starts chanting his name. "Amith, Amith, Amith!"

The dream is broken by an explosion of thunder. Karishma is startled from sharing Amith's picturesque dream with him. Shaneel stares at the upheaval in the skies above. The storm is not calming down. It seems like things are only going to get worse.

The rain falls harder and at a much sharper angle than before. The wind has picked up, causing the rain to penetrate the canopy of leaves and shower the shivering kids.

Shaneel moves closer to the tree trunk, but Amith just looks into the sky, annoyed by the inconvenience of the rain. Amith starts pulling bark off the branch he sits on and tossing it into the air to see which direction the wind will take it. He grabs a rather large piece, maybe big enough to defy the wind, and tosses it sideways like a Frisbee through the air. But as Amith watches its trail through the air, a movement in the distance catches his eye.

Dark shadows are moving around in another tree. Amith squints to make them out and sees small, humanoid figures, similar to the kids in size. After careful examination, Amith grins.

"Look, Shaneel, your arch enemies!"

Shaneel's eyes follow the path of Amith's pointing finger toward the distant trees . . . and suddenly fill with anger. In the trees sit the most wretched creatures known to man, creatures so full of themselves, so arrogant, and so beguiling that they disgust anyone having to deal with them. In that tree is the very same gang of monkeys that threw feces at Shaneel.

The monkeys catch sight of the kids too, but more importantly of Shaneel. No longer upset by the weather, the monkeys jump up and down in excitement because now they have a show to pass the time, and tonight's main attraction is Shaneel, the boy who was pelted in the face with their poop.

The monkeys howl with laughter as they taunt Shaneel by slapping their cheeks and wiping their faces with their hands, simulating Shaneel's response to the revolting experience.

Shaneel is getting very annoyed.

"They must also be hiding from the rain," Karishma says.

"They might be safe up in that tree, but wait until the rain stops. I'm going to get back at them," Shaneel snorts as he raises his fist in the air.

"Are you going to hit them with your poop?" Amith says, laughing from his perch on top.

Shaneel just sits there, powerless and infuriated by the situation. In the other tree, the monkeys continue their rampage with their crude antics and heckling.

"You stupid monkeys, I'm going to get you!" Shaneel swears.

The monkeys howl louder right back at Shaneel.

"Hey, they're making fun of me!" Shaneel screams.

A loud crack thunders in the air. Everyone stops for a moment, even the monkeys. The monkeys stare back at Shaneel and at the sky, but soon the mocking starts once more. The monkeys start getting wilder and wilder, shaking the branches they sit on.

Suddenly, another thunder blasts through the air, but this time lightning comes crashing down near the tree the monkeys are sitting in. The force sends the monkeys jumping out of the tree, and they cry out as the treetop catches on fire.

"Ha, ha! Karma!" Shaneel yells out.

The monkeys disappear into the fields, fleeing from the flaming tree. Amith stares at the monkeys, and then something makes him worry.

"We have to go!" Amith says.

"Why?" Shaneel asks.

"The lightning hit a tree," Amith explains.

"Yeah, so?"

"WE are in a tree!"

Amith quickly scurries down the tree. A moment passes as Karishma and Shaneel stare at each other before the reality of the situation sets in, and then they too quickly move down the branches after Amith.

The storm clouds roar again, readying for another lightning strike. Once on the ground, Amith points to the tree line at the jungle.

"Over there!" Amith screams, and the kids take to the open field.

The storm clouds seem to snarl in anger at the sight. As the kids get farther and farther into the field, the storm appears angrier and angrier. Vein-like lightning flashes through the clouds, and soon loud cracks of thunder fill the sky and rain shoots down in bullet-sized pellets.

Amith and Shaneel are in the lead, and they rapidly slice a path through the field, taking whips and scratches from the blades of grass as they go. The much slower Karishma lags behind.

The kids continue to run as the thunder roars dangerously overhead. All of a sudden, a blinding light fills the air—must be a lightning strike! The boys stop. It was close, too close.

Shaneel and Amith look around, trying to find where the lightning struck, but there's nothing to be seen. Then they realize that something's missing: there's no sign of Karishma! The realization shoots through their minds as they start screaming her name.

"Karishma, Karishma!"

Suddenly, the thunder calms and the storm subsides. The clouds retreat into the jungle ahead, leaving a trail of burning trees and soaked earth behind from its wrath.

Amith and Shaneel continue looking for Karishma and calling out her name as they expand their search. There's still no sign of her, only grass.

After what seems like eternity, they finally find her. Karishma lies face down in the mud, with her muddied arms out in front of her. The nearby ground is heavily charred.

For the first time, Amith starts to tear up. Shaneel stands frozen in shock; the boys can only stare. Suddenly, she moves.

Quickly they rush to help her stand. She's fine—no burn marks or wounds, only frizzled hair that stands straight up on end from the static electricity that ran through it. The lightning didn't hit her, but it must have been close. Luckily, no harm was done to her.

"I'm okay," Karishma says, smiling.

The boys stare at her for a moment in relief—and also in disbelief. Then they notice her hair standing straight up as tall as the grass that surrounds them. The boys start to snicker.

"What?" she asks.

The boys go into full-blown laughter. Karishma just stares at them, wondering what's so funny. Shaneel tries to hold in his laughter, not wanting to offend Karishma, but he can't help himself and starts to snort. The snort launches volleys of laughter.

"What?" Karishma demands now, perturbed by the boys' heckling.

Soon the boys are rolling on the muddy ground in laughter with tears of joy and amusement streaming down their faces. They only stop to point at Karishma's hair, which starts their hysterical laughter again.

"Stop laughing at me!"

They try, but the sight is too fantastic for them to stop.

"I almost died, okay?!" she says, pouting with her arms crossed defiantly.

The realization of how dire the scenario was, and the resulting outcome, only makes the situation even more hilarious to the boys. They fall to the ground, filling the air with their laughter and tears.

In hopes of ending the amusement, Karishma starts walking through the grass—her hair standing up like a flag to guide the way. The boys snicker and snort their way to a standing position and follow her into the tree line and the waiting jungle, not knowing that what they just experienced was only a taste of the real storm that was brewing.

CHAPTER 32

The Belly of the Beast

HERO TRAINING TIP #17

"A hero is never afraid to do what's right."

~Karishma

THE NIGHT WAS TOUGH; it was cold and wet, especially since they couldn't get a fire going in the wet mud. It was very uncomfortable with many bugs and noises to keep them awake. But Karishma was awake for another reason: her guilt was haunting her.

It had been a long, hard journey walking, climbing over rocks, and trudging through the thick foliage to get this far since morning. The weather might have let up, but the jungle hadn't. The kids are covered with scratches and cuts from their nature lessons, yet they still venture forward.

Karishma's conscience grows heavier and heavier with each step. She knows it's her fault that they have traveled so far into the unknown. It's inevitable that they will need to turn back, but she doesn't have the heart or the words to tell the truth. The fear of abandonment and rejection by Amith are hard to bear, even for a tough little girl like Karishma. She knows that she is leading them astray for no reason. She worries that she should admit she doesn't know how to read. And most of all, she hates that she is giving Amith and Shaneel false hope. Then again, she wonders if false hope is better than no hope at all.

Karishma stops to take a break, her little head full of concerns and worries that are way too grownup for her.

"Are you okay?" Shaneel asks, concerned.

Karishma pulls the book out from her satchel and opens it. She stares hard at the scratches that are words, but nothing makes sense to her. A terrible realization sets in. Karishma tosses the book down in aggravation.

"Karishma, what's wrong?" Shaneel tries to comfort her, but she wants none of it. Instead, she squats down and just stares at the book.

"Hey, Karishma! We have to be going!" Amith howls from up ahead.

"Wait a minute, bhai," Shaneel yells back.

Shaneel sits down next to Karishma, his heart full of genuine concern, while up ahead, Amith pouts and paces back and forth impatiently.

"Come on, let's go!" Amith shouts.

"I said wait, man!" Shaneel answers back.

Unable to look at the book any longer—unable to face that lie and unable to face Shaneel—Karishma shifts her gaze blankly to the trees up ahead.

Shaneel looks at the book and then Karishma, but he is unable to decipher the truth. So he follows Karishma's gaze and stares at the trees. They sit like that for a moment, staring into the oblivion of reality, and then Shaneel speaks.

"Is it because you almost died?"

There is a long pause as Karishma takes in the words. They break through the barrier of her blank stare. Shaneel might be right; she never focused on her actions before her close call with the lightning. She thought her actions were innocent and no one would get hurt, but now things are different. The reality of consequences to actions has become very evident. This isn't playtime anymore; there are no parents to scold them in their wrongdoings, to let them off with a warning or some minor punishment. What's left now are only dire consequences. There is a price to be paid for their acts, and Karishma is not sure if they are ready or willing to pay the cost. Someone could get hurt because of the lie she told just to be accepted. The harsh truth is that someone could die because of her.

With that final thought, Karishma bursts into tears. She tries to hide her face in her hands, embarrassed that she is unable to cover the truth of her emotions.

What will the boys think of her if they see her break? Will they think she is just a little girl, weak, fragile and unable to toughen up through boy hardships? They will think all these thoughts and they will be right, because at this moment, all those thoughts are true.

Her heartbreaking wail stops Amith from pacing, and he watches closely with concern.

"Karishma, what's wrong?" Shaneel says quietly. He puts his hand on her head and gently strokes downward. It is what his parents do when he is upset. It is also the way Karishma comforted the wounded deer—fitting, since Karishma too seems wounded.

Karishma sputters some words, but it's hard to make sense of them.

"It's just . . . because of me . . ."

"No, Karishma. You are a big help," Shaneel says calmly.

"Yeah. Without you, we wouldn't know what the book says," Amith adds, walking over to them.

Karishma opens her mouth, about to relieve herself of her haunting burden, but she is stopped by something. It's as if the truth sits on the tip of her tongue, but it's stopped by Amith's presence.

Karishma breathes in deeply as she readies herself to spit out the truth and hit the two boys with the stark reality of her lie, to destroy Amith's hopes and dreams. But for some reason, staring at Amith's face, it gets stuck again, on the tip of Karishma's tongue.

"Come on, Karishma," Amith says. "Let's go and save my mom." Amith gives her a confident smile, trying to get her mind off her worries, not knowing that he is only making matters worse, especially since his eyes are full of perseverance and hope. Karishma knows that the truth will break his confidence and his faith, and in doing so, it will break Amith. That is something Karishma doesn't have the heart to do.

So the truth jumps back down into the hatch it came from. It travels back into the deep pit of her stomach, unable to escape. It waits, angrily churning and burning, now heavier than before. Karishma wipes away her tears. She knows it's no use; her lie will be the end of them, and she doesn't have the strength to reveal it.

For now, she must follow through and continue. She must continue down a path that leads to nowhere, a path that could be dangerous and might never lead them back—a path that may be empty but full of hope.

Karishma pulls herself together and stands up. Shaneel watches her with a heart full of genuine concern. But Karishma has a concern of her own: the concern of why she can no longer reveal the truth. Is it the fear of telling the truth, the consequences of what may come, or the love of Amith?

It is an answer that she has not figured out yet, and when she does, maybe it will change everything, or maybe it will be too late. She walks toward Amith, her footsteps heavier and slower than before. He leads the way as he always does but stays close to Karishma, helping her along.

Shaneel watches the two disappear into the foliage. He looks down and sees the book Karishma left. He picks it up, puts it in his backpack, and follows behind them.

CHAPTER 33

The Lake

THE KIDS SIT RELAXING in front of a small pristine lake. It was a pleasant surprise to stumble upon this magical gift of nature, as the kids spent most of the morning wading through thorny vines and dense vegetation. Now as a reward, the cool, crisp feeling of pure water tickles their fingertips as they wash the grime and dirt from their hands.

The water's edge is lined with jungle trees that grow tall into the sky, twining their vines together and creating a ceiling of greenery and bark. Only a small opening breaches the high leaves, acting like a skylight sending a circle of light to reflect off the surface of the water and illuminate the air in luminance. The entire area is well lit since the wind can hardly penetrate the thick wall of trees, leaving the water's surface to act as a perfect mirror to the radiant light. An aroma of jasmine and gardenias, mingling with the fresh scent of a recent rain, fills the air in an intoxicating way that only adds to the allure of this magical place.

"This is great. What luck!" Amith cries out joyfully.

Shaneel looks over at him with a pleased nod. He sits down at the edge and starts washing the scratches he collected during his tussle with the shrubbery.

Karishma crouches nearby, playing with a twig that she swirls in the water. She watches as the ripples break the faultless surface of the lake and blur her reflection.

The kids sit back and enjoy the splendid spectacle in front of them. It is a beautiful sight to see nature at work. They feel very privileged to be able to witness this secret of the jungle. They can see small ripples along the edge, near the roots of the trees. The leaves slowly drop their collected rainwater into the heavenly little lake, appearing as many hands working together to create this gift. It looks so cool and extremely inviting—it would only make sense to enjoy its full glory.

Amith can't help it. He gets up and jumps in.

Shaneel watches in shock at first, worried about what might be in there, but he can't help but wonder how it feels as he watches Amith splash and laugh in the magnificent water. Soon Shaneel jumps in too. Karishma watches them, still standing on solid ground, her feet firmly planted.

"Hey, Karishma! Come on!" Amith calls, expertly swimming in circles around Shaneel.

"Yeah, Karishma! The water is really nice!" Shaneel yells, rejuvenated by the much-needed bath.

Karishma was never a good swimmer and not knowing how deep the water is, she decides that it would be smart to stay on shore. Then again, it would be such a perfect dip in this humid weather, just to cool off a little. Before long, Karishma gives in to her urges and she too decides to get in the water, although not nearly as quickly as the boys.

She slowly dips her feet, getting the courage to move farther in. Soon half her body is submerged and after a little more courage she goes all in. Once fully afloat, she paddles around slowly, trying to get to the middle of the lake near the boys, who now are having a water fight, undoubtedly trying to find out who is the water hero of some sort.

The kids play in the water, laughing and forgetting their worries and enjoying the splendor of just being kids. All is perfect. But as the world has taught them well, nothing is perfect for long. A faint thump echoes through the jungle.

The kids look at each other in bewilderment. The thump sounds off again.

"What's that?" Karishma asks. She stops swimming and scours the wall of trees with her eyes, trying to locate its origin. The sound gets louder and louder as it draws nearer.

Still it is hard to make out the source of the sound; it could be from any direction. The kids gather together in the center of the lake out of fear.

Soon the ever-growing sound of bushes being trampled reverberates through the air. Amith and Shaneel start swimming to the other side, leaving Karishma in the middle.

"Karishma, come on!" they call to her.

Karishma turns around to look and starts paddling over to the boys, but her skills as a swimmer are mediocre at best. She struggles but only gets a little less than halfway. Then, the sound of rustling leaves and breaking branches fills the entire oasis.

Karishma starts paddling frantically, but her tiny arms and legs can't move fast enough. It isn't long before she sees what's making all that noise.

The huge creature crushes everything in its way—leaves, twigs, and branches disappear into the ground with each giant footstep. The trees part with ease, like a beaded curtain, from the enormity of the creature as it makes its entrance. The mighty elephant stops and stands at the edge of the lake, and then it sees tiny little Karishma.

Karishma has never seen such a sight as this in her life. She has seen smaller, trained elephants that were used to haul heavy goods, and she has even heard stories of people riding them. But to see such a creature right in front of her eyes, such a majestic and powerful creature with a size unmatched by any in the animal kingdom, as well as any she has witnessed before, is awe-inspiring and frightening.

Karishma had seen statues of these majestic creatures with their trunks raised into the air and had heard stories while growing up. She once asked her dad what it meant and was told that it was a symbol of good luck when their trunks were held up in the air and a symbol of bad fortune when they were pointed down. Right now she hopes that was a lie, since the trunk of the elephant she sees in front of her is down.

Karishma is filled with fear, not knowing what her next move should be. She is helpless and at the mercy of the creature. Amith and Shaneel watch in panic, while trying to make their way to her without alarming the creature.

Before they get close, the elephant shifts its gaze to them, and it doesn't look happy. The elephant lifts its trunk into the air and blows a trumpet-like warning, sending the boys paddling back to their corner of the lake.

It's a stalemate, but it doesn't last long. The elephant takes a giant step into the water. Its enormous tree-trunk-like legs sink about six feet into the lake bottom, and still its body is above the water. Karishma stares at the elephant in shock. She is certainly no match for the elephant if it decides to attack.

The elephant raises its giant head in a circular motion, loosening the muscles that make up its short but very powerful neck.

Doing that reveals the elephant's long ivory tusks, which curve to a point and are dripping water, making them shine like sabers.

Karishma's eyes widen as she sees the tusks up close, each as long as her entire body. Thoughts start to rush through her mind again, compiling all the data she has acquired in her short life. She remembers that elephants are known to be gentle creatures but can be fiercely territorial, and that they have been known to trample people to death just because of a bad mood. The question on Karishma's mind is, what mood is this elephant in?

The elephant brings its head back down, letting its tusks pierce the water's surface, and stares at Karishma. She can't help but hold her hands in front of her, waiting for the inevitable assault.

The elephant rears up its trunk and bellows out a great cry, spraying water from its spout. Then it sinks its trunk back down in the water and starts to drink.

A great shockwave of relief rushes through Karishma's little body; she is almost paralyzed, and she has a hard time keeping afloat. She starts to sink, but quickly kicks her legs when the water reaches her mouth. The action sends her floating again, but unfortunately, toward the elephant's sharp tusks.

Karishma screams in fear. This must be it, she thinks. This is the price she must pay for her lie, for letting the boys travel on a journey of false hope. Now she will have to pay with her life. Maybe she deserves it. All these thoughts race through her mind as she rapidly drifts toward the tusks.

The elephant turns its head, and using its trunk, sweeps Karishma carefully to the side before she can get hurt. The elephant stares at her as Karishma paddles around, trying to get under control. Karishma looks up at the elephant in disbelief.

She smiles to show that she is okay but almost sinks again in the process. The elephant looks at her disinterestedly, then goes back to drinking.

The boys stand near the water's edge in awe, staring at Karishma wading at the elephant's side. She looks at them and smiles an "I'm okay" look. The boys look at each other in astonishment.

Karishma turns her attention back to the elephant. Its thick and rough grey-brown skin moves up and down as the elephant takes in huge gulps of water. She reaches out.

"Karishma! No!" Amith and Shaneel yell together.

But it's too late! Karishma's hand is on the elephant's skin. The elephant quickly rears its head up, reacting to her touch. In a moment of anger, it raises its tusks toward Karishma.

Karishma quickly cowers, covering her face and looking away, regretting her action. There is a moment of silence as the kids all wait for the worse to happen.

But to everyone's shock, nothing happens. Karishma slowly lowers her hands and opens her eyes, only to meet the elephant's gaze with hers. The elephant looks at her as if deciding what to do to this tiny annoying creature. It raises its trunk out of the water and points it at Karishma as if smelling her. Then a massive jet of water shoots out, drenching Karishma in elephant spit and regurgitated water. Then the elephant returns to drinking.

Karishma turns to the boys, holding out her hands and wondering why. They burst into laughter.

It isn't long before the elephant drinks its fill. It steps out of the lake with its mighty legs and walks off in the direction the kids had come from. It breaks through the tree line and wades into the jungle as easily as when it arrived.

The kids watch as the elephant makes its exit and disappears into the jungle behind them. Then they turn their focus to the opposite direction and stare at the passage the elephant created when it came through the jungle. They exchange glances, all wondering one thing: if the elephant came in from the direction they are heading, what other great beasts could be ahead? Because they are now certain—they are truly in the wild now.

CHAPTER 34

No Turning Back

HERO TRAINING TIP #18

"A hero is courageous."

~Karishma

THE WAY IS AGAIN ARDUOUS, the uphill path is full of broken branches and thorny vines. A passage like this would pose no threat to an elephant, with its long stride and tough skin. But for the kids' short legs, it continues to be a source of pain and torture.

Nevertheless, the kids move forward—Shaneel and Karishma lagging behind, as Amith continues to make his way vigilantly ahead.

Soon the trail gets rougher, as they encounter steep overhanging rocks that make it difficult to move ahead. Before long, they have no choice but to go back or climb up. It's an easy decision for Amith, and he is the first to crawl up a rather large towering overhang. He makes his way easily up the side. At the top, he looks back and offers his hand to those below.

Karishma is next to go. She tries to jump up, but she's a little short—in every sense of the word. Luckily, Shaneel comes to the rescue—he can boost her up. She gets up on Shaneel's back and steadies herself on the wall with her hands before she attempts to reach out for Amith's hand hanging from above. She is barely able to grab it, and he tugs her up the rest of the way.

When she gets on top, she struggles to get solid footing and almost falls. Amith quickly pulls her close, and she falls into his embracing arms. As she feels the beat of his heart, strong and proud and full of courage, she closes her eyes and wishes this moment would last forever. Amith quickly moves back, but there is something different: he is blushing.

Amith moves ahead, embarrassed, and Karishma blindly follows behind. A moment passes as the two disappear into the jungle.

"Hey!" Shaneel yells from below, completely forgotten by the others. He yells again, but no one answers him. He has little choice but to find his own way up. He looks around and sees a root hanging out from the dirt. He gives it a tug—seems sturdy enough. He clutches the root and starts to struggle up the rock.

Shaneel slips many times, but true to his nature, he doesn't give up. He knows that eventually he will succeed. It is his persistence that has kept him in the same league with Amith, even when he was outmatched. It is his persistence that has let him accomplish the same physical acts that the stronger, more athletic Amith does with ease. Shaneel doesn't give up. He can't, if he wants to be a hero one day. It is that motive, that singular thought, that guides him up the steep climb, and before long Shaneel makes it to the top. He brushes the dirt off his clothes and storms forward to catch up with the other two.

Shaneel has taken abuse from Amith for a long time. He's taken the hits, the cheating, been the lap dog. Now he no longer wishes to play that role. Karishma will never respect him in that role. She will always go for the hero, like all the girls do in the movies. She will always go for Amith.

¤ ¤ ¤ ¤ ¤

Shaneel comes barging out of the jungle at the cliff where Amith and Karishma stand. He's poised and ready to give them a piece of his mind for leaving him stranded. But before he can say anything, he stops. Few words can truly describe the beauty that lies before them. The vision leaves Shaneel speechless.

This is an isolated area of the jungle, away from the sprawling humanity that breaches the other regions. Instead, this part teems with a life of its own. It is a tapestry painted by nature, filling its canvas with green hills and towering mountains as far as the eye can see. The sight is almost worth the strenuous hike they've made up the mountainside. It is an absolutely breathtaking view, a sight unmatched by any the kids have ever seen before, because it is a sight that few have ventured out this far to see.

It is an exhilarating experience to witness this marvel, and the kids are filled with feelings of fascination and inspiration, which are only intensified by them being together and sharing this moment. For just like the branches and trees and vines that are woven together in front of them, so are the kids' lives. Each is connected to the others in a masterpiece of destiny.

From the high vantage point, the kids can see relatively far, at least as far as is allowed by the heavy fog that is rolling in over the never-ending jungle. The fog is thick and heavy, filling all the nooks and crannies of the jungle as it creeps forward. It resembles smoke, pearly white at the top and coarse grey at its soul. It moves over the beautiful terrain, its tendrils grasping the land below and covering the sight from human eyes—as if the land is a secret—like another sign to the kids that they're not supposed to be there.

Karishma stands still, in awe at the impressive sight. The vastness of the jungle and the fog seems to go on forever. There is no end, yet Amith will march an infinite walk until the end of eternity to get what he's looking for. There is nothing that she can say to stop him now, at least nothing that she is willing to say.

Shaneel is overwhelmed as well. He is a little mesmerized at the sight, a little angry at being left behind, and a little curious about what's ahead. All those feelings cause his stomach to churn as he watches the dire fog roll in.

There's a coolness between the kids now. It's not just their feelings; even the warmth of the sunshine is fading. The icy crisp air that accompanies the fog soon brushes against the kids' skin and sends chills through their bodies. Before long, the exhilaration they felt at the sight vanishes completely and is replaced with the dread of walking the steep path to reach below.

Nonetheless, however dangerous the path, however grave the situation, it won't stop brave Amith—not today, not when he thinks he is so close.

"Doesn't look that bad," Amith says with sarcasm. He flashes his broad smile and starts galloping down the steep hill into the grey haze of the fog.

¤ ¤ ¤ ¤ ¤

Amith makes quick progress down the steep hillside, but when he reaches the bottom, he lets out a sigh of relief. For even he had some trouble keeping his balance on the way, but he made it. He wipes the sweat from his brow and looks up, way up, to see the other two, appearing and disappearing as the fog slides against the cliff like waves.

"Come on down, yaar!" he yells from below.

Karishma looks concerned. The climb down looks terrifying, and she doesn't have the courage to take the first step. Shaneel notices.

"Karishma, it'll be okay," Shaneel says encouragingly.

She closes her eyes and shakes her head no in disagreement.

"Do you want me to go first?" he asks her.

Karishma is uncertain, but finally she nods her head yes.

Acting with his heart, not his brain, Shaneel takes his first step down the hill. He turns around and gives her a smile to signal that everything is okay, but the smile quickly fades—and suddenly Karishma's fears come true.

A loose mound of dirt under Shaneel's feet gives way and sends him tumbling uncontrollably downward. He disappears from Karishma's sight, being absorbed into the fog's grasp.

Shaneel's journey down is full of thorny bushes, broken tree stumps, and pointy rocks, all causing nicks, scrapes, bruises, and cuts with each bump taking an increasing toll on his body. There is no way to prepare for the next hurdle, as Shaneel tries to stop his fall. The fog hides the next obstacle, only revealing it just before Shaneel crashes into it. Shaneel loses consciousness.

Shaneel's body comes barreling out of the cloud of fog, over the cliff, and crashes onto the ground, right in front of Amith.

A shockwave of terror and fear jolts through Amith, and he is petrified by the sight. The journey has given him many worries and many concerns, but Amith has just brushed them off, his faith acting as his impenetrable armor. Now, that resolute armor has finally cracked, as he sees Shaneel's motionless body lying in front of him.

Still standing above, Karishma is shocked and confused. The worse thing is not seeing what you fear, but rather not knowing if your worst fear just came true. This has never been more real for poor little Karishma. She panics and screams "No!" from the top of the cliff.

Her cry seems to wake the jungle from sleep. A thunderous rumble is heard far in the distance, near the monolith-like mountains—maybe an echo, maybe something else. A gust of wind rustles the leaves into trembling and startled birds fly out of the quivering jungle canopy. Even the fog seems to shrink away in fear.

As the fog retreats, it reveals its hidden nightmare below. Karishma sees Shaneel lying on the jungle floor. She can't contain herself at the sight and begins to sob as her heart fills with anguish. The blame, the remorse, the guilt—it all hits her, and she single-mindedly charges down the hillside. Her mind fills with thoughts; every move, every notion, every action they took in this jungle is because of her.

Fueled by adrenaline and concern, Karishma makes her way down without falling. She runs to Shaneel's side, crying hysterically. She knows that it is her fault that they are here, her fault that he put himself at risk, her fault that he took every step, and now her fault that he took his final one.

Amith stands still frozen, unable to process what he has just witnessed.

"Help me, Amith!" Karishma yells.

But Amith is unmoving, still in shock. He has never imagined that this could happen. He has always felt that they are somehow immortal, that the clutches of death could not reach them. He always somehow believed that they could never be hurt, that they are just like the movie heroes. He always saw the heroes succeed in the end and win against unimaginable odds, even when it was tough—but in the end they always survived. Those thoughts seem childish now, they seem like a dream conjured up by stupidity and naiveté. This is what grownups must know. It is why they worry; they know that they are, in fact, just mortal and at risk to be hurt by anything and everything, at any time. It is why they are afraid, and it is why Amith is now too.

It takes a moment before Karishma's words penetrate Amith's stupor and he finally regains his senses. He jumps to aid his fallen comrade. He kneels down and puts his hand under Shaneel's back, pulling him up off the jungle floor and into a seated position.

Shaneel is out cold, but his chest is moving—a good sign. Karishma pulls Shaneel's body closer. She lays his head in her lap and examines his many cuts and bruises.

Amith watches, horrified, to see the person closest to him—next to his mom—lying unconscious and possibly dying on the ground right in front of him. Shaneel did it all in the name of Aunty, Amith's mom. Even for a tough boy like Amith, it is hard to see Shaneel in this condition. They had shared so many experiences together and although they were not connected by blood, they considered each other brothers. Amith cannot bear to think of being left alone in the world without his best friend to stand by him.

"What do we do?" Amith yells hysterically.

"We have to take him home!" Karishma answers back.

It knocks the wind out of Amith when he hears those devastating words. His mind starts to spin from the harsh choice that he has to make, one that he never expected to face. He takes a few steps back, his heart in agony over the decision.

"Amith!" she yells again, but he is lost. He is lost in his thoughts, lost in his worries, and lost in his indecision.

Amith has not prepared for this. He always has a plan to fix things, to win any issue that presents itself through persistence and sheer will. But now he holds two futures in his hands, and choosing one will mean failure of the other.

On one hand, if Amith keeps moving forward, on his quest, he might lose his friend, a friend he grew up with, one he shared the most important moments of his life with, and a friend who has always stood beside him, even when the odds were against him.

On the other hand, if Amith goes back, he will lose the chance to save his mom, the very essence of his life, the driving force of every step he takes, and the woman who taught him to be good when bad situations occur and to sacrifice his own well-being for the sake of others.

Now those very life lessons that he learned from her haunt him. Can Amith be good? Certainly a horrible situation has occurred, so what *is* "being good"? How does he give up what he wants, when he wants both? What does he do? Does he save his mom or save his best friend, his brother?

Either way, he must sacrifice one for the other. And in making that decision he will also sacrifice his conscience forever. There will be only sleepless nights from this day on. The turmoil, the upheaval, and the unrest seem to last forever, but just a single moment can change all of that.

Then Shaneel coughs—the first sign of life! Amith couldn't have wished for anything more, but it gets even better. Shaneel slowly opens his eyes.

Yet, the first sight Shaneel sees is not Amith, but an angel. It is a face that watches him, full of concern and love. It is a face that Shaneel has admired since the moment he saw her when they were very young. It is the angelic face of Karishma.

Karishma breaks into a smile that brightens the dark sorrow of the situation. Shaneel sits up straighter under his own strength—Amith gets up and walks off to the side.

Shaneel looks around, trying to adjust to his new surroundings. He doesn't recall how he made it down the hillside. He just remembers the cliff—seeing the dreadful cliff with the menacing fog rolling in and Karishma's face. If that was to be the last thing he saw in life, it wouldn't be bad. But he sure is happy to see her again.

Shaneel looks over to the trees and sees Amith hunched down with his back to them. There is a pause as Shaneel wonders why everyone is so serious. Finally Shaneel speaks. His first words are "Amith, are you okay?"

There is such tenderness in Shaneel's voice. He's not worried about his own pains, but focuses on his friend, Amith, which only makes things worse because Amith doesn't respond.

Amith just sits there quietly, his eyes fixed in terror and his face covered with tears. He is glad that everything is okay, but he knows that now everything has changed, because the choice he made . . . wasn't Shaneel.

CHAPTER 35

Instinct

LIFE SEEMS MORE INTENSE in this part of the jungle. The trees seem larger and the bushes thornier; the bright colors are brighter and the darks much darker. Everything appears as if in a vivid painting.

And yet, the overwhelmingly elegant beauty seen from the cliff above is in actuality a tough, harsh terrain. Even the very ground hinders each step, its mud clutching at the soles of the kids' feet with an iron grip. Even the smallest things that would seem safe otherwise have an aura of danger about them. One would be unwise to touch or eat anything unrecognized in the normal world, and especially here because this isn't like the normal world. This is the heart of the jungle, the untamed wild. It is a place where the kids don't belong.

Shaneel walks with a slight limp and is still sore from his tumble down the cliff. Karishma walks ahead, carefully clearing the path of branches and twigs out of concern for Shaneel.

"How are you feeling, Shaneel?" she asks.

He wants to tell her the truth, to let her know that besides a few aches and pains, he is relatively fine, but there is something more that he wants. Shaneel looks at his ripped shirt and remembers the attention she had given to the injured deer by using his shirt as a bandage.

"Well, my arm hurts a lot," Shaneel lies, as he feigns an injury. "Ouch!"

Karishma stops to look at Shaneel's arm. He holds out the bottom of his tattered shirt, offering it to her with a grin. She smiles back and instead, tears a strip of cloth from the hem of her dress. Then she looks back at Shaneel with those beautiful, round brown eyes and says, "This won't hurt, I promise."

Karishma reaches for Shaneel's arm and carefully wraps the strip of cloth around it and then ties the ends together to make a miniature hammock. She slips the tied end over Shaneel's head and gives him a smile and a thumbs-up sign.

Shaneel moves his arm, now secure inside his custom-made sling. It feels snug and surprisingly comfortable.

"Wow, you're good at this," Shaneel says, impressed.

"I want to be a doctor," Karishma says as she adjusts the sling at Shaneel's shoulder.

"You can't be a doctor!" Amith says, interrupting the conversation.

Shaneel watches as Karishma's smile quickly vanishes. She knows that what Amith says is true. Doctors don't exist where they live—at least, not real doctors. There is no real medical school for them to attend, and even though her family is considered some-what well off, there isn't enough money in the entire village to pay to attend college somewhere else.

Shaneel sees the sadness on her face as her dreams quickly fade because of Amith's remark. It is so much like him to do such a thing, so unfair, so unjust.

"Hey, don't tell her what she can't do!" Shaneel snaps.

Amith stops walking, shocked by Shaneel's comment. He turns around and stares back at him, feeling more bewilderment than anger, more surprise than unease. This isn't the Shaneel he has grown up with. This isn't the Shaneel he has played games with in the streets. This is a different Shaneel.

A moment of silence fills the air, even the jungle noises seem to stop.

Then Amith lets out a deep sigh and shrugs before moving on. Shaneel starts following, but he stops and looks back at Karishma. She's smiling at him.

Shaneel smiles back, wondering who said that. He never spoke harshly to Amith before, even when he knew Amith had cheated to win in their fantasy games. He always took the higher road. This was something different. It was instinct that caused him to defend Karishma and to finally stand up for himself. It was instinct, and it sure felt good.

CHAPTER 36

Starfruit

HERO TRAINING TIP #19

"A hero never picks on anyone."

~Shaneel

THERE IS A MOLDY SMELL IN THE AIR, a smell that reeks of dead moss and wet vegetation. Yet, even the stench of decay doesn't stop the kids' stomachs from grumbling. The supplies they brought with them are long gone. No more bread, no more rotis. To make matters worse, they haven't seen any berry bushes for quite some time. The water they gathered from the trees at the lake is running out, and there is no grand oasis to cool them off in this dreadfully humid weather.

"Is there anything in there?" Amith asks.

Shaneel rummages through his backpack. "Nothing."

"My stomach hurts," Karishma says.

"I know, Karishma. Stop whining," Amith says, annoyed. "We are all hungry."

Shaneel doesn't like Amith's tone.

"Maybe we should turn back," Karishma says, trying to manipulate the situation into an escape plan.

"We are not turning back!" Amith yells.

Shaneel quickly stands up eye to eye with Amith. "Don't yell at her, Amith," he says.

"Areh, what's with you?" Amith snaps, staring right back.

"Nothing is with me, Amith. I just think you shouldn't yell at Karishma all the time," Shaneel says, holding his ground.

The tension in the air is unmistakable. It makes it hard to breathe. Never have the two collided like this before. They have fought before, but only the way brothers bicker. This is something else entirely.

"Don't!" Karishma yells, getting between the two. "Look!" she says, pointing up to the treetops.

Amith and Shaneel back away and turn their attention to the jungle canopy. They see a very familiar sight in the very unfamiliar terrain: a tree bearing starfruit high above.

Starfruit is known to be bitter, but it is one of Amith's favorite sweet dishes that his mom cooks for him. It isn't just the treat itself that makes it taste so delicious—it is the whole process of making it.

Amith remembers those rare occasions when his mom would bring a starfruit home. It is an odd-looking fruit with many edges that are shaped like a star. It was always a pleasant surprise having the fruit, since Amith's mom would sometimes wait for days before preparing it. It was like the tension in the plot of a good movie building toward the ending—this time slowly escalating to a climax of sweet, juicy fruit yumminess. When the harvest day finally arrived, she would quickly cut up the fruit into thin slices. But Amith's mom wouldn't let him taste the fruit then since it can be quite bitter—she would make him wait. She would marinade the fruit slices in a coconut bowl, full of sugar, spices, and a lemon, and wait until it was the perfect temperature outside.

Only she knew when that time was, and it was always agonizing for Amith to wait for it.

When it was time, his mom would ask Amith to take the slices and lay them out on a flat rock to bake in the hot sun. The sun had to be at a precise temperature on an unusually hot day for it to bake correctly. Then they would sit together, outside on those scorching days, and make sure that no ants or bugs crawled up on the rock, allowing the starfruit to bake untouched. When it was fully baked, his mom would gather the pieces up in the same coconut bowl and mix them with more herbs and spices. Then she would give two to Amith, take one for herself, and package up the rest of the starfruit to save it for another time. It was a delicious treat that satisfied and rejuvenated them on a hot day. Amith always looked forward to it.

As Amith thinks back on it, he knows that although he loved the fruit, eating it wasn't the best part. The best part for him was sitting outside on an unbearably hot day and keeping the bugs away from the baking fruit with his mom.

"Haven't had starfruit in a long time," Shaneel says, his mouth watering from the thought of the juiciness.

"Yeah, now all we have to do is find a way to get it down," Karishma says, pouting.

An idea sparks in Amith's imaginative mind, and he starts looking on the ground, rummaging through some rocks. After he collects a few choice rocks, he says in an overconfident tone to Shaneel, "Watch this." Amith rears his arm back, like a major league pitcher does preparing for the game-winning throw, and hurls the rock toward the fruit. It travels like a bullet to the tree.

It's a strike. Amith misses the fruit and the rock disappears into the jungle canopy above.

"I'm watching, man, but I don't see anything," Shaneel remarks smugly.

"Shut up," Amith barks.

Again and again, Amith launches his missiles like rockets toward his target. Each time he fails to hit the mark. Amith grunts in irritation and kicks the ground. All the effort causes his stomach to grumble more. Even Shaneel is too hungry to make a comment. The kids stare at their prize, hanging just thirty feet up in the tree.

"We should try something else," Karishma says.

There is a moment before Amith thinks of another idea. He looks at the tree, then at Shaneel. Shaneel has the same idea. He raises his supposedly injured arm, carefully wrapped in the sling, and smiles.

"Looks like you're going up this time."

¤ ¤ ¤ ¤ ¤

After much effort, Amith makes it halfway up the tree. He doesn't know if it's the shape of the tree trunk, the slippery bark, or the combination of both that makes it extremely hard to climb. If it wasn't for the few branches that give Amith a moment of rest to gather his strength, he might not have even made it up that high. It hasn't been an easy climb.

"Hey, hurry up!" says Shaneel, heckling from below.

Karishma is not amused. "Stop being so mean to him," Karishma says in Amith's defense.

"Don't worry, Karishma. I'm just giving him some of his own medicine," Shaneel says and quietly snickers.

"Come on, scaredy cat. Climb faster," Shaneel yells.

"I'm climbing!" Amith yells back as he scales another few feet.

Shaneel watches in amusement. Usually when it comes to climbing, Amith has an uncanny, spiderlike ability to climb any surface. Most times, he leaves Shaneel lagging far behind and watches as he struggles to catch up. But today the tables are turned. On this day, Shaneel finally has the pleasure of watching Amith struggle.

Amith makes another move up, gripping with an outstretched arm and pulling himself up, but the recent rain and mossy surface causes his grip to slip. Amith slides down a few feet before bear-hugging the tree with his arms and legs stops his descent, and he lets out a relieved sigh.

"Up! You have to go up, not down," Shaneel yells from below as he launches a pebble toward the tree.

"Shut up, man," Amith yells back as he repositions himself for another move up.

Shaneel snickers. Karishma shakes her head. She has no interest in the boys' bickering or their egos. All she wants is to eat some fruit.

Amith stops. He has made some good progress, but now a patch where the bark has been stripped off is in his way. To make matters worse, it's full of moss which makes it impossible to grip. To move ahead, Amith has to leap up with a thrust of his legs and grab onto the clean bark above the mossy area. Amith takes a moment as he looks down and then up to judge the situation. He thinks to himself that it hasn't been an easy climb, but it's an easy trip to the ground. But worrying about that won't move him upward—he has to get focused. Amith closes his eyes and begins chanting to himself, "Who's the hero? Who's the hero?"

Amith opens his eyes, but he doesn't see the tree anymore. It no longer exists in front of him in reality because he is no longer in reality—he is now in his fantasy. What stands in place of the tree is a satellite. There are wires that stick out, shooting sparks of blue electricity that contrast with the pitch blackness of endless space. To touch it would be death by electrocution. The only way to make it is to use the lack of gravity to his advantage. He can use the momentum of his leap and launch himself over the damaged wires, higher up into the safe zone, a safe area which holds the control panel for the entire satellite, the fruit of his mission.

"What's he waiting for?" Shaneel whispers to Karishma.

"I don't know. He looks like he's meditating," she answers back.

Amith ignores his fear and concentrates. He knows this mission must be accomplished. He knows that the fate of the galaxy hangs in the balance, and the only one who can save it is the brave genius astronaut known as Amith. He was chosen from 70 billion men to command this mission, and if he fails, his arch nemesis will laugh at him from inside his space station.

"Stop wasting time," Shaneel heckles from below.

There he is, taunting him from his evil space station of death. Amith concentrates, his eyes lock, and a look of determination crosses his face. He cocks his head side to side, working out all the kinks. He loosens his muscles for the ascent. He takes a deep breath inside his space helmet and pushes himself up from the satellite. He kicks with his legs, and helped by a thrust from his space pack, he is propelled forward. A smile shines on the brave hero astronaut's face, knowing that the entire galaxy will cheer him when he returns. Suddenly, the thrust from his space pack starts sputtering. The smile quickly fades. Amith is going right toward the wires.

Amith's eyes open wide as he grabs the mossy part of the tree. The moss is, as he feared, slippery and wet, and it quickly pulls away from the tree before Amith can get a solid grip. He slips off.

"Amith!" Karishma and Shaneel yell out.

First, Amith hits the branch right below him. He scrambles, trying to get a grip, but the moss from the tree still covers his hands and chest and makes it extremely hard to get any traction. Nonetheless, Amith does hold on for a second, but he slips off again. Then he smacks his side against the next branch, knocking the air from his lungs and sending him in a spiraling plunge toward the ground. The rest of the way is unobstructed by branches, and he lands with a thud on the mushy ground below.

Shaneel and Karishma cringe at the crash and quickly run to Amith.

"Are you okay, man?" Shaneel asks as Amith rolls on the ground, moaning and trying to breathe.

"Shut up," he grumbles.

Karishma and Shaneel help Amith struggle to his feet. Amith stands up and finds no major cuts but some bruises here and there. "I'm sorry, Amith," Shaneel says. "I didn't think you were going to fall."

Amith tries to push Shaneel to the ground.

Shaneel quickly catches himself by hugging Amith with both arms. This only infuriates Amith more.

"Areh, saalaa!" Amith curses Shaneel in Hindi as he pushes Shaneel away.

Shaneel is done being the victim, the loser of the duo, the one who always takes the fall and ends up being the bad guy. It's time for him to fight for himself. It's time to take Amith down. It's finally time for him to be the hero.

Shaneel walks back up to Amith, and they glare at each other, face to face. It's a showdown, only this time it isn't any fake Western movie fight. This fight is for real, and it's been a long time coming.

"Stop!" Karishma yells, stopping the boys from throwing punches. She looks at the two of them, for once at a loss for words. She doesn't have anything more to say after that; she just knows that she doesn't want to see them hurt each other. But before she knows it, they are ready to pounce again. Karishma thinks quickly to come up with something fast.

"The book . . . I just looked at the book, and it says to go that way," she stammers as she points west of the direction they were headed. The boys still stare at each other, neither one wanting to back down. This is a matter they want settled now.

Karishma quickly walks up to Amith and stares at him with her only weapon: her large brown eyes. She gives him her softest, most convincing look and says, "We have to find the cup, okay?" Then she looks deeply into his eyes and adds, "For Aunty."

The words hit Amith like a sledgehammer, and his anger instantly subsides. He steps back, picks up his fallen red scarf, and wraps it around his neck once again. Nothing will stand in the way of him saving his mom, not even Shaneel.

Amith starts walking in the direction Karishma pointed.

Karishma lets out a sigh of relief at having her lie, for the first time, do some good. She looks at Shaneel with regret and then turns and follows Amith.

Shaneel watches the two make their way down the new path. He starts to follow, but he stops after a few steps. He thinks to himself for a moment, then takes off his backpack, puts it on the ground, and opens it. He reaches inside and pulls out the book.

CHAPTER 37

Campfire

HERO TRAINING TIP #20

"A hero stands up for others."

~Shaneel

AN EERIE SILENCE HAS TAKEN OVER THE JUNGLE. There aren't any birds or chirping crickets. There isn't even a wind to rustle the leaves. There is only an overwhelming quiet, a stillness that would make anyone uneasy. It even seems as if the moon senses what is to come and is hiding. Tonight there is nothing but complete darkness. Tonight the children are truly alone.

The small campfire that the kids made is the only light in the blanketing darkness surrounding them. The flames struggle to breathe for life, and only offer warmth to those who sit closest to the dancing tongues.

Amith rolls to one side; he's asleep, but his stomach grumbles, saying, "I'm hungry." It is a constant reminder of his failure to get their food—the starfruit—for tonight.

Shaneel and Karishma sit nearest to the fire. They are both awake. Although Karishma's eyes are heavy, Shaneel is as alert as a fox.

Karishma sits staring at Amith, then she looks over at Shaneel. He seems disturbed. "Shaneel, are you okay?" she asks.

There is no answer, only the crackling and spitting of the fire as it fights for life in the moist wood that Shaneel feeds it. There is a pause as she tries to make sense of his mood. She reaches for his hurt arm, but he pulls it away.

"How's your arm?" she asks him.

"It's fine," Shaneel answers coldly.

Karishma is bewildered by Shaneel's attitude. Well, at least she got a response this time, she thinks to herself. She wonders if it's something she said, something she did wrong. Maybe she shouldn't have gotten between the boys; maybe she shouldn't have broken up the fight. Why is Shaneel mad?

"Shaneel, I'm sorry."

This gets Shaneel's attention. He turns to her, looks at her for a moment with interrogating eyes, and then asks, "For what?"

Karishma doesn't know how to respond. She doesn't know why she's sorry, but she is. She's sorry for this mess, she's sorry for being helpless at times, and she's sorry for what happened to Amith's mom. She is sorry for a lot of things.

"For not being a bigger help in finding the cup?"

There is a pause before Shaneel returns his gaze to the fire. After a moment he says, "What if we never find it, Karishma?"

Again she doesn't know how to respond. They never will find it, because Karishma doesn't know where it is. She's never thought about that before. It was as if Amith's hope and determination to find the cup was enough for her, but now it's not.

"We will find it," Karishma answers.

Shaneel returns his gaze to her; Karishma meets his stare. There is a pause as they just look at each other. Shaneel realizes that her words say one thing, but her eyes tell an entirely different story. They reveal what she has been hiding.

Karishma's eyes widen with worry. He knows. "It's late. You should sleep," Karishma says as she quickly looks away and stands up.

Shaneel returns his stare to the dancing flames.

Karishma moves over to her makeshift bed of gathered leaves, lies down, and snuggles herself into a ball to protect herself from the cold. She closes her eyes.

"Karishma . . ." Shaneel says softly.

"Tomorrow, Shaneel." Karishma closes her eyes tight, trying to force herself to sleep, but it's not working.

"Karishma?"

She doesn't respond.

"How did you know where to go next?" Shaneel asks.

The air is still, as if the world has stopped breathing. Karishma opens her eyes again. There's no more hiding from Shaneel—it's time to tell the truth. To absolve herself of her guilt, her burden that she has carried all this way. It is time to finally let it go.

But . . . "I read it in the book. It said to go this way," she lies.

There is a pause as the dwindling fire crackles, fighting to stay alive.

"When did you read the book?"

"Yesterday," she lies again.

The fire takes new life as it jumps and absorbs another piece of wood, quickly engulfing it. Shaneel doesn't say anything. He just watches the flames.

The silence is harmonious to Karishma. She wishes that she was deaf, that she couldn't hear. She doesn't want the silence to leave.

"I have the book, Karishma."

The fire crackles as the wood starts to burn again. The piece of wood must have looked drier than it actually was. But the quick burst of energy was its last strength and now it's fading again. It won't be long until the fire burns through all of it and there is nothing left.

"Oh! I mean, I read it the day before."

The fire still dances on the edges of the bark.

"I had the book then too, Karishma."

The fire goes out and only the hot embers remain.

Karishma sits up and stares at the burned out campfire, only the embers glowing in the dark.

For a long time, nothing is said. Everything is out in the open now. They both know where they stand. They both finally understand the situation they are in—and the lie that surrounds them. Everything seems more real than it has ever been before.

"Do you even know how to read?"

Karishma doesn't have the strength to lie again. She just hangs her head.

"Oh, God," Shaneel says as he runs his hands through his hair, down to the strain that has lodged in his neck. He looks over to her. Her eyes are full of tears and she breaks down.

"I just wanted to play with you guys," she sobs.

Shaneel listens.

"You two wouldn't let me play, and then Amith forced me. He told me to read and I don't know how. But he made me do it!"

She quickly covers her mouth with her hand, not wanting to awake Amith. She looks at Shaneel, who stares back.

"So you lied?"

Tears stream down Karishma's cheeks at the question; then she nods her head yes.

Shaneel gets to his feet. "We have to tell Amith."

"No!" Karishma says loudly, stopping Shaneel in his tracks. Amith, still asleep, turns as if he is having a nightmare.

"We can't," Karishma whispers softly.

"What do you mean, we can't?" Shaneel glares at her. "He thinks you know how to find the cup."

"Yes . . . but he doesn't need to know," Karishma glances again over at Amith. "Not yet."

"Then when?" Shaneel insists.

She looks back at Shaneel. "I don't know."

"Karishma!"

"Okay, I'll tell him . . ." Karishma starts to plead. "I will tell him everything, but not now, please! I will . . . I really will."

Shaneel sits back down, slumped over.

"Promise me you won't tell him," Karishma pleads.

Shaneel looks at the dying embers in the pit. "I don't know, Karishma."

"Promise me!" She stands up, staring at him. Shaneel looks away, but she's not backing down.

"Okay, fine . . . I promise," Shaneel finally says.

"You swear?"

"I swear," Shaneel says reluctantly.

"And you'll never break it?"

"Come on, Karishma."

She looks at him with intensely fierce eyes.

"And I'll never break it," Shaneel sighs.

Karishma continues her stare.

Shaneel finally caves in. "Never, okay?"

Karishma smiles and walks over to Shaneel. She gives him a hug and a kiss on the cheek. "Thank you," she says, then goes back to her bed. Within minutes, she falls asleep.

But Shaneel can't fall asleep so easily. Karishma's burden might be eased, made lighter for sharing it with someone, but for Shaneel, his burden has just begun.

He sits alone in the dark, staring at the last remaining embers. They twinkle bright before starting to dim, dying into the darkness. Shaneel looks around for a branch or a twig, but there is nothing to be found. He looks at the makeshift sling around his neck and takes it off. He looks at Karishma and remembers the care she put into making it, the piece of her dress she tore instead of tearing his shirt. It's beautiful and very thoughtful, and it is full of the love she showed him. He sets it aside and takes off his tattered shirt. He holds it over the flame and sees Amith on the other side of the fire, tossing and turning. Thoughts rush through his mind—all the moments they have shared—but it stops on one image. It's an image of his smiling Aunty Rheka. That image lingers in his mind.

Shaneel grabs the sling next to him and tosses it into the fire, then he puts his dirty, tattered shirt back on. He moves from the fire and lies back against a tree trunk, closes his eyes, and goes to sleep.

The embers in the fire pit lick at the sling's edges and slowly build into a small fire. It grows and grows and finally consumes the sling.

CHAPTER 38

Alone

"OKAY KARISHMA, WHICH WAY NOW?" Amith stands impatiently waiting for the next set of directions.

Karishma looks around. Thick vines hanging from trees and large spiderlike plants surround them. Karishma seems more confident than before. She smiles and points northwest.

"That way."

Amith quickly heads off in that direction. Karishma starts to follow but then stops and looks back. Shaneel is staring at her. There is disappointment in his eyes. She looks away, ashamed.

"I'll tell him, okay? Just . . . when the time is right."

Shaneel doesn't respond. Instead, he follows after Amith, leaving Karishma alone with her thoughts.

She hoped that since last night things would become easier. She thought that sharing her burden with someone would lighten the load, but it seems heavier now than ever. She dreamed that maybe it would help justify her lie to herself, that it was in some way okay to pretend, to go on a false journey based on belief. She thought that maybe it would be possible to keep her friendships. But instead of losing her friendship with Amith, she is now losing her friendship with Shaneel.

Nothing has changed for Karishma; she is still doomed. She still has to tell the truth eventually. Shaneel put her to the test last night, and she failed. Now, she has no choice but to continue until the right moment comes along. The question is, when the time comes, will she destroy a friendship or will she keep hope alive.

Suddenly, she realizes that she hasn't heard anything from the boys for a while. They haven't called for her. They haven't waited. They've moved on. Which way did she tell them? Which way did her lie send them?

Karishma starts running down the path where she thinks the boys set out just moments before. No sight of them! They're a lot faster, and normally she has to struggle just to keep up. She starts to panic. Has her greatest fear come true? Is she alone? Or even worse, has Shaneel told Amith?

The jungle seems awfully alive right now. The trees seem larger than ever, like giants that spiral up and into the heavens, covering all but glimmers of sunlight. Her little legs keep moving as she hurries forward past bushes and tree trunks.

She asks herself, did the boys go this way? Or did they veer to the left? Did she point in this direction? It seemed like the easy way, but there are so many trees, so many rocks, and so many ways to get lost. Suddenly she stops. The world is spinning and she can't remember which way she came from. In fact, which way is she headed? But most importantly, which way did the boys go?

For some reason, the sounds of the jungle seem more frightening now—the bugs crawling and chewing on plants, leaves quivering in the wind, and even the butterflies' wings seem to flutter too loudly. The air becomes muggy, and it's harder for Karishma to breathe. She's surrounded by nothing, but she feels trapped. She needs to find another place, someplace open, someplace else, someplace where she is not alone. She has to move on, and she has to find the boys.

Karishma starts running, her tiny feet beating the ground as fast as her heart beats in her chest. She brushes leaves and bushes aside and sprints ahead. She can feel the wind, the crisp breeze coming from up ahead as she runs toward it. Some green plant blocks her way, but she knows she will be in the open if she can get past it. She plunges through.

She feels the wind on her skin. Then she sees them, she sees the boys. She can finally breathe.

Shaneel and Amith stand in a small open area on a hill. Shrubs, dirt, and gravel cover the slope, but only for a short distance before the jungle starts right up again.

"Amith!" she calls to him.

Amith is silent. He just stares into the jungle, searching for something.

Did Shaneel tell him? Did he break his promise to her? Did he betray her or did he save her from herself? Karishma walks cautiously up to the boys, but they pay no attention to her. They each stare into the distant emptiness of the jungle, into the mass of emerald green in front of them.

"Shaneel, what's . . ." Karishma starts to ask, but Shaneel quickly hushes her by putting his hand over her mouth.

He gives her a stern look and whispers, "Shhhh!"

Karishma nods and Shaneel lets go of her.

Amith looks around as if he is trying to solve a complex math problem in his head. Could his problem be whether to keep Karishma or not, or could it be what to do to her as punishment? Karishma cringes at the thought. What will happen to her? She is in the middle of nowhere, and the only thing she has is them. Without them, she is lost, she is alone. She must apologize. Now is the time.

"Ami…"

Amith spins around, angrily silencing her with his stare. "Shhhh!" he whispers with a finger to his lips. "Listen," he says, looking back into the jungle.

Karishma listens. She doesn't hear anything, just the chirping of the birds far away and the wind that softly caresses the land and pushes the grass into waves. She hears the gentle sound of gravel against dirt when they move — just the usual lullaby of the jungle that seemed so terrifying just moments before. Now those same sounds seem to calm her.

Then Karishma hears it, a sound she didn't think she would ever hear in a place like this. A sound not made by nature. Then she hears it again.

It is a faint *ding* sound. The sound chimes again — this time it's louder. It's coming closer. One more time it chimes, but this time they hear a hum after it. The kids exchange looks; they all heard it clearly this time. The question is, what is it? And what is it doing here?

Moments pass before they see anything. At first, a speck of vibrant orange appears, an orange that does not belong to the jungle. It steps out and walks across the clearing. Then the next one appears, and then the next, and the next. A chain of monks walk in a single file, walking with no sound but their footsteps in the dirt, walking in silent prayer. They walk in unison, each foot striking the ground at the same time, as if they are part of a giant centipede, all linked together with one singular thought.

Then the kids see it: the source of the sound. One monk holds a bell. From time to time, he rings it, and the ding echoes across the valley. During these times, the monks hum in harmonious unison as in response to the tone. But just as the sound of the bell fades, so does the monks' song. They continue to walk and each time the bell chimes, the monks respond to the bell's call.

Amith and Shaneel have seen the monks before, traveling through their village when they were playing. These men look just like them, but their robes seem aged and holier than those of the phony street monks that the boys tried to expose. These monks must be the real ones that the con artists imitate while scouring the towns and looking for easy prey. These are the real monks that most have never seen. These are the truly pure and the ones who some say don't even exist.

The monks walk past the kids as if they are not there. They walk deep in their prayer and follow only the path forward, a path through the clearing and into the jungle to the east. They walk until the first one vanishes into the jungle. Soon the line of orange fades away into the green of the trees, and the bell becomes silent. Just as quickly as they came from nowhere, they disappear, again into nowhere.

The kids watch to see if the monks will return, but there is no sign of them. They are completely gone and have left no trace that they were ever there. The kids exchange glances to check that they all saw the same thing, if what they saw was real. After a few moments, they are still unsure, but there is no time to waste. It's time to move again.

"Karishma, what did you want to say?" Amith asks, while Shaneel watches intently.

Karishma looks at Shaneel and then at Amith. His eyes are soothing. She doesn't feel so alone anymore; now is the perfect time to finally reveal her secret.

"It was that I . . . it was . . ."

She looks again at Shaneel. He is waiting for her answer, even more eagerly than Amith, but she is too afraid.

"It was nothing," she says and holds her head down.

"Okay, well, let's go then. No time to waste," Amith trumpets, as he gallops his way down the hillside.

Karishma knows better than to look at Shaneel. She can feel his questioning, disapproving eyes on her. But she has to look. She has to know.

To her surprise, he isn't looking at her. Instead, he stares at the path where the monks disappeared. He grabs the straps of his backpack and then follows Amith, with not as much as a glance at Karishma.

Karishma stands there, watching him make his way down the hillside behind Amith. She looks down at the ground and kicks some dirt with the tip of her toe. Then she stares at the boys. She is glad she has found them, and she is glad they are together again. But now she knows it doesn't matter. Because she knows her worse fear has already came true. She is truly alone.

CHAPTER 39

Choices

HERO TRAINING TIP #21

"A hero never leaves anyone behind."

~Shaneel

THE PATH IS GETTING MORE TREACHEROUS with each step. It seems as if the entire jungle is fighting back and hindering the kids' progress. And now that Shaneel knows the truth, every task seems like a pointless obstacle to overcome. Every thorn, every rock, and every slip makes Shaneel want to scream out the truth. But for Karishma's sake, he bites his tongue.

Amith pushes a big branch out of the way, and when he lets go, it swings back behind him, striking Karishma in the arm. She falls to the ground into a bush.

Shaneel helps her get up, but the bush she landed in was full of thorns. And now, Karishma is bleeding from all her little cuts. Shaneel starts plucking the thorns out, one by one. She lets out an "ouch" for each one. Finally he can't take it anymore.

"Amith, stop," Shaneel says.

Amith is still busy trying to make his way up a steep, slippery trail.

"We have to stop, Amith." Shaneel lets out a deep breath, as if he had been holding it the entire time. "We should go back."

Amith stops in his tracks, feeling mortally wounded by Shaneel's words. He doesn't turn around. He just stares in front of him into the jungle ahead.

Karishma looks at Shaneel. She knows he's right. She knows it's gone too far. They need to stop, but she can't be the one to do it. She can't destroy Amith's hope. She can't destroy Amith, so Shaneel must.

"What?" Amith finally speaks.

Shaneel gets up from where he was sitting next to Karishma. "I said we should go back."

"Why would you say that?"

"Karishma is hurt, Amith. We need to go back."

"Karishma is fine. Aren't you, Kafie?"

Kafie. Amith has never called her that before. He has heard her parents call her that. It is the nickname her parents use when they hold her in their arms—what they call her out of love. She is instantly wooed by his words.

Shaneel jumps in before Karishma can respond. "Karishma is not fine, Amith. None of us are. We're hungry. We don't have any water. And we don't know where we're going."

"Did you forget, Shaneel?" Amith spins around. "We have the book."

The book. Karishma has been waiting for those words to be spoken. The words have haunted her the whole trip. They have filled her with regret from the beginning, and now that regret has spread to everyone else. It is like a disease that she knows will only end with sorrow. Karishma looks down in embarrassment.

"The book . . ." Shaneel wants to say more but stops, and just stares at Karishma. She looks so sad, waiting for the assault of the truth and the damage it will do to her. Shaneel lets out another sigh.

"Forget the book, Amith! At least, let's go back and see if the cup is where the monks are."

"The cup is this way, Shaneel. Not that way. Now shut up and be a hero for once," Amith turns back around and starts walking into the jungle ahead.

Shaneel yells back, frustrated, "Going out into the middle of nowhere on a wild goose chase is not being a hero!"

Amith stops again.

There is a long pause between the two as no words are exchanged. Then Shaneel calms down and starts to speak again. "Amith, we're not getting anywhere. Who knows how far we have to go? Who knows how hurt we will get?"

Amith doesn't respond. He just stands there with his back to Shaneel and stares at his feet.

Shaneel continues. "Listen to me, Amith. I'm sure our parents are worried. We need to go do the right thing." Shaneel walks over to Amith. "We will never find it. Listen, no one is going to blame you if . . ."

Before Shaneel can finish, Amith spins around and jumps at Shaneel, screaming. He knocks Shaneel down, knocking the wind out of him.

"Coward!" Amith screams, as he punches Shaneel in the face.

Shaneel tumbles to the side, knocking Amith off. He tries to catch his breath, but Amith comes at him again. Shaneel pulls away from Amith and gets some space between them. Amith just stands there, bent over, his hands clenched into fists, and stares back with wild eyes.

The air above them churns, and the clouds start to rumble. The wind starts howling its presence as Amith begins screaming at Shaneel.

"You're scared, Shaneel! You are always scared. You don't think you can do anything."

Shaneel breathes slowly for a moment and then murmurs, "I don't want to fight you, Amith."

"Coward! See, I knew you were scared. You will never be a hero, Shaneel!"

Shaneel stands up. He's dirty, and his half-torn shirt is lying on the ground. "We're not heroes, Amith. We're kids. We can't do this . . ."

But before Shaneel can finish, Amith screams, "Whose kid am I, Shaneel?"

Shaneel is heartbroken. No response will work.

Amith is crying now. "You don't want to save my mom!"

"Yes! I want to save Aunty!" Shaneel yells back.

"No, you don't, Shaneel. You're a coward. You don't want to save anyone but yourself," Amith cries.

"That's not true," Shaneel says.

"You're selfish! You're a selfish coward!"

Shaneel tries to shrug off the words, but they hit a nerve. "I'm not a coward," he mutters back.

"Coward!"

"I'm not a coward, Amith," he says louder.

"Coward! You're the biggest coward I've ever seen."

Karishma knows this has gotten out of hand and she has to do something. Shaneel can't take this abuse for much longer.

"Amith!" Karishma yells, trying to stop him.

"Shut up, Karishma!" Amith snaps at her.

199

"Don't tell her to shut up, Amith," Shaneel yells, moving forward.

Amith walks up to Shaneel and says, "I'll do what I want to."

They lock eyes. One boy is full of determination and desperation; the other, love and frustration.

"Coward," Amith continues and pushes him.

With that final insult, Shaneel can't take it any longer. He tackles Amith to the ground, but Amith is ready and fights back.

The boys wrestle on the ground, each trying to gain the upper hand. Shaneel clamps one leg down around Amith's waist and pushes him to the side. Amith is too sly and slips out, putting Shaneel into a position where he can get on top of Shaneel. He starts raining wild punches down on Shaneel—many miss but a few hit. Shaneel tries to protect himself, but Amith's punches come from every direction.

Shaneel has to think quickly. He kicks his legs up and pushes Amith over him. Amith tumbles off. Shaneel pushes off with one leg and lunges at Amith. This time Shaneel catches him square in his shoulders, knocking him down, and Amith lands hard on his back. Then Shaneel sits on top of Amith and starts landing a barrage of punches on him. Amith covers up and tries to escape injury, but it's no use—Shaneel has him outmatched. He lands one punch and then another, each punch a precise, well-executed one, each punch thrown at Amith for a different reason. One for being more athletic than him, another for always cheating when they played, and another for yelling at Karishma. Shaneel lets out a primal scream as he tries to knock some sense into Amith, over and over again.

Finally exhausted, Shaneel stops his berserk-like barrage and sits back, taking deep breaths. He glances over at Karishma and sees her staring back at him. Her eyes are full of horror, full of tears, and most of all, full of guilt. She knows that she is the cause of this. She knows that it is her lie that started this.

Shaneel's heart instantly melts. The savageness he felt quickly dissipates. He looks at Amith, still under his hold and whimpering. He's helpless, hurting physically from the cuts, bruises, and gashes all over him, but more importantly, he's hurting emotionally. Shaneel knows more than anything that, although he might not have broken any of Amith's bones, he just broke his heart.

Shaneel takes a deep breath and moves off Amith. Amith lies there breathing heavily, still recovering from their fight. Shaneel gets to his feet and brushes the dirt off.

Meanwhile, Karishma rushes to Amith and starts tending to his wounds. Shaneel stares at them. For a few moments he watches Karishma as she rips pieces of cloth from her dress and dabs Amith's cuts and gashes, just like she did for him. Shaneel lets out another deep sigh, although this one seems painful.

He walks back over to Amith and says, "Fine. If you want to go that way, go. I'm going this way." Then he kneels down next to Karishma. "Karishma?"

Karishma doesn't reply, just continues treating Amith.

"Karishma, come with me," Shaneel pleads.

Karishma stops and looks at him with her sad brown eyes.

"Please, Karishma."

She knows Shaneel is right, that she should stop this while she can. If she goes with Shaneel, maybe Amith will follow them. But she knows Amith. He's like her, and he won't give up. He'll move on and on, even if he's all alone.

Shaneel looks into her eyes, full of sadness.

Karishma has to choose. She looks away.

Shaneel stands up.

"Fine." Shaneel starts walking but then stops. He takes off his backpack, opens it, and grabs something from inside. "Here," Shaneel says as he tosses the book on the ground. "It's no use to me."

With those final words, Shaneel walks away into the jungle, back the way they came.

CHAPTER 40

God

HERO TRAINING TIP #22

"A hero never loses hope."

~Amith

JUST WHEN THEY THOUGHT THE GEMS of the jungle were behind them and only harsh unforgiving obstacles remained, the jungle gives them another surprise. Amith and Karishma stand in the presence of beauty that is overwhelming.

It's an enchanting meadow sprawling with flowers. The flowers seem to bleed from one color to the next in a river of rainbows. Its evolving color palette even includes the carefully laid stone path running down the center, which starts dark and lightens as it travels toward the other side, mimicking the surrounding perennials.

On the other side, a stone platform stands as a monument to the meadow's serene beauty. It's man-made, but nestled seamlessly into the dirt and erected with intricate precision and accuracy. It seems natural, as if it had been there since the beginning of time.

Even the steps leading up to the platform are made of faultless white marble that reflects the clouds, making it appear as if it's a pathway to heaven.

On top of the platform, pillars of intricately carved stone support a marble roof. Inside the large, carved-out stone rests a shrine, serving as a holy praying spot for the statues of deities stationed inside.

It is a magical sight indeed. It feels like a place of worship, a place to slow down and focus on the important things, but all Amith can think about is, I wish Shaneel was here.

"Shaneel would have liked this," Karishma says, as if reading Amith's mind.

"I'm glad he's not here," Amith says as he starts walking down the path toward the shrine.

Karishma follows.

In a perfect world, Karishma could see this as a place for her wedding, a place that exudes holiness, romance, and friendship—the trinity of life. It would have been perfect. But Amith's words sting and destroy any dreams that could have come from this picturesque place.

"Do you think the monks did this?" Karishma asks, trying to change the mood.

"Maybe. It looks really old," Amith replies, taking in the surroundings. There is a long pause as Amith looks around, carefully investigating the setting. Suddenly he is filled with excitement.

"Maybe this is it!" he cheers, and starts running down the path and up the steps.

The sweet words fill Karishma's ears, as if Amith had just saved her from her fate. Maybe this *is* it. Maybe the cup is real, and this enchanting place holds a magical device that can save anyone with a mere sip from it. All of the struggles they faced will have been worth it. Maybe the lies she told weren't lies but hidden truths that are finally revealed at the end of the journey, that this was the right way to go all along. Maybe, just maybe, the whole journey that started as a dream and turned out to be a nightmare is finally over.

Those words play a song of hopeful emotions in her heart as she watches and expects Amith to come back, triumphantly holding the holy cup in the air. It would be a perfect moment that could belong at the end of the best movies.

She smiles as she watches Amith rummage through the altar. But her smile starts to fade as he takes longer. The cup would be an easy thing to find, she assumes. If it is that important, it would be right in front of everything. Then her smile disappears as Amith stands up. He holds nothing in his hands. She frowns as he walks back down the steps, his head sunk into his chest and his face full of disappointment.

She should have known better. Hope is hope because it doesn't come true. Life is never like the movies, and that's why people watch them—they hope their lives will become like the movies, with the picture-perfect ending that makes their journey through life worth it. But she knows now that it may not happen. She has lost the naiveté she had when she started this adventure. She knows that living, sometimes, is not worth the journey.

"What's wrong, Amith?" Karishma says, as she walks up to him.

Amith has never looked so distraught. His perseverance has always shown through, but now there is utter gloom on his face. Amith sits down on the steps, puts his elbows on his knees, and rests his face in his hands.

"It's not there," Amith says, defeated.

"We'll find the cup, okay?" Karishma sits next to him.

"Maybe Shaneel was right," Amith mutters in a low voice.

Karishma changes the subject. "What's up there?"

Amith lets out a sigh in frustration. "Just some stupid statues," he mumbles.

Karishma whispers, "I'm sorry."

"It's not your fault."

There's a pause before she responds. "Yes, it is."

Amith looks at Karishma.

She doesn't say anything, just slowly pats Amith on the back.

"No, it's not," Amith says, taking a deep breath. He looks up at the sky and stares at the clouds. "It's God's fault," he finally says.

"Amith!" Karishma says, startled. "You shouldn't say bad things about God."

Amith looks at Karishma and asks, "Why?"

The place is filled with quiet once more. Karishma doesn't know how to respond. She doesn't know why. Her parents always told her not to say such things, not to get angry, to always be appreciative. She always accepted that, and never thought about why. It was what everyone believed, so she went along. All she knows is that God is always watching and grants things to those who pray.

"Because . . . because God is always listening," she answers.

Amith thinks for a moment, then says, "My mom prays . . ."

Karishma is silent.

". . . and look what happened."

A chilly breeze sends a shiver through Karishma. She doesn't have anything to say.

Amith adds, "And if He's listening, I hate Him!"

"Amith!" Karishma yells, shocked at Amith's blasphemous statement.

A moment of silence settles between them, as Amith returns his stare to the clouds. After a while he turns to her and says, "Don't worry, Karishma. He doesn't hear me."

Amith looks up but he doesn't see anything, just empty dark clouds that seem to be gathering together.

Karishma sits silently.

"We should go," Amith says, getting up and stretching. "Looks like it's going to rain again."

Karishma looks at the clouds. They're darkening and closing in.

Amith walks out of the beautiful meadow and into the treacherous jungle.

CHAPTER 41

The Storm

THE HOWL OF THE WIND is like that of a raging monster as it gains speed—very fitting for the monstrous storm brewing above. This storm is unlike anything they have encountered before.

Amith sprints down the path. The gusting wind slices through the canopy of leaves above and a large branch breaks and falls, just barely missing Amith. He stops in his tracks. That was close, he thinks.

Amith looks back, but doesn't see Karishma. "Karishma!" he calls out.

There is a small pause before he hears her reply. "Amith!"

They can't see each other. The scream of the wind is alarming, and leaves and debris blow all around, quickly covering everything. The kids are cut off from their sight, smell, and touch—only sound remains.

"Where are you?" Amith yells.

"Over here!" Karishma calls back.

Amith backtracks, following her voice. After a few minutes, he finds her. She's all right—covered in dirt and scrapes from many falls—but she's all right. She gives him a weak smile.

"We should hurry," Amith says. "Looks like it's going to be a bad storm."

Karishma nods. They try to make their way forward. They can hear the approaching storm above, its thundering rumbles boom like a marching army.

"I've never seen a storm like this before," Karishma says.

"I have," Amith responds without even thinking. He stops and pauses for a moment—he doesn't know why he said that. He's never been in a storm like this before but oddly, this all seems too familiar somehow. Then it hits him.

"We should hurry," he barks back to her as he hurries forward.

"Where?" Karishma yells, breathing hard from jumping over all the broken branches and debris in their path.

Amith stops again and looks at her with a seriousness he hasn't displayed since his fight with Shaneel. "In my dreams."

There is an uncomfortable silence, then the wind begins to howl through the jungle. The kids look around as the whole jungle creaks under the weight of the storm.

"Let's go. I want to find the cup before it gets worse." Amith turns to run up the path.

"Amith!" Karishma calls out, stopping him in mid-step.

He turns around. "What?!"

Just then a thunderous roar blares through the air as a warning of the coming torrential rain.

"Great!" Amith says. "We're too late." He quickly takes cover under some branches that offer a little shelter, but it won't do. It's of no use against a storm like this. Amith starts moving again.

"Amith!" Karishma calls out again.

Amith doesn't listen but continues to look around for better shelter. "We have to find something to hide under," he says.

"Shaneel!" Karishma yells.

Amith stops and turns to look at her, a look of resentment on his face. "What about him?" Amith says with venom in his tongue.

Karishma doesn't know why she thought of Shaneel. "I just hope he is okay."

Amith shrugs it off and walks slowly forward, violently slapping at the twigs and branches that get in his way. He hates the fact that she's thinking about Shaneel at a time like this. He hates the fact that she's worried about Shaneel's well-being or what is happening to him. More importantly, he hates the fact that he is also worried about Shaneel.

"I don't care what happens to him," Amith says with malice.

"Amith, don't say that!"

Amith lets out an angry sigh. "I can't believe he's being such a coward."

"He's not a coward. He's just worried," Karishma tries to explain.

"Worried about what?" Amith yells. He doesn't want to hear any excuses about why Shaneel won't stand by him when he needs him, why Shaneel won't be there to help him save his mom, or even why Shaneel left him. Shaneel's gone and that's all Amith needs to know.

"He's worried about himself. He doesn't care about anything else. He's selfish!" Amith yells, as he still looks for shelter.

"He cares about you!" Karishma says loudly over the howling wind.

Amith lets out a sarcastic laugh. "If he cared about me, he would've come with us."

They stop and sit under some low-hanging trees for a moment as the thunder warns of an assault of rain. Amith watches as the first huge drops dash down from the sky and strike the ground.

"He's a coward."

Karishma looks at Amith with concern. "Amith!"

Amith doesn't respond—he's too involved with his assessment of the storm.

"I have to tell you something, Amith."

"Not now, Karishma. We don't have time. Let's figure out what to do next."

Karishma sits silently watching the storm clouds twist and turn in the sky. Amith stares at the book in Karishma's hands. She's been holding it ever since Shaneel gave it to her, close to her heart, wrapped up in her arms when she walks, held like a baby being protected from the wilds. Now she holds it in one hand, only her fingertips holding it.

"What does the book say?" Amith asks.

Karishma looks at Amith, then the book in her hand, but she doesn't know what to say. She's tired—not of the journey but of the lies and deceit. She wonders what she can say next.

"Come on, Kafie. Where next?"

"Amith . . ." she says, trying to muster some courage.

Amith is getting impatient. He grabs the book from Karishma and opens it. He flips through the pages, but none of it makes sense. He opens to a page with many scribbles and holds it in front of her.

"What do we do next?"

Karishma looks at him and then the book. She looks away.

"Come on, Karishma! Look!"

Karishma doesn't look. She doesn't want to see the book anymore.

"Look at it and tell me what we need to do next. Come on! It's going to be raining very hard soon," Amith says with a touch of desperation.

". . . I don't know."

"What?"

"I don't know what it says."

"Look at it first!"

Karishma grabs the book from Amith's grasp, closes it, and then hands it back to Amith. "I can't read."

Amith stares for a moment before he reacts. He laughs in disbelief. "Stop, Karishma. This is no time to joke."

Karishma isn't laughing, and Amith's smile disappears. "I can't read, Amith," she says again.

Amith is flabbergasted at what he is hearing. "But you said . . ."

"I know."

Amith looks at Karishma, confused as he holds onto the book. He wants to say something, but no words come out. He thinks to himself and absorbs what Karishma said, and truly processes the situation. Suddenly, it hits him hard, like a ton of bricks, like he is falling from a ceiling with no floor below, into a world that is not his own.

All the questions that should have come to mind earlier start to form. All the things he should have asked, and all the things he should have known. He never questioned Karishma's reading ability. Maybe it was the fact that at the time he needed to believe. He needed to have hope, he needed an answer and she was it. He never stopped to wonder how she learned to read before him. He never stopped to think where she learned to read, or even if her parents knew how to read. He never stopped, only moved forward. There was no doubt, only blind faith, but that won't do now because for the first time his eyes are open, and he can see clearly.

"What do you mean?" Amith finally asks.

He knows the answer but he doesn't want to hear it. He just wants this to be a dream. One of those times when nothing is real and there aren't any consequences, only a kid's imagination at work. But he knows that he cannot pretend any longer, that it has long been time for him to grow up.

Karishma states flatly, "I don't know what it says."

Amith sits staring at the book in his hands. It seemed so precious before, sacred. It was a symbol of everything he was trying to do. It was a symbol of him becoming a hero, for saving his mom, for looking ahead and not looking back. The book was hope. Now it is just a book.

"Amith?" Karishma says, concerned.

He doesn't say anything—just stands there, frozen.

"Amith, I'm sorry."

The rain starts to pour.

"Amith, we should get under something," she says as the rain intensifies by the second.

Amith doesn't move. Instead, he bends down and sits right there, in the middle of the now muddy trail. He pulls his knees up and wraps his arms around them. There is no point in going anywhere now. There is nothing to do. There is no hope, so why try? So, for the first time, Amith doesn't try. Amith just sits.

Karishma stands nearby, watching Amith. The skies crackle above and the pelting rain comes down harder.

"Amith?"

The first lightning slithers in a flash across the sky.

"Amith, we should find some shelter."

Amith doesn't respond. He stares blindly at nothing.

"Amith, please talk to me."

Amith turns and looks at her. "No." Then, Amith's face turns angry. "No, I don't care. I know you're lying."

"I'm not lying, Amith," Karishma says.

"Yes, you are. You're just like Shaneel." Amith says and gets up. "You're a coward. You just don't want to help me."

Another roar of thunder rattles above and another bolt of lightning sneaks across the skies.

"I'm not lying, Amith."

"I don't care what you say. I'm going to save my mom!" Amith starts walking off.

"Amith!" Karishma calls, reaching her hand out to him.

Amith smacks her hand away. "Get away from me!" he yells. He turns around to face her eye to eye. "I don't need cowards following me around."

Karishma starts to cry. "I'm sorry."

It doesn't have the slightest effect on Amith. "I want you to get away from me. I want you to go as far away as you can."

"Amith, I—"

"Go find Shaneel. You two deserve each other, two cowards together." He starts walking again.

Karishma makes another plea. "Ami—"

Amith spins around to face her once more. There is vengeance in his eyes. "Leave me alone!" Amith snaps.

Shaken, Karishma takes a step back. This is her fear incarnate, what she knew was coming and never wanted. Karishma stares at Amith as her eyes fill with tears. They blend with the rain that streams down her face.

He walks up to her. "I never want to see you again. You can die for all I care. I hate you." Amith turns and starts walking down the path again. He looks back to see Karishma still standing where he left her. "Go away!" he says, glancing over his shoulder. And with that, Amith turns his back on her.

Karishma turns and starts to run in the opposite direction of the way Amith is heading. She doesn't know where she is going, but she knows she can't be here anymore. Not if Amith doesn't want her.

She's gone. Amith knows it. He heard her footsteps when she ran off sobbing, but he doesn't care. She deserves to feel that way for not helping him save his mom. She deserves whatever she's going to get.

The thunder cackles above and the downpour rages from the sky, drenching Amith.

Then he stops. He slumps over onto the ground and starts to cry. He has lost his reason to move forward. He has lost everything that he thought he was fighting for: his friends, his way, and even his hope.

But he can't give up. It's not possible to stop. He must get up and move forward. He must get up and take the next step. Hope or no hope, he must save his mom. It's his duty as a son.

Amith gets up and pulls himself together. He wipes the tears from his eyes, but they are replaced by rain. He hitches up his drenched shorts and rewraps the heavy, sopping wet red scarf around his neck. The burden on his shoulders eases. He breathes in deeply and locks his eyes back on the path. This isn't the time to break down. This is not the time for regret. This is the time to grow up and move forward. And so Amith soldiers on.

But after only a few steps, Amith is stopped in his tracks. He hears a scream. It's Karishma!

CHAPTER 42

Faith

"KARISHMA!"

No answer.

"Karishma!" Amith calls out again.

Nothing.

"Karishma!" Amith screams, as he dashes through the downpour, but still, there is no answer. All he hears is the cry of the jungle in the storm and the howl of the wind.

The rain bullets down in a continuous torrent that stings his skin, but Amith doesn't care. He races through the jungle, jumping over knocked down branches, running through bushes, and making his way to where he thinks the scream came from, but he's not sure. He's not sure of anything anymore. There is only one thing on his mind and that one thing is to make sure Karishma is okay.

Amith is sorry for all the things he thought about her, all the hate that he bottled up and unleashed at her all at once. He is sorry for everything bad he ever said to her, and for all the times he didn't let her play when she was left on the outskirts of his world looking in. Amith understands now, very clearly, because he too feels alone. He was left alone by Shaneel and now, Karishma. Even though he caused it, it's a dreadful feeling, and one he would never like to feel again. That's what she must have felt all the time, every day when she saw them playing. She had no one. Amith knows now—that's the reason she did what she did. She lied to him because she didn't want to feel that loneliness anymore. And all Amith wants right now is to be next to her.

Amith comes barreling out of the bushes to a sight he feared most, a sight that makes him feel like his heart has been ripped out of his chest. There she is, only a few steps in front of him, lying on the ground.

What could have done this? What villainous entity would dare attack adorable little Kafie, a child who shouldn't be here in the first place, a precious little thing given to this world who only sought the companionship of friends. Her intentions were good, even though her actions might not have reflected it. And here she is, lying on the ground. What or who would dare commit a violent act against her?

Then Amith sees it. He's not sure what it is exactly and has to take a second look, but he sees its tail as it slithers back into the jungle: a snake! Oh God, don't let it be a cobra, he thinks to himself.

"Karishma!" he screams as he rushes to her side.

She's not moving. He doesn't even know if she's alive. He tries to recall a movie where this happens, but no movie comes to mind. His education never taught him beyond the necessities of life—how to build a fire, what fruit is safe to eat, where to get the best deal on rotis, and the normal routine of the living poor—but nothing of medicine, nothing to cure someone who was sick, and nothing to save someone from certain death. Amith screams at the top of his lungs.

"Ma-duth!" the Hindi word for *help*.

He yells, "Ba'-chouh" the Hindi word for *save*.

Then he cries, "Kōi bhī," the Hindi words for *anyone*.

But there is no answer. He is all alone. He sinks down into the mud and pulls her into his arms. "I'm sorry, Kafie," he whispers.

With only the empty wail of the wind to keep him company, he is left to himself. He sits, filled with guilt, staring at her corpse.

Why did he say those things to her? Why did he make her run off alone? Why does he always push away everyone who is close to him? He doesn't want to be alone! He hears all these thoughts inside his head.

He pleads once more, "Karishma, wake up . . . please."

She doesn't move, but he thinks he sees her eyelashes flutter. It could have been the wind, but at least it's something. Maybe there is still hope.

The cup! he thinks to himself. That's the answer, it has always been. But unless he finds it in the next few minutes, there is no chance, there is no hope. The real question is, where to look?

He was so certain he would find it just moments ago, but now he has no clue. He doesn't know which way to turn, which way to go, or how to find it. He doesn't even know what to do with it. Amith's eyes fill with tears now that the shock has subsided. He must figure out something—and quickly! But what? What can he do?

Then he remembers the way the heroes act in his favorite movies. No, this is not the time to give up—this is the time to take action. Just like before, this is the time to be a hero. He can't let it end this way. This will not be the ending to his movie. He must find a way to save her.

Amith picks Karishma up in his arms. She's a little thing and wouldn't have been a problem for an adult to carry, but there's no adult here. All she has is Amith. He is her only hope. So he starts walking with her in his arms.

Despite her small size, she is heavy for him; her dead weight makes each step a struggle. He has to brace himself with all his strength just to keep from falling. Even worse, the rain has made the ground slick, and he has to make sure not to slip. Plus, the vicious weather only adds to the challenge. Amith falls and slumps over her lifeless body. How will he ever be able to carry her all the way back to town? And which way is town? Think, Amith, think! What can you do?

The shrine! It's the only answer he can come up with. That's the only place left. He knows that there's nothing there, but at least it's a safe place—and he remembers which way it is. That's all he has, and that's all he needs. He tries to pull her up, but she falls back down. He thinks of all the heroes who so effortlessly carried the maiden away. All the heroes who would toss evildoers left and right, all the heroes who would have the strength to do what he needs to do now.

Amith braces himself by spreading his feet apart and rooting himself into the ground. He pulls her up a few inches and gets her into a sitting position. A few more inches, and he gets her standing on her own feet but balancing her weight, trying to keep them both from falling.

He takes a deep breath, bends down into a squat, and then stands up, lifting her limp body into his arms. He can feel the small tendons in his back strain, the lean muscles quiver from the pressure, but he is not going to give up even if it destroys him.

Amith takes a step, then another. Each one just as difficult as the last, and each one making him want to stop and give up. But he keeps taking steps . . . until he slips and falls. Karishma lands near some rocks. Luckily, Amith is able to take the brunt of the fall, and she doesn't hit her head. He just sits and stares at her for a moment.

The storm continues to rage and circles like an animal in the sky, mocking him and his feeble attempt. It knows that Amith is down; it knows that he has nothing, and today it will break him.

The wind shrieks in Amith's ears, and the rain smacks against his skin. They tell him to stop, to give up, to tuck his tail and run away, like animals do when they know a storm is coming. They beckon him to give in, to lie down in defeat, but Amith doesn't. He won't. He never has, and he never will. His mom didn't raise him like that. The very thought of his mom's face puts a small smile on Amith's face. In this dire situation, with the world crashing down around him, even the smallest comfort makes a difference. And this gives him strength.

Amith stands and lifts Karishma up once more. Before long, he has her all the way up in his arms again. He takes a step forward and then another and another, and before he knows it, he's running. He doesn't know where the strength came from, but it doesn't matter. Because right now, he knows that even the storm can't stop him. Amith runs.

¤ ¤ ¤ ¤ ¤

God only knows how many steps Amith took before he makes it to the shrine. He rushes down the path through the little meadow and into the sanctuary. It's the only place that seems safe, the only place that can repel the wrath of the storm above.

Amith gets Karishma's body under the shrine's roof before he collapses, exhausted, on the ground. He lies on his back, his arms spread out, looking up at the ceiling that gives them shelter from the onslaught of rain. He can hear the rain beating against the roof, while outside the wind shrieks, the thunder roars, and the clouds rumble in fury.

There is no place left for Amith to go. If it wasn't for the shrine, he wouldn't be able to survive the angry storm raging dangerously outside.

Amith takes his eyes away from the menacing storm and sees the smiling faces of the deities, standing inside the stone monument. They seem to be the only things here with him, bearing the storm's assault, and they do it with a smile.

For the first time, Amith feels comforted. He joins his hands together, like his mom always does, stands in front of the statues, and pauses. He is at a loss for words. He doesn't know what to say. He wishes he had listened to his mom's words, to the songs that she sang in front of their tiny altar. He wishes he felt the same devotion and faith she had in them. He has to say something, but what?

"Bhagavaan," (*God*) Amith stutters. He takes a deep breath, finally letting go of his control and following his heart. "Please save Karishma. It's not her fault that she's here."

The sound of the rain striking the marble roof is deafening, as if the storm is trying to interrupt his prayer. But Amith says what he has to say.

"It's my fault," Amith continues, turning his attention back to the deities. "I just want to save my mom. Don't punish Karishma for it." Amith pauses to keep from crying. "If you have to punish someone, punish me instead. Please let her stay." He looks over at Karishma and their surroundings. It's just the two of them. He turns back to the deities. "I don't want to be alone, Bhagavaan. Don't take her away from me. Please, Bhagavaan."

A comforting feeling comes over Amith, but he stops anyway, unable to continue. His eyes well up with tears and he wipes them away. He starts to stand up since he's finished with his little

221

prayer, but he stops. There is something he forgot to do. He tries to remember—it's something his mom always did. He looks up and sees the bell hanging from the ceiling. His mom always ended her prayers with a ring of the bell. He should do the same.

Amith reaches for the bell, but he can't quite touch it, even on his toes. It's hanging too high above him, just out of reach. He jumps and tries . . . and misses. He jumps again and again, getting closer and closer, but still no luck. Amith crouches and leaps into the air. It's a hit!

The bell unleashes a deafening ring. Amith listens to the echo traveling through the jungle, cutting through the storm and calling for an answer to his prayer. Amith gets an idea.

Amith crouches and leaps again, ringing the bell as hard as he can. He leaps and slaps it vigorously, over and over again, until his fingers become sore. With each ring, the storm gets worse and worse, as if angered by Amith's scheme. It blasts more thunder, as if trying to drown out the bell's ring. But Amith is persistent, and he keeps at it until finally he can't do it anymore and has to stop from sheer exhaustion.

He breathes heavily, standing bent over with his hands on his knees supporting his upper body from collapsing. A tiny smile creeps across his face. He is satisfied with his effort because he knows that even the rage of the storm couldn't block the sound of the bell, the sound of his prayer's end. Something, someone should have heard it.

Amith thinks about the monks for a moment, how they had magically appeared out of nowhere and then disappeared without a trace. Were they a warning sign, a notice from the heavens to stay back, otherwise you will never be seen again? Were they even real, or was it a sight conjured up by his creative mind? Maybe he just dreamed everything. Questions and doubt flood his mind, and he is no longer sure.

He waits for a few moments, but there is no response to the bell. Maybe it is a trick. He waits a little while longer, and still nothing. And then he feels more doubt. Even if the monks are real, they could be far away by now and might not have even heard the call of the bell.

Then Amith is overwhelmed by fear. He looks back to see Karishma lying on the floor. One thing is for certain: he can't wait here to find out if anyone heard the bell. If he is going to save her, he needs to find help. But the weather is still harsh, and the rain hasn't let up—it continues its devastating attack.

The storm knows Amith's chances. It knows that there is no escape from its rage. It knows for certain that Amith must find help to save Karishma. The only way to do that is for Amith to venture out into its claws.

Amith lets out a deep sigh and readies himself to leave the safety of the shrine. As he takes his first steps down the marble steps, a roar of thunder laughs through the clouds. The storm knows it has Amith cornered.

Amith takes a deep breath as the rain bombards his skin and then he runs down the path, back into the depths of the jungle, and into the fury of the storm, with only a single hope.

His hope is that somewhere, someone, something has heard his call for help. The question is, who or what? But something *has* heard the call and now lurks and prowls in the foliage of the trees. That something has taken great notice of the kids' arrival and has been watching their every move. Now it is ready to make a move of its own . . . and help is not what *this* something is here to give.

CHAPTER 43

Hero

HERO TRAINING TIP #23

"A hero never runs."

~Amith

SHARP GUSTS OF WIND cut through the jungle canopy, sending leaves and debris flying through the air. Rain collects into small streams, making the ground as slippery as ice. And the wind blows so hard that the entire jungle shakes from its presence. It is a miracle to not lose one's way, let alone to gain ground in this storm. But still, brave little Amith endures and proceeds through the dripping trees and slimy mud to find a way to save innocent little Karishma.

"Ma-duth," (*Help*) Amith cries out, as he makes his way into the jungle. The ferocity of the storm has only grown wilder as the torrential rain drowns out Amith's calls for help.

"Ba'-chouh!" (*Save*) he screams. These are hardly the words that are spoken by a destined-to-be hero, but Amith has abandoned all childhood fantasies and dreams of saving the day. He just wants to save Karishma at any cost.

"Help!" Amith yells again. But the storm's growls and rolls of thunder deafen everything around. The storm draws nearer, knocking down branches and pushing mud down dirt paths—anything to hinder Amith.

He dashes past a blur of trees with creaking branches, bushes with poisonous berries he was told to never eat, and thorny plants that leave a gash on his skin even when he only slightly brushes against them. It makes no difference. Even battered and bruised, Amith moves forward. To him there is only one thing that matters and that is to save Karishma's life. Not even losing his own is of any importance now.

It is clear that the storm is chasing him. It's waiting to make its move, ready to pounce. But Amith can't turn back now. He must keep moving forward. He must fight to gain ground, even if he has to fight the storm.

Then Amith hears something: a growl! Not like the storm, not like the wind, not like anything he has ever heard before. It is a haunting sound that causes all the hairs on the back of his neck to stand up.

Amith spins around to look, but he doesn't see anything. The path he carved through the trees behind him is empty. He squints and moves stealthily, examining the horizon for any sort of movement. Could it be the elephant? He hopes so. Could it be something else? He hopes not.

He doesn't see anything. Amith has no choice but to dismiss his thoughts as a trick of the mind and continue to move ahead. The storm is playing with him, he thinks. It wants him to go crazy before he dies, maybe lose all hope. Maybe it wants him to slow down and let Karishma die, so he'll be left with her blood on his hands. But Amith won't let that happen, he won't give up. If the storm wants a fight, then Amith will give it everything it can handle. Amith spins back around to run, but instantly, he stops in his tracks.

Coldness seeps through his body, as if all the air and warmth has left him at once. He is stuck to the spot, his feet planted, but everything inside him feels like it's turned upside down, falling in place with no motion or direction to guide it back into place, all because of what he sees: two yellow eyes staring back at him. They are full-moon-shaped circles, each with a lifeless sliver of black slicing the yellow in half. They stare at him, unblinking, unmoving, searching inside Amith's soul. Amith is immediately taken back to the market, where he saw this sight before. There, he had stood frozen in the middle of the street, entranced by the very same image that is in front of him now. He is taken back to the memories of the man who was brought to the hospital, missing one arm. He is taken back to the warning he heard when the man suddenly sprang to life, clutching Amith's arm. He wishes he would have listened then, because he hears those words clearly in his head now, repeating over and over: Tēndu'ā! Tēndu'ā!—the Jaguar, the Jaguar.

The jaguar's body is bent slightly forward and its back is arched, while its powerful legs are clutching at the ground, with bent knees, ready to pounce. Its mouth is gaping open, showcasing the two yellowish fangs in its lower jaw, shimmering from the saliva that's rolling off its long tongue onto the dirt. Its muscular front legs end in huge paws with claws that grip the ground with razor-sharp, fang-like nails. Its thick, powerful, catlike frame is covered with dark spots that have just a hint of yellow to separate them from the abyss-colored black fur. Even the rain doesn't dare strike the creature but instead, it glides off its perfectly smooth, lean, muscular body as if caressing it.

The jaguar fixes its eyes on Amith: its next meal. It lets out a growl and licks its lips. The storm above agrees and grows deathly silent while watching the scene. The jaguar begins circling Amith, inspecting him, waiting for the perfect time to strike.

Amith is horrified, wishing this was just another dream, a made-up fantasy that he was playing with Shaneel. How good those times were, always winning even when he shouldn't have. Those images come back to him in quick flashes. Amith sees the showdown with Shaneel, where he had him dead to rights with no way out. He sees the clever way he tricked Shaneel and turned the tables on him to win. He sees the many times that he should have lost and Shaneel should have won. Amith sees his life. He doesn't like it. Then Amith sees Karishma, wanting to play Amazon and make Amith her cowboy husband. That memory is quickly replaced with a picture of her now, lying on the shrine floor. Then Amith sees his mom.

Instantly, he's brought back to reality, back to the task at hand, back to his fear incarnate staring right back at him.

Keeping an eye on the jaguar, Amith searches the ground for something to use—he finds nothing but a lot of mud, leaves, berry bushes, and trees. Wait! He gets an idea.

Amith slowly crouches down. The jaguar halts its circling and watches curiously, moving its head down and slightly forward to observe Amith's every move. It sees Amith reach for a bush but the jaguar doesn't move, just watches. It sees Amith pick off a handful of the poisonous berries from the bush. Still it makes no move. It watches and waits.

Amith cautiously tosses the berries in front of the jaguar. It looks down at them, taking its eyes off Amith for a second. It moves closer and sniffs the berries. Then slowly it rears its head up to stare at Amith again. It snarls, showing its wicked teeth. It knows what Amith is trying to do, and it's not going to work. This is no ordinary jaguar.

Amith has no choice. He knows there's no way out. All he can do is delay—maybe delay his death just long enough for someone to hear his cry and even if they can't save him, to save Karishma. Amith knows that he must do exactly what he did that first day, when he saw the jaguar at the merchant stand. It is the same thing he did the day when the man in the hospital warned him. And Amith now knows that this is what the jaguar has been waiting for all along, that this is what it had been watching and conserving its energy for. That today, Amith must do what everyone does when they face death. They run.

The bushes and trees seem to fly past, as Amith sprints through the jungle. The jaguar chases him effortlessly, striding on its powerful legs as easily as Amith has always been able to do everything. It runs past bushes, turns past trees, and easily dodges the branches, twigs, and everything else that Amith tries to throw in front of it.

The storm continues to churn above, seeming to be watching the event like a spectator in a coliseum—just waiting for the inevitable to happen.

The jaguar lunges, but Amith feels it coming from behind and quickly veers to the right. He can't take the time to look around to see if it worked, but then he hears a crash. Maybe it bought him some time. But before Amith can even take a moment to breathe, he hears that snarl right behind him again, closer than ever.

This continues for a few minutes, as Amith quickly makes his way through the dense jungle, just like an expert marathon runner. He dodges trees and hurdles over rocks, and when he feels the beast springing at him, he quickly zigzags in another direction to try to throw it off, never looking back with only a flash of his red scarf zipping through the green blur of the jungle.

Still, no matter how many bushes he crashes through, vines he dodges, or sudden changes in direction he makes, Amith can hear the beast getting closer and closer, that snarling just breathing down his neck. He knows it's only a matter of time before the jaguar overtakes him, before he finally loses. Then it happens. Amith makes a quick veer and is caught.

The scarf around Amith's neck snaps sharply as the jaguar yanks hard enough on the end with its powerful jaws to make Amith slip in the mud and go sliding across the ground, crashing into a tree. Amith spins around as quickly as he can.

The world comes to a halt and the storm bellows a triumphant roar of thunder. The only thing Amith can see is the black, cloak-like skin of the beast lunging in the air at him, claws out like sickles and ready to slash him. It's as if time has stopped, as if death has come to claim its inevitable prize.

The jaguar comes crashing down as Amith quickly rolls to the side, fighting for his life, and the jaguar's claws barely miss him. Amith again feels the strain on his neck. He looks to see that the jaguar has a firm bite on his red scarf, and it's not letting go this time.

Amith tries to pull at his scarf but before he can even grab it, the jaguar yanks on it with its powerful neck and sends a choking Amith flying into the bushes. The vines and thorns tear his skin as the jaguar tugs on the scarf, dragging Amith out of the bushes and across the muddy ground.

Amith gasps for air as the very same red scarf that allowed him to live as a hero begins to strangle him, bringing him closer and closer to death's jaws.

Desperately working his hands around the tightened noose on his neck, Amith tries to undo the scarf. The jaguar notices and yanks hard again, but Amith is able to unwrap it just before it breaks his neck.

Amith takes quick, deep breaths, trying to force the air back into his lungs as fast as he can. The jaguar doesn't make a move. Instead, it stands ready, gazing at Amith while chewing on the red scarf in its mouth and grinding its teeth in fuming rage. Suddenly, the jaguar shakes the red scarf ferociously, shredding it into tiny pieces.

Amith watches in horror. It might be just a scarf to anyone else, but to Amith, it is something much more. It has been a part of him for as long as he can remember—a sort of security blanket. It travels with him wherever he goes, always accompanying him on his adventurous treks. It has been closely attached to him, like an arm. Now it's gone, and with it all the security that it brought.

A freezing gust of wind flies through the jungle, sending a chill through Amith. The next thing he knows, the beast is flying in the air at him. Amith quickly rolls to the left and barely escapes being mangled as the beast hits the ground.

The beast snaps its jaws, but Amith blocks it with a nearby stick. He uses the stick again as the jaguar comes in for another bite. It's another successful block, but Amith knows this won't last for long.

The jaguar's temper builds, and the storm's rage grows with it. Thunder crackles overhead and lightning snaps in the sky. The jaguar snaps again and Amith blocks, but the jaguar hits its target.

Luckily, his target wasn't Amith this time but the stick. The jaguar tugs the stick away and flings it into the air.

Now there's nothing between him and the beast—smart creature. At least it gives Amith some satisfaction to know that he was bested by an intelligent creature and not a mindless one. But it's hard to find any comfort while the gaping jaws of death are snarling in front of one's eyes.

Amith takes a deep breath and the world suddenly slows down. Amith thinks about the happiest moment he can remember: he sees himself sitting outside with his mom, fending bugs off their starfruit that's baking in the hot sun.

The creature gazes at Amith while licking its lips, knowing that its meal is just seconds away. Their eyes meet for the last time, and then Amith closes his eyes and whispers, "Sorry, Ma."

The jaguar closes in for the kill.

The next moments happen in a flash. The storm screams as blood flies into the air. The weight of the beast crushes Amith as it squirms on top of him. He can hear the sound of flesh being pierced. He can even feel the saliva drip on his face in long strands.

Strangely, Amith feels no pain. Death must be painless. After a point, he guesses, maybe you don't feel anything. Maybe in death, all you take is the misery of your failures. Because death knows that, that is pain enough for a thousand lifetimes. How Amith wishes he could feel physical pain and not the regret and misery he feels. How he wishes he could stop thinking and just blank out of existence, but Amith feels no pain, only regret. Then another moment passes as Amith realizes that he should have at least felt something from the bite. But yet there is nothing, nothing but the cool drip of the saliva.

Amith slowly forces his eyes open. To his shock, his eyes meet the jaguar's. Strangely, the jaguar doesn't look menacing anymore but has only a blank stare. Its mouth is gaping open—the jaw juts out, its teeth just inches away from Amith's neck, and its tongue hangs out of its mouth—and it lies flat on Amith's upper chest. They both lie there for a moment. The jaguar makes no move and its head just lies lifeless on top of Amith.

But it makes no sense. Amith can see all the blood on his chest. He remembers it pouncing at him. He remembers that it attacked him. He remembers that it was very much alive when he closed his eyes. Then Amith finally realizes—the blood isn't his!

Amith quickly pushes the jaguar's head off him and scuttles backward until he can't move anymore with his back against a tree. Now he can make out what happened.

A long spear is embedded into the jaguar's body, piercing it almost all the way through. It's poorly made but very effective. On one end, he sees the jaguar's dead corpse, and on the other a sight that Amith thought he would never see again. And he hears those same familiar words that, this time, stop him from trembling in fear.

"Who's the hero?" Shaneel asks, standing over the dead carcass of the jaguar, his hand still on his makeshift spear.

Amith smiles back.

"You're the hero!"

CHAPTER 44

Heaven and Hell

IT IS A STRANGE FEELING to be walking when one shouldn't be. Amith almost doesn't believe that he is alive. He feels as if this is all a dream, some fantasy he made up and now he can't get out of. For how can one be at the brink of death and come out better than he was before? This must be a lie. This must be some sort of heaven.

Shaneel walks with Amith, at his side, wearing a valiant smile on his face. It seems that their previous misfortunes have disappeared. There is a confidence to Shaneel's step and sureness in his eyes that he's never had before. This is not the Shaneel of old. This is a new Shaneel.

As he walks, Shaneel rubs his finger on one of the jaguar's fangs that he took as a trophy, a proof of battle. And now that he finally has a real one, it makes him realize just how fake the one the vendor was selling really was.

Amith can feel the rain pelting him relentlessly, the way it taunted him before, but it makes no difference now. It feels comforting, like tears of the storm crying at its loss. Even the lightning tantrums above them seem like fireworks being set off in celebration, like the ones during Diwali, his favorite Indian festival.

The storm's howling and moaning doesn't affect this dreamlike trance for the boys. They feel like kings. They feel like champions. Most of all, they truly feel like heroes. All is surreal, every step, every breath, every move they make until they reach the meadow with the shrine. Suddenly, the euphoria they felt is broken. The storm quickly regains its monstrous presence—it's not over yet. Where is Karishma?!

Amith runs toward the shrine. He reaches the top step, but he doesn't find what he's looking for. There is no sign of her body. She is missing! No, this can't be heaven, Amith thinks. This must be hell.

Shaneel catches up. "Where is she?"

"I don't know . . ." Amith struggles to say the words. ". . . I left her here."

Shaneel's eyes widen as he too has the same worries as Amith.

They search the meadow, frantically looking for any sign of her, but they find nothing. No trace, no evidence, not even the little satchel she carried.

The situation becomes dire as they extend their search to the nearby jungle. She could have run off somewhere, delirious from her wound. It could be anything, and they have no clues. Then they are overtaken by fear. Did something find her? Who or what took her? Was there another jaguar? Every unfortunate outcome crosses their minds as they search the jungle high and low looking for her, but still nothing.

The storm above crackles with thunder. Lightning once again slithers its way across the sky. It launches gusts of wind and fires down rain. The boys walk side by side, sulking, back to the shrine.

They're exhausted and drenched from the freezing cold rain. Their hunger doesn't help either, and they no longer have the spirit to continue. They start shivering and sneezing fiercely.

It looks like the storm has another trick up its sleeve: it's made them sick. Having a sickness in the village can be a death sentence, but out in the middle of nowhere, it's only a matter of time until it overtakes them.

The storm must have had this planned all along, attacking them physically, then mentally, and now emotionally. And in the end, it's finally won.

With their hearts broken and spirits undone, they don't have the will to fight on. They sink down onto the floor of the shrine — it protects them from the rain, but it's too late. The storm has done its damage.

Soon fever sets in, followed by chills. Amith turns around and curses the deities who stand in their shrines, smiling at the boys. He wonders if he means anything to them at all, and thinks that it was cruel for them to save him, raise his hopes by bringing Shaneel back, and then smashing them by taking Karishma.

He curses and curses, even when Shaneel begs him to stop. Amith won't have it. If he will die this day, he will spend his last breath telling the gods how cruel they were to him.

It seems their fate had already been sealed, from the moment they began the journey, and it is now coming close to an end. They had escaped death's grasp with the jaguar and instead fallen into one from another part of nature.

The boys begin to tire and close their eyes as the world becomes hazy. Amith looks up to give the gods his final insult, but he hasn't the spirit, he hasn't the strength. He is too tired, too drained.

He wonders, how many times have they escaped death's grasp? With each dire moment, they went to death's doorstep and taunted him to take them, only narrowly escaping his grasp by the slightest of margins. But they know, no matter how far they go, that death always takes its prize in the end. Maybe this is finally their time. Maybe they taunted him one too many times, and he has finally opened his door.

The boys soon pass out on the cold marble floor. Above, the deities sit in their sanctuary, idle and unmoving, staring at the boys with welcoming smiles as the boys enter a dream, maybe their last.

CHAPTER 45

Being Dead

HERO TRAINING TIP #24

"A hero never dies."

~Amith

THERE IS SILENCE HERE, PURE PEACEFUL SILENCE. The howling of the wind is gone. The piercing cold has been replaced with embracing warmth. The dark churning skies have been changed into decorated vaulted ceilings.

Amith stares at the blissful flames that dance in the chamber, filling the place with the crackle and sweet smell of wood burning. Amith sits up and removes the warm, wooly blanket that is covering him.

The place is completely empty around him; the only sign of life is Shaneel, who is also rolled into a blanket and sleeping. There is a green leaf on his head, one that Amith is not familiar with. It seems to be wrapped around his head like a crown. Amith touches his head and discovers a similar one on him as well. He removes the leaf and examines it. It has some purple residue on it, which smells like honey. He tosses it in the fire. It crackles as it slowly burns, giving off a grey smoke. Amith stares into the dancing flames.

This is it. He has finally done it, he thinks to himself. He has entered the afterlife. He failed in his goal and was blinded by his ambition, which ended with the people closest to him perishing. And this is what is left. His true body must be frozen on the floor of the shrine, left for the gods to mock him. But this isn't as bad as Amith had thought.

It's nothing like what he imagined. He has heard stories of reincarnation, stories of Heaven and Hell, even stories about when the time comes you cease to exist and just vanish. None of those seem to be true. If this was Heaven, his mom would be beside him, along with Karishma. If this was Hell, Shaneel wouldn't be here. And if he just ceased to exist, he wouldn't be here at all. What a wonder it is to die, Amith ponders, as he teases the flames with his fingers.

Amith sits for a long while, allowing the flames to fill him with warmth. He thinks about his life, how he never truly became a hero, how he never truly helped anyone. He thinks about what it is to be a hero, to risk one's life for another out of love. Shaneel did that for him. He killed a jaguar. Amith has never done anything so grand. He did vanquish a seven-armed alien with a death ray once, but that's not the same. In a way, he always knew he was pretending and that the dreams he created weren't real, but there was something to them, something that made them more, much more. To live like someone else for a moment, someone who isn't afraid, someone who has the strength, someone who truly has courage. He doesn't know if he was that person in real life or only in his dreams, all he knows is that he wants to be.

Amith moves his hands closer and closer to the flames. Hmmm, he wonders. Amith puts his hand in the fire. Ouch! He quickly pulls it out before the fire can do any permanent damage.

I guess you still don't get powers when you die, and you still feel pain . . . a lot of pain, he thinks. Too bad. Being fireproof, even in death, would be kind of cool.

The burning sensation fades quicker than Amith expects, although if he had any hair on his arm it had certainly disappeared by now.

Shaneel starts to toss and turn inside his blanket, and Amith turns his attention to him. Before long he wakes, and the first sight he sees is of a smiling Amith, welcoming him to the afterlife.

"What happened?" Shaneel asks, still half asleep.

"We're dead," Amith replies and smiles back nonchalantly.

Shaneel quickly jumps out of his covers, shocked at the words. "What?!"

"Yeah," Amith says. "Don't worry. It's not so bad."

The words don't calm Shaneel at all. Instead, his mind races with too many questions to complete. "Where . . . what . . . how? . . ."

"I think we died in the meadow, on the floor of the shrine," Amith answers.

Shaneel is silent for a while as he sits next to Amith and stares into the dancing flames. A long time passes before he says anything. "So . . . we died?"

Amith nods his head yes.

They sit quietly for a long time and then Shaneel says, "Like, dead, dead?"

"Yup."

Another quiet moment passes between them.

Shaneel looks himself over and then, sitting forward, at the flames. "So—"

"Don't bother, I already tried. No powers."

Shaneel returns to sulking next to him, disappointed. "Oh."

"Yea, I know."

Another few silent moments drift by.

"Well, that sucks."

"I know."

The stillness between the two is broken when they hear footsteps outside. They rush to the door of the room they are in and peer out. They are amazed by the sight they see.

They have seen what beauty nature can produce, what wonders the earth can provide, but this is something entirely different. There is a wonder to this place that surpasses all that they have seen before. Long hallways of intricate stonework with beautifully patterned pillars along each side hold up arched rooftops, decorated in carved marble and gold so vibrant they appear to be miniature suns. The gigantic hallways stretch far around the whole compound, encircling a lawn of lush, pure green. Between the encircling hallways and the lawn, pools of glowing blue water reflect the clear, cloudless sky. It's for sure that they are dead because, in reality, nothing this beautiful can exist.

There are doors along the hallways, each leading to a room as intricate and beautiful as the outside but void of distractions. The boys explore a few and find them similar to the room they had been in: mainly empty, just a few pots here and there. The only difference is that there aren't any fires in the fireplaces.

All of a sudden, a loud bell sounds, disturbing the tranquility. For the first time, Amith and Shaneel see someone else besides themselves—a group of monks come out of a distant room and enter the hallway, walking toward them. They walk side by side, each in silent prayer.

"Hey!" Amith and Shaneel yell.

They get no response and the monks continue to walk toward them. Amith starts flailing his arms up and down. "Over here!" he screams.

Again, nothing. The monks are getting closer.

Amith and Shaneel shoot each other bewildered looks as the monks approach. They both start waving their hands but still get no response.

The monks pass, each with their heads held down and in silence. They show no sign that they see the boys and continue their walk down the hallway. Soon they disappear into one of the rooms.

"Why aren't they talking to us?" Shaneel asks.

Amith thinks for a moment and gets an astonished look on his face. "I think I know."

As Shaneel anxiously awaits Amith's theory, Amith turns and looks Shaneel straight in the eyes and says, "We are ghosts."

"We're what?" Shaneel yells in bewilderment.

Amith nods his head. "Yup. We died. And now, we are ghosts."

"Ghosts?"

"Yeah."

"Us?"

"Yeah," Amith says in an assuring voice.

"That can't be," Shaneel says and starts walking away.

"Okay, have you ever seen a ghost?" Amith asks.

Shaneel stops to answer. "No."

"Have you ever heard a ghost?" Amith says as he walks up to Shaneel.

"No."

"There you go," Amith says, and he walks off as if he solved the case.

Shaneel ponders this for a while, then runs up to Amith.

"I've heard that ghosts make noises, like 'boo.' They should be able to hear us."

Amith comes up with another answer. "That's because it's our punishment."

"Our what?"

"Our punishment, yaar."

Shaneel looks confused. "For what?"

"Because of what I said back at the shrine, you know, to the gods." Amith points up. "Now they are punishing us by not allowing anyone to ever hear us talk, ever again." Amith gives a triumphant nod.

Shaneel looks at him, trying to decide if he's playing a trick on him. "So they can't hear us?"

"What do you think? Didn't you just see what happened?"

Shaneel contemplates the idea for a moment, realizing that Amith's conclusion makes absolute sense. It is the only logical solution. "I guess you have a point."

Amith smiles in agreement. "I always do," Amith says, smirking as they start to walk down the hallway.

"I knew you shouldn't have said those things," Shaneel mutters, irritated with Amith but still walking beside him.

Amith nods his head in dismal agreement.

Suddenly Shaneel stops and says, "That's not fair. Why do I have to be punished because of you?"

"Because we're friends, yaar."

Shaneel lets out a deep sigh at Amith's comment.

". . . and because you didn't stop me," Amith says as he continues down the hallway.

"What?!" Shaneel catches up to Amith. "I tried!"

"Yes. But you didn't succeed," Amith responds prophetically. Shaneel thinks it over. Amith is right. He wasn't able to stop Amith from saying those things, and at times he even felt the same way. Maybe you don't have to say those things, just feel them. There is little difference in saying it in your mind or saying it in real life, because God can hear both. Maybe this was his fault as much as Amith's. Shaneel remembers what a priest had said once at a pooja (an Indian prayer), "To stand in the presence of God and witness sacrilege without doing anything about it is just as bad as committing the act yourself." Shaneel never knew what those words meant until now. This was as much a punishment for him as it was for Amith.

They continue to walk down the hallway, stuck in a debate about their new circumstances. They stop when they hear their stomachs grumble.

"I'm hungry," Shaneel mutters.

"Maybe that too is our punishment," Amith answers confidently, now on a roll. "We will spend all of eternity never being able to eat anything . . . ever," Amith continues in a dramatic speech.

At that very moment, a door opens and a monk walks out of the room. Behind him sits a table full of food. It looks like a feast with all sorts of vegetable curries, warm aloo roti, rice, eggplant gobi, and other vegetarian delights just waiting to be eaten.

The kids are so enthralled with the sight that they do not notice that the monk is smiling at them. The monk even holds the door open as the boys stumble in like zombies, intoxicated by the smell. The monk closes the door behind them as the boys attend their feast.

The first thing Amith does is head straight for the aloo roti—his favorite. He grabs it with both hands, tearing it into chunks and eating the bite-size pieces. The cooked potato inside the tortilla-like shell melts in his mouth the moment it touches his tongue. Before long, it quickly fights the pain of hunger into submission.

Shaneel, on the other hand, jumps for the rice. He quickly finds an empty bowl and fills it half with rice and half with an assortment of curries. He is the type of person who likes to taste everything, even if it's all at once.

The boys sample all the different dishes, even the ones they usually hate such as eggplant gobi, which tastes surprisingly as good as the best curry on the table. They don't know if it's their hunger or the memories of having dinner at home, but this quickly becomes one of the best meals they have ever had.

"This is great," Shaneel announces while taking a big bite out of a vegetable poori.

"I know," Amith barks in agreement, spraying food from his mouth. Their manners have flown out the window.

Soon the boys are stuffed to the brim, and they lick their fingers clean. They get up and head back down the hallway, each carrying a piece of warm naan bread. It's nice to know that even death has its perks, they think.

"That was amazing."

"Yeah," Amith says and smiles as he leans on Shaneel, letting him carry part of his weight.

But something stops them dead in their tracks. A room stands with its doors wide open, and their mouths hang open at the sight of what's inside. They see something they thought they had lost forever, something that instantly brings them joy. They see Karishma.

CHAPTER 46

Alive

"KARISHMA!" The boys yell in unison as they jump up and down in excitement.

Karishma lies on a bed in the corner. She is covered with a white sheet, but her hurt ankle is uncovered. It's heavily bandaged with purple and green leaves. The purple seems similar to the ones they had on their heads; the green is unfamiliar.

"Is she okay?"

"I don't know."

"Do you think she died too?"

"I don't know."

The boys just sit there, watching her lying in bed. Their unblinking eyes stay fixed on her, as if they don't want to lose sight of her ever again.

"What do we do?"

"I don't know."

"Areh, can you stop saying that!" Amith barks at Shaneel.

The boys start arguing. Then, whether it's from the sound of their familiar squabbling or the concern they have for Karishma, she begins to wake up.

She rolls to one side and her eyes flutter open. "Shaneel?" she says as she makes out the hazy figures of the two squabbling boys. They stop instantly and quickly turn to her.

"Karishma?" Shaneel says, as he rushes to her.

Karishma's eyes lock with Shaneel's as they both show relieved smiles.

Amith watches.

"What happened?" she asks, still drowsy.

"We're dead," Shaneel says.

Karishma looks shocked. She looks at Amith.

Amith nods confidently.

Then she bursts into laughter.

"What?" Amith asks.

Karishma snorts between chuckles. "We're not dead, stupid," she says.

Amith looks confused—so does Shaneel.

"The monks brought me here, and they bandaged my leg," Karishma explains.

"They can see you?" the boys say in amazement.

Karishma looks confused and then bursts into laughter again. "Of course they can see me!"

Amith and Shaneel are still bewildered. They exchange looks of disbelief.

"They can see you too, dummy," she continues between giggles.

"Then how come they didn't say anything to us?" Shaneel asks as Amith nods in agreement.

"Really?" exclaims Karishma.

"What?"

"Don't you know anything about monks?"

Shaneel and Amith shake their heads no in unison. Besides the "kung fu" stuff they've seen in movies, they genuinely have no idea.

Karishma stares at them, now feeling rejuvenated. "They've taken a vow of silence."

Amith and Shaneel still don't understand what she's saying.

Karishma looks at them in amusement. "It means they are not supposed to talk."

"Oh!" Amith and Shaneel nod their heads at each other, their mystery finally solved.

But then Amith starts to wonder again. "Why?" Amith asks in curiosity.

Karishma gazes at them, silent for a moment. Then she starts to reply, but she doesn't know the answer, she hadn't thought of that before. It *is* a wonder why monks don't talk. Maybe it's their religion, or maybe they have bad breath, or maybe they are worried that flies will get in if they open their mouths. They were humming when the kids first saw them, so maybe they can make sounds but not say words. Or maybe those were different monks who only hum during prayers or with a bell. If she sees the monks again, she'll ask even though she won't really get an answer, maybe a hum at best, and a hum is no closer to yes than it is to no so there isn't any way to be sure. She ponders and ponders, but nothing that makes sense comes to mind. Instead, she just shrugs her shoulders with an "I don't know" look.

"Well, where are we then?" Shaneel asks.

"I don't know," Karishma says.

"It doesn't matter," Amith says. "Let's just go home."

"Right," Shaneel agrees.

Karishma gets out of bed with the boys' help.

They head toward the door, but Amith stops everyone. "Wait!" Amith turns around. He starts to think. He saw Karishma badly wounded, lying there in the shrine, almost dying. The monks must have done something to heal her, they must have used something.

"Karishma, how did they heal you?"

Karishma tries to think but her memories are foggy. The only thing she remembers is seeing a monk's smiling face and then falling asleep.

"I know you were bitten by a snake. You were really sick," Amith continues.

Karishma thinks again but nothing else comes to mind. About the trip to the shrine or from the shrine to here, she has no memory, only that she kept falling asleep when the monks were bandaging her.

"I don't know," she responds.

"Karishma, what happened exactly?" Amith asks.

Karishma remembers drinking something, and them giving her water. "I don't know. They just gave me something to drink."

"What was it?"

"I don't know, but it was bitter. It made me feel better, but then I fell asleep."

Amith looks confused, his eyes wandering around the room searching for clues. Then he sees something.

"Karishma, what did they give you the medicine in?" Amith asks, not moving.

Then Karishma recalls seeing something gold. She could feel the weight of it on her lips when she drank from it. "I don't know. It was something in a heavy gold cup. They made me drink from it."

"Then what?" Shaneel asks curiously.

"Then I started feeling better."

Shaneel pauses and thinks about it for a minute. Could it be true, could this be what the boys had been searching for this whole time? They were right here when it was used. Can the monks be hiding such a treasure? "Amith, do you think? . . ." Shaneel says with his eyes growing wide.

Amith doesn't respond. He is lost in thought.

"Maybe it does exist," Shaneel continues and turns to Karishma. "I mean, who better to hide it with than monks—and especially ones that don't speak!" Shaneel continues, as he begins to figure out his little puzzle. "Very clever way to keep a secret," he mutters as he rubs his chin with his thumb, "and a temple is a perfect place to hide it."

"Hide what?" Karishma asks curiously.

"Amith was right all along!" Shaneel exclaims.

Still Amith says nothing.

"The cup they used, it was the magic cup that can heal anyone, just like in the movie," Shaneel says.

Karishma's face lights up. Her lies weren't told in vain; she did lead them closer to the cup.

"There's hope for Aunty!" Shaneel screams in excitement and starts to celebrate but quickly stops. His face turns deathly serious as he kneels down to Karishma. "Karishma, where did they take it?"

"I don't remember."

"Did you see anything before you fell asleep?"

Karishma thinks hard, but nothing comes to mind. Karishma shakes her head no.

"Do you know where it could be?"

Karishma looks down at her feet in sadness.

"I know," Amith interrupts.

"Where?" Shaneel asks.

"Look." Amith says.

Amith points to where he's been staring the whole time, his eyes still frozen on the spot. Shaneel and Karishma look to see where Amith is pointing.

Right there, sitting on the table in front of everyone, are some purple and green leaves, and next to that are a mortar and pestle. The pestle resembles a small brass rod that is blunt on one end for crushing herbs—something the kids have never seen. The brass mortar, on the other hand, resembles something much more familiar to Amith. It resembles a golden cup, the one from his dreams.

CHAPTER 47

Magic

THEIR TRIP BACK WAS AS QUICK AS LIGHTNING. What took them days to travel on foot, they made in a single night. They were led by one of the monks. He was very nice and packed little but a healthy smile. He didn't speak, but led them through the jungle with ease, always guiding and telling them with a stern finger when they were headed the wrong way.

There were no signs of the storm. It must have retreated back into the nightmare from where it came. There were only clear skies and cool breezes to accompany them on their journey as they traveled farther and farther out of the heart of the jungle.

The monk led them to a road, similar to the one that they had traveled along through the jungle before. It wasn't long before a truck appeared, making its rackety way toward them.

When they turned to look, the monk had disappeared. It made them wonder if he was ever there or just some sort of spirit of the jungle. It could easily be unreal and imaginary if it wasn't for the proof that hid in Shaneel's backpack.

The approaching truck driver stopped, surprised by the kids being out this far, just to make sure he wasn't delusional. Turns out it was the same truck driver who had argued with the farmer before, but he didn't look so menacing now. The driver pushed open the door and motioned for the kids to get in. Apparently, "the Butcher of Children" is a pretty nice guy.

As they traveled, they began to talk—the truck driver was happy to answer all of their questions. The kids found out that he was one of the few drivers to come out this far. He would pick up farmers' harvested bounties and take them into town, as well as carry supplies back and forth. When they asked why the farmers are so far away, he told them that the soil in the jungle is much more fertile than the land on the hills and yields a variety of crops that can't grow on the hills. More than anything, the truck driver was intrigued by how the kids came to be out in the jungle. So he asked them how they managed to come out this far, the question that had plagued him since they met.

The kids told him their story. At first, he thought they were delirious or sick from being in the jungle. When Shaneel spoke about the tussle with the jaguar and how they escaped death by defeating it with a makeshift spear, the driver was almost certain that they were lying. But once Shaneel showed his prize, a gleaming real jaguar tooth, to the driver, he believed them.

The rest of their story excited and impressed the truck driver. Several times the story almost made him lose his focus on the road. He even oohed and aahed when the kids told him about the storm. Apparently, he heard the violent rumble of thunder, but the storm did not venture from the depths of the jungle. The driver said it was one of the reasons why the farmers choose the areas they do, because they know that the weather deep in the jungle can be deadly for their crops, as well as for themselves. The driver was extremely surprised to hear that the kids had actually lived through one.

The rest of the journey, the truck driver told about the strange sights he has seen on his journeys into the jungle—from rare birds to large snakes. But he has never seen a jaguar and hopes he never will. Jaguars are the king of the jungle in these parts, and a sighting is always fatal. He was ecstatic to hear that a little boy like Shaneel actually fought one, and even won.

They drive and drive, and it seems as if the green trees are blending together like an emerald blanket flowing in the wind as they weave along the curvy road.

The kids peer out the windows as they pass through the dense jungle. They see all sorts of things that they have grown familiar with: huge trees, small berry bushes, thorny plants, delicious bananas, and monkeys, those infernal feces-throwing monkeys. Shaneel was compelled to roll down the window and make a monkey face with his tongue sticking out at them as they passed. The monkeys, in return, taunted him back by making human faces.

It is a pretty uneventful journey, until the truck suddenly squeals to a stop. The kids almost fly through the windshield when the truck driver hits the brakes. Luckily, the truck driver put out his arm to brace them and prevent any injury.

"What is it?" Amith whispers.

"I don't know," Shaneel says, looking over the high dashboard. "He stopped for some reason."

"Well, would you look at that?!" the truck driver says.

Karishma crawls up and stands on the seat. Her eyes open wide and her jaw drops open as she looks.

"Karishma?" Shaneel asks.

She doesn't respond.

"What is it?" Shaneel asks, as he too gets up to look at what's going on.

"Amith, you're not going to believe this!" Shaneel says as he gawks at the sight.

Amith sits up and looks over the dash.

A deer crosses the road with her young. She snuggles her fawn close, as she makes it to the other side.

"So?" Amith says.

"Amith, look at her leg," Shaneel says.

Amith looks.

There in front of his eyes, he sees what the commotion is all about. One of the deer's legs is bandaged—with the same bandage that Karishma ripped from Shaneel's shirt and wrapped on the dying deer several days before.

The kids stand in shock as the deer crosses the road, but before it disappears into the jungle, it looks at them as if saying thanks.

The kids look at each other in disbelief. Finally their eyes fall on the backpack. Amith unzips it and peeks inside. The cup is still there.

"Wow, that's amazing," Shaneel says.

"It's working," Karishma whispers.

Amith zips up the backpack and sits down. The truck starts up and heads down the road once again. Amith stares through the window, and the jungle trees continue zipping past. He thinks of his mom and smiles.

"I never had any doubt."

CHAPTER 48

Home

THE NEXT STOP IS ONCE AGAIN A FAMILIAR SIGHT: the farmer's house. As the truck driver pulls closer, Karishma starts to tremble in her seat, afraid that the farmer will remember them and pull out his gun to finish the job.

The truck parks in front of the farmer's house, and the farmer comes out to greet the driver once again. Amith and Shaneel get out to stretch their arms and legs while Karishma stays in the truck, hiding behind the delivery truck's massive doors. She takes little peeks from inside, peering around the edge of the window, each time getting a bit braver and taking a better look at what's going on.

The farmer walks right past her, and he doesn't look the same either. He doesn't appear any less threatening like the "Butcher of Children" did, but he truly looks like a changed man, as if something spiritual has come over him. He wears a huge smile and carries his shoulders high, like he is free of the burdens of the world. The farmer greets the truck driver with a big hug, who himself is mystified at the new rejuvenated persona.

Before the driver can cancel his contract, the farmer ushers him around the fields, which also look changed. There are rows of water running through the fields, and the dry dirt is now as fertile as ever. Some greenery has even sprouted, which wasn't there before. It is so strange to see it now, so different from eight days ago.

Shaneel plays with a stick he found nearby. Normally, it would be a task for Amith, but brave little Shaneel has become quite good at thwarting off evil. Amith stands near the rear of the truck, hugging the backpack with his prize and salvation inside. He looks at the ground and sees the running water and small sprouts of vegetation starting to grow again and smiles.

Shaneel stops and looks at Amith. "Amith, what is it?"

"The cup," he replies.

"What about it?"

Amith points to the ground.

Shaneel looks at the ground and realizes that it is just like in the movie. The knight used the Holy Grail to bring back the dead, heal the land, and cure the maiden from her sickness. It has done all three! The magic power of the cup is real, and it is happening right in front of their eyes.

The driver finishes his meeting with the farmer, and as the driver gets ready to leave, they are both smiling. Whatever quarrel was between the two of them seems to have been healed by the cup too.

The driver starts up his clattering engine, leans out the window, and yells, "I got to say, it's a miracle."

The words bring a smile to the farmer's face, as well as Amith's. Amith then turns to Shaneel with determination on his face.

"Let's go save my mom," he says, patting Shaneel on the back and heading back to the truck.

¤ ¤ ¤ ¤ ¤

The ride back to the village seems like an eternity. Time ticks by a second at a time as if it will never end. They finally get there, but it is night. The kids burst out of the truck the moment it stops rolling, waving their goodbyes to the driver.

Shaneel goes straight to his parents' store where they will soon be closing. Karishma runs to her house where her family is probably upset and worried sick. Amith, carrying Shaneel's backpack, runs straight to the village hospital where his mom waits for him.

Amith flings open the hospital door. No nurses or doctors are inside, just the same sick people as there were before.

He runs past the hospital beds, one after another, running toward his mom, who is surely waiting for his heroic arrival. It's time to do what she had raised him to do. It's time to finally be the hero he promised her he would be.

Amith finally reaches her bed. He smiles as he sees her and stops to catch his breath. He walks over, ready to tell her about all the things that he has seen, all the things he has done, and all the things that they can do, now that they have the cup.

Amith sits down on the vacant bed next to hers. For a moment, he just watches her, debating if he should wake her, pull her out of her dream. She seems to be sleeping so peacefully. Maybe he should wait till tomorrow when she has gathered some strength, or leave the cup for her as a surprise. He debates and debates, as he stares at her, trying to decide when would be the perfect moment. But he can't wait any longer, there is magic to be done.

He pulls Shaneel's backpack up into his lap, slowly unzips it, and pulls out the magical healing cup. He holds it high, like he has done in his dreams, and looks over at his resting mom.

"Ma," he says, "I told you I would save you one day." Amith gets off the bed and stands up with the cup in his hands. "I have brought you the cup—it's supposed to be magical," he says as he stands next to her. "Anyway, Ma, it was so hard getting it. You won't believe me," Amith says as he acts out his adventure, "but there were monkeys, elephants, a big storm, and a giant jaguar that tried to eat me. I think it was the same one that attacked the man who came in here."

Amith turns his head to look for the man who was attacked, but there's no sign of him. When he sees him, he'll have to let him know. "Okay, I don't see the scary jaguar guy," Amith says as he looks around, "but he will be happy to hear that Shaneel got revenge for him."

Amith turns his attention back to his mom.

"Anyway, Ma, the jaguar was sooo big, but Shaneel saved me with a spear, just like in the movies. And then Karishma got bitten by a snake, and there were monks, and a temple, and some other things."

Amith can barely breathe as he rushes to say it all. "But I got it, Ma. I found the cup and brought it here so I can save you." Amith holds out the cup. "It's supposed to heal the sick, and it's very powerful. It brought a deer back to life, and healed Karishma, and made plants grow right in front of us."

Amith's mom doesn't respond.

Amith puts the cup down, waiting impatiently. He tries to think of what to do. "Oh, the monks made Karishma drink from it. That's how it must work on humans," Amith says loudly as he rushes to the table on the other side of the room.

There is a bucket of drinking water with a small, clean metal bowl sitting next to it on the table. Amith grabs the bowl and scoops up some water and fills the cup. He grabs the cup—it's even heavier than usual—and slowly walks back, holding onto the cup with both hands to be sure to not spill a single drop of its magical healing liquid.

He places the cup on the side table near her bed. Then he sits next to her to examine her. She looks like the same beautiful mom he has grown up with, the same one who fought ants off their starfruit, the same one who greets him with that beautiful loving smile every morning. She looks rather pale, but it could be just because it's night and the moon isn't very bright.

Amith grabs the cup and brings it to his mom's dry lips. He pours a little into her mouth. Then he sits back on the vacant bed, waiting.

After a few moments pass, nothing happens. Amith gets back up. He grabs the cup again and pours a little more, then goes back to his bed to sit and wait. This time he waits with a smile. He waits and waits, but nothing is happening.

Amith sits there, wondering how to make his mom recover faster. She must need a full dose, he thinks. He goes back over to her bed and pours some more, until he realizes that the cup is empty. That must do it, he thinks, and jumps back onto the empty bed next to her.

Amith sits with his legs dangling, kicking them back and forth in anticipation. He thinks of all the things he will say to her, what great stories he will tell her, what great adventures they will go on. He plans and plans, beaming with a powerful radiant smile, waiting for her to wake up, for that perfect moment to come. He waits and waits until the night slowly passes.

CHAPTER 49

Fall

THE SYMPHONY OF THE OCEAN FILLS THE AIR as the waves glide onto the sand and retreat back the way they came. The wind is gentle and the sky is clear, but the sun is going down and quickly chills the air over the sand.

There are people here, most of the village folk. Shaneel is here with his family clutching him in their arms, as is Karishma with hers holding on to her shoulders tightly.

Amith is here too. He stands alone at the shoreline, his eyes dull but full of dying hope. He stares directly in front of him.

The people talk and say things in a language Amith doesn't understand, yet they announce it to the world as if it means something. The villagers listen in respect to those mysterious words, but Amith doesn't. He just stares at the wooden bed waiting for him.

He never expected to see this sight so soon again. If it wasn't for his mom standing next to him during his first trip to the beach, he wouldn't have been able to handle it the first time through. She's still with him, but not standing next to him clutching him in her arms, like all of the other parents do. Instead, she lies waiting on the bed inside the wooden pyre.

The villagers shed their tears as the shaman says his prayers, but Amith doesn't cry. He knows this is not the time for tears. There is no need for it. This time is for waiting and seeing, for allowing the heavens to work their wonders, to allow the cup to work its miracle like he knows it can. It saved everyone else, why not his mom?

So Amith waits eagerly with great anticipation because he knows there is no world so cruel as to take everything from him, to take the one meaning in his life that drives him, the one reason he wants to be a hero, the one thing that guides him, the reason for his living.

Amith's eyes lay fixed on his mom, waiting for the cup to work its magic. He even put the cup right next to her, lying on the wooden bed, along with the remnants of his red scarf just for the added magical kick. Yet nothing has happened so far. His mom still lies asleep.

Finally the shaman is quiet, the villagers hushed, and even the ocean goes silent. A shaman dressed in ceremonial garb gives him something. Amith grabs it without even realizing what he holds.

But soon the realization hits, and it hits with great horror as the shaman takes out a match and lights the torch that Amith holds. A terrible look of fear covers Amith's face, and for the first time, his eyes fill with tears—but he doesn't let them out. There is still hope. Amith tries to force that powerful smile to give him strength, but it doesn't come; it's been ripped away.

The gloom-faced shaman looks at him and nods his head. He doesn't speak any words, but Amith knows what he wants him to do. He just doesn't want to do it.

Amith stares at the village folk as he wanders aimlessly on the sand. The villagers look sad, but there is a sense of gladness from them. They're glad that they aren't in his place, that they don't have to endure what Amith will now have to endure, that they don't have to feel what Amith has to feel.

Amith looks at Karishma with her family. She's filled with sorrow, her face scrunched up and streaming with tears. He looks at Shaneel, who desperately wants to be at his friend's side but is being held back by his parents who nod their heads at Amith, just as the shaman did. How he wishes they would do something different. Instead of nodding, he wishes they would shake their heads no. Tell the world that they are crazy and to stop this insanity. How he wishes for all those things, but they don't come true.

Before Amith knows it, he has somehow wandered up to the pyre. He still feels lost and is looking for an answer. But no answer comes because what answer could explain this? Amith stares at the bed; he can't bring himself to look at his mom, not so close, not like this. So he focuses on something else.

The wooden pyre, it's a sight to see. The wooden frame made of intricate branches looks like it was woven together with utter love and care. He has heard that it was built by Shaneel's and Karishma's families. Normally, that would be a resounding symbol of friendship and love, but right now it looks extremely frightening and betraying. Why don't they see what he sees, why don't they know what he knows? The magic of the cup will work. Why don't they believe?

Amith gets a headache just looking at it and quickly looks at something else: the tattered remains of his red scarf, the companion that hung on him as he had his adventures, the gateway to his imagination and joy but now it's gone, gone like his childhood. Maybe, in the future, it will bring some use to his mom, maybe it will bring her the same fun and joy it brought him. All those memories it had made must hold some sort of power, some sort of meaning that would empower the cup.

Finally Amith focuses on the cup. Its brass-like exterior still gleams bright, just like his dreams. It's the same magical cup that he entered the depths of the jungle for, the same magical cup that he risked life and limb for, and the same magical cup that made bonds with his friends that can never be broken. And yet, all those experiences he went through, all the moments he created, he would gladly exchange for a few more days with his mom. They pale in comparison to her glory, her love. He would even gladly give his life in payment.

How he wishes he could go back and pay that penance. What an easy choice that would have been, to give his life so his mom would be okay. If he could, he wouldn't be able to feel this pain, this remorse, or this empty hole in his life. But who is Amith kidding—he is no longer a kid, he can't be. He knows better now. He knows that the magical cup is no more magical than the pretend scenarios he used to conjure up. No more magical than the movies he used to watch, and no more magical than the dreams he used to have. He knows now, in fact, that the cup is just a cup. With that, Amith finally brings himself to move his eyes to his mom.

She's as beautiful as always, lying there sleeping comfortably on the bed, dressed in the white garments. They move and sway in the wind like wings of an angel. And the ocean winds send strands of her hair dancing in the air, reaching for the sky. There is a peacefulness about her, something he had not noticed before. Maybe because she doesn't have to struggle anymore, she doesn't have to hurt or be sick, and she can finally rest in peace.

"I'm sorry, Ma," Amith says as he looks at her a final time. He looks at the dancing fire on top of the torch in his hand. Then he looks back at his mom. "I'm sorry I couldn't save you, Ma," he says.

Then Amith lights the wooden pyre. It starts to burn, releasing long threads of smoke twirling into the heavens. The flames gather strength and spread over the entire bed, over the pieces of his tattered red scarf, over the golden cup, and over everything else. The fire soon turns into a blaze and smoke rushes into the dimming sky. The stars start to shine, the ocean begins to roar, and Amith finally mourns.

CHAPTER 50

Rise

AMITH WALKS DOWN THE FAMILIAR PATH of the alley, but today he is all alone, left to the sorrow of his life and the emptiness each day will bring him. Out of nowhere, Amith hears a familiar voice.

"Amith!"

Amith turns to look. It's Shaneel. He is glad to see him. They haven't seen each other since his mom's funeral.

Shaneel smiles as he walks toward Amith, but before he can reach him a group of voices call out from around the corner.

"You, boy!" they call out.

Shaneel looks shocked as he turns to see a mob of people rushing toward him.

"There he is!" yells a man who is missing one arm.

Shaneel disappears into the crowd that fills the alley. Before he knows it, Shaneel is riding up in the air on the shoulders of the people, laughing as the hands tickle him while passing him from one person to the next.

"He's the boy who killed a jaguar with his bare hands," a voice says.

"He's a brave boy for being so little!" someone yells.

"Our hero!" a few people cheer.

Amith watches in disbelief as Shaneel rides along on the crowd's shoulders, from one side of the alley to the other and back again, being shown off like a trophy.

Shaneel is smiling from ear to ear as he hears the words he's waited his whole life for.

"Hero, hero, hero!" they start to chant.

Those words bring a joy that he thought he would never be able to attain, a goal that a mere young boy would never be able to accomplish. Now Shaneel's dream has truly come true, that perfect moment that he always wanted is happening and it is happening now. All he needs now is for Amith to join him in the celebration.

He looks around to where Amith was standing, but he doesn't see him. There is no sign of him, only the empty alley wall up ahead, where they used to sit and watch movies, dreaming together.

¤ ¤ ¤ ¤ ¤

Amith runs down the street as fast as he can before he has to stop. He puts his hand against the wall to brace himself from falling and takes deep breaths, hyperventilating.

He doesn't know if his heart is going to burst from the sprint or from seeing Shaneel being hoisted up as a hero. Is he wrong to think the way he does, to feel jealous and angry at his friend for achieving what he always wanted? For getting everything that he ever wanted, when Amith has nothing? He knows he should feel proud and happy—that's what a good friend would do—but he doesn't feel that way and he doesn't know why.

All Amith knows is that he doesn't want to feel any more pain, at least not now. He goes over to a pile of debris, wooden boards, and old crates and kicks it in frustration.

Suddenly it moves and he hears something. Is it his imagination? Is it one of those dreams? By now, he knows better than to dream. He knows better than to hope.

Amith shakes the thought from his head and starts to walk away, but something stirs behind the crates again. Something beckons him to stop. He does.

Amith looks up into the heavens, wondering what to do. He doesn't know. He just stands there for a moment and finally he can't help it. He turns around and goes back.

Something is moving behind the pile of discarded goods. Amith takes a look. There's a mound of clothes piled up and a large blanket covering something. It smells bad and is attracting flies. Amith takes a closer look. All of a sudden, the blanket moves. Amith jumps back. He knows it's not his imagination — something is in there. Amith pulls the blanket off.

A sick old man is lying there. His frail bones show through his paper-thin skin, his hands are trembling and his lips quivering. The man looks starved and in pain. He has tears in his eyes but even though he doesn't let them out, Amith can see them. Amith has gained a power from all of this. He can sense when someone is in pain like he is, when someone is lost like he is, when someone has no hope.

Amith tries to think of something he can do and looks to the heavens again for an answer. After a moment, something comes to mind. Amith reaches inside his pocket, pulls out something, and hands it to the sick old man.

The sick old man looks down. It's a piece of starfruit. He quickly gobbles it down. Amith then puts out his hand, offering help. The sick old man looks up at Amith.

Then Amith does the one thing that has always comforted him in his life. The one thing that he knows will keep him strong and give him strength, even when the entire world is against him. The one thing he knows to never forget. Amith looks at the sick old man and smiles.

HERO TRAINING TIP #25

*"Sometimes no matter what you do,
you cannot change what is going to happen.
But what's important is that you tried
and did the right thing. Okay?"*

~Amith's Mom

THE END